Opal

Her Covered Bones

Chapter 1

An early morning heat haze shrouded the distant escarpment, promising a warmer than expected spring day ahead. Jenny lifted her coffee to her lips, savouring the rich, dark bean flavour and caramel syrup sweetness.

'I don't know how you can drink that.'

She glanced at Nick's curled up lip and shrugged, knowing he drank his espresso neat. He wasn't the first person to cringe at her signature coffee. Her work colleagues shared his opinion, but she didn't care. She'd always had a sweet tooth.

Glancing out from the new veranda, she admired the unique, rugged landscape – noticing for the first time how the old vegetable garden at the back of the dry, crisp lawn obscured an otherwise perfect view.

'You might want to move that vegetable garden now the renovation is nearly finished.' Jenny lifted her mug toward the rusty galvanised iron and steel droppers holding back a few tons of dirt and weeds.

The old William Creek homestead burnt down earlier in the year – all because Nick helped her keep two witnesses safe. She was the cop. It wasn't his job, but he offered his home as a refuge – more to keep her safe, she knew.

She still fought with the guilt. They were all lucky to escape the inferno, set by a former police detective trying to cover his tracks.

Fortunately, the old stone survived the blaze, but every bit of timber turned to ash. Nick's neighbours rallied together to help rebuild the heritage farmhouse and it was almost complete.

Jenny realised Nick was still silent. Lowering her cup from her lips, she studied his face as his eyes focussed on the garden. His expression was one she rarely saw these days. Steely blue eyes looked over the yard, sad, cold, distant.

'I'm sorry. It's none of my business what you have in your back yard. I was just thinking about the view, from the back doors, now you relocated them and all that,' she rambled on.

His eyes flicked to hers.

'It's okay. You're right. It's time.' He drew a deep breath, sprang to his feet, drained his coffee cup in one long gulp, placed the empty cup on the table and strode toward the machinery shed.

'Where are you going?' She finished her drink, popped the cup on the cedar table between the new Jack-and-Jill seat they picked up in town, and followed him.

'No time like the present.'

He strode away with the long gait that Jenny, even at six foot, struggled to keep up with.

'Nick. What's up?'

He stopped, turned and reached for her hand in one smooth motion.

'Nothing.' He pulled her close. 'You got me thinking. You're right. It's time to move the old veggie patch. It's in the wrong place now.'

'But it means something to you. I can see it does.'

Jenny ducked her head to draw Nick's eyes to hers. His face twitched as he sucked in a deep breath through his nose, making his nostrils flare.

'Mum planted it. It was her thing – growing stuff. That's why it was overgrown. Your cousin Melanie did some weeding and planted that lime tree while she was here, but…'

'I'm sorry Nick. Leave it be. We'll put a new sleeper wall around it, weed it, replant it, make it pretty, but it should stay.'

'No.' He carried on toward the shed, dragging her along with him. 'You're right. It's time. Mum's not coming home anytime soon.'

Nick's mum disappeared the day his dad died. Ron Johnston was thought to have committed suicide, until Jenny's friend Penny, a forensic scientist from Adelaide saw a photo and did some digging into the case.

The case was reopened as a homicide, and Ron's body was exhumed, but so far, the case was as cold as a frozen fish. But it wasn't only Ron's death that upset Nick now. His mum, Patricia was never found. The idea she may have killed her husband and run off was too hard for anyone to bear, so the subject rarely came up.

Except now. Jenny had put her foot squarely in her mouth when she suggested they dig up the garden Nick's mum planted.

'Nick. Don't do this on my account.'

He let her hand go as he slid one of the side doors on the shed open to reveal a green tractor, front-end-loader with a covered cab.

'It's okay Jen. Truly.' His lips softened. 'I'll use the tractor to pull the side down, but maybe we can save the lime tree Mel planted. It's just starting to bear fruit and I don't mind a slice of lime in my Corona occasionally.'

Jenny laughed. 'Don't let Marj hear you say that. I don't think she even serves it in the motel bar. I can hear her now.' Jenny lifted her hands in air quotes. "*Not having any of that foreign crap in my place.*"

'I won't tell if you don't.' His lips curved and his face relaxed. 'Here. Take this to put the lime in.' He handed her a large black tub. 'It will do for now. I'll find a new spot for the lime tree later.'

Jenny put her hand on his as he reached for the tractor door to hoist himself up into the cab.

'Please don't do this because of me.'

'I'm not Jen. Sam and I need to move on. I have to admit, it would be easier if we knew what happened to mum and who killed dad but…' His shoulders sagged as another sigh escaped his lips.

'We'll get answers. I got answers to what happened to Melanie and Aunt Carolyn didn't I?'

She smiled, but deep down she wondered if that were true. Sure, she found Melanie – well in reality Melanie found her.

Thankfully, her cousin and aunt weren't dead as she always feared, but still, there were so many unanswered questions about why Melanie ran away. Who the father of her child was and was she raped or simply hiding a teenage pregnancy?

'Take the pot and the shovel. I'll meet you over at the garden.'

Nick pushed up into the cab, closed the door and started the motor.

A puff of black diesel smoke made Jenny vacate the closed in space, shovel and pot in hand.

The tractor reversed out, and stopped as Nick selected a forward gear. Jenny jogged to keep up. By the time she got back to the rear of the homestead, the loader bucket was already full of twisted iron and star pickets.

Jenny picked up the pace, then halted. Squinting, she tried to make out what she was looking at. Was it the root system of the lime tree? Surely not? Melanie only planted it last month. It couldn't have grown a tap root *that* thick.

'Nick!' She shouted, dropping the shovel and pot and sprinting toward the tractor. 'Nick!' She waved her hands to stop him from digging the bucket in for another load, but he didn't stop moving forward.

Drawing alongside the cab, she saw his ears were covered in sound deadening earmuffs. Reaching out, she grabbed the door handle and jumped up on the sidestep of the cab. Nick saw her as her fist thudded home on the glass.

Braking, he pulled the earmuffs from his ears, rested them around his neck and opened the cab door as Jenny sprang back down.

'What's up?'

She pointed to the open side of the metre high vegetable garden. Nick's eyes turned to follow her finger. At first, his eyebrows dipped, then shot up, then fresh frown lines reappeared.

Pulling the stop on the tractor, he jammed the footbrake on, flung the door the rest of the way open and jumped down.

'Have you or your family buried a pet in the garden?'

She knew she wasn't looking at a buried pet, but she was clutching at straws, trying to think of an explanation. Any explanation other than the obvious one.

He shook his head and stumbled forward.

'Nick. Don't touch anything.' Jenny followed him, dragging him back by the arm. 'Please. Let me get someone out here.'

She never met Patricia Johnston. She couldn't be upset over a woman she never met, but as Nick's whole body began to shake, hot tears stung her eyes.

When he fell to his knees, a knot formed in her stomach. The sensation of having swallowed a rock made her nauseous. Biting her lip, she desperately tried to keep her emotions under control. Nick needed her now, more than ever.

‘I’m going inside to call Sarge.’

He didn’t answer. She dropped to her knees next to him.

His eyes were fixed on the discoloured bone jutting from the rich, dark soil.

‘Nick.’ She whispered. He didn’t respond. ‘Nick. Listen to me. This might not be what we think.’

She knew it was, but she needed him calm.

He began to sob. The sound tore at her heart. Wrapping her arms around him, she held his face to her chest as his whole body heaved.

Patricia Johnston’s body was buried in the homestead vegetable garden for nearly ten years. Another few minutes wasn’t going to make any difference.

Chapter 2

Jenny's legs wouldn't sit still. She fixed her gaze on the side mirror and watched as red dust flew into the air and hovered like mist.

Glancing over at the driver's seat, she studied the grey-haired man next to her. An unlit smoke hung from his lip. His eyes remained focussed on the road ahead. The deep lines on his dark skin made reading his expression difficult, but he didn't seem anxious.

'Thanks for driving Al.'

He nodded – his eyes stayed focussed on the road. Al and his son Ed were back from the weekend break and Jenny was thankful for their help.

'Mrs B. will look after the boys.'

She spoke for her own peace of mind. Al remained silent. Jenny's leg continued to jiggle.

'Did you ever wonder why Patricia went missing?'

Al's eyes finally left the road and found hers. What she mistook for the old jackaroo's stoic expression, she realised was in fact, him maintaining his composure.

'Never believed she left.' His eyes were back on the road.

'So you thought she was dead?'

Al shrugged.

Now wasn't the time to question witnesses. Penny and her forensic team were flying out to the station after picking up Sarge in Coober Pedy. As if on cue, a Pilatus PC 12 circled overhead.

The light, single-prop plane was used by the Royal Flying Doctors and the regional South Australian Police for emergencies.

William Creek Station was now the site of a double homicide, all be it a decade old case. It didn't matter. In Sarge's book, that required an immediate response. The plane flew low over the road, lining up with a graded runway a few kilometres from Nick's homestead.

As Al drove over tufts of saltbush, the four-wheel drive lurched. Jenny ignored the rough ride – her mind drifting to Nick.

For more than ten minutes, he sobbed out a decade of anxiety. Left to take over the family farm at nineteen, he learnt to bury his pain deep. When Jenny first met him, he was distant, cold, all business. But since they started working together to find Melanie and discovered his dad was murdered, he let his guard down and opened up to her.

She only hoped this wouldn't pull him away again.

Hopefully Sam would keep him focussed. Nick's brother was his opposite in so many ways. Openly friendly, a little bit cocky even, but he was only nine when his mum disappeared. She knew the news of her death would hit him the hardest.

That's if the body was Patricia's. Maybe this was something else entirely. Maybe they were dealing with a serial killer and Nick's dad was one of many victims?

The four-wheel-drive stopped at the end of the rough runway. Jenny watched as the police aircraft touched down, bounced, then began to slow.

'Need to get the grader out.' Al observed.

'Thanks for helping get Nick to the pub.'

'Ed will watch 'im.'

Al's son was a sweet guy. About Jenny's age, he grew up around the William Creek Station and worked there since he was sixteen. Sam grew up with Ed. Nick treated him like a brother. If anyone could help Nick and Sam now, it was Ed and Mrs B. at the William Creek Pub.

Jenny shoved her tan Akubra on, adjusted it and stepped out of the vehicle, thankful she carried a spare uniform in her car on the weekends. Coober Pedy was a small town, with a short-staffed police department. Four officers covered the entire area, seven days a week. She never knew when she might be called back to work.

The loud prop wound down as the door on the aircraft popped open. Jenny sucked in slow, even breaths, telling herself to keep her emotions under control. While Nick was falling to pieces, she managed to keep it together, but now Nick wasn't here and Penny, one of her best friends, was about to step off the plane and offer her sympathy.

She didn't want to fall apart.

The face that appeared in the doorway wasn't Sarge, or Penny. The woman was medium height with short cropped brunette hair, and large brown eyes which quickly disappeared behind aviator sunnies.

She wore tailored dark grey pants, black Doc Martin boots and a high neck tee, with cut off arms showing sculpted golden tanned muscles.

The woman casually disembarked, throwing a shoulder bag over her head and across her body as she approached Jenny.

'You must be Constable Williams.'

The woman held her thin hand out. Jenny grasped it and shook, fighting the temptation to salute afterward. This woman was obviously not part of Penny's forensic team.

'I am. And you are?'

The woman's lips curved.

'Direct. I like it. I'm Detective Sergeant Grave.'

Jenny was speechless.

The woman smiled knowingly.

'I've read your record Constable. My attendance isn't a slight on your investigative ability.'

'I wasn't….' Jenny protested.

Detective Grave put her hand up. Jenny stopped speaking.

'This case has links to too many people in town, you included. I'm here to oversee the investigation.'

Jenny nodded. She didn't like it, but it made sense. Nick was her boyfriend. Detective Grave might not know he was away at university when his dad was killed, and his mum went missing.

Was he a suspect?

She bit her lip to avoid asking any stupid questions, surprising herself.

'Got it.'

'I've heard good things about you Constable.'

Jenny was about to delve deeper into that statement when Penny appeared with a bag in each hand.

'From me of course.' The forensic scientist grinned mischievously.

'I'm surprised it was all good then.' Jenny resisted the urge to hug her friend. With a detective on board, it would be unprofessional, and she was afraid of what her emotions would do if her friend showed any sympathy.

Penny dropped her bags with a thud, stepped forward and grabbed her shoulders firmly.

'How are you doing?' She studied Jenny's eyes with an intense stare.

'Don't ask.' Jenny looked away, but Penny pulled her close, wrapping her arms around her, pulling her into a firm bear hug.

Penny was Jenny's height, but a broader build. There was no getting away from the embrace. Still, as tears stung her eyes, she tried to wriggle free.

'Seriously. I'm fine.'

Penny finally let go. Jenny waved her hand and swallowed hard.

'But Nick was a mess. Sam is going to be devastated.' She hurried to divert the unwanted attention.

'We don't know it's their mum yet. Let's keep an open mind.' Penny stepped back and collected her bags.

'I'm sorry about that.' Jenny glanced at the detective, her cheeks flushed, her eyes still damp with tears she failed to suppress.

'Don't be. There's a reason women live longer than men.'

Jenny lifted an eyebrow.

Grave chuckled.

'We let our emotions go more often. It's not always pretty, and its often not nice for anyone on the receiving end, but it certainly lets out the stress. This is all a shock. Even if you didn't know the victim,' she glanced over her shoulder at Penny, '*possible* victim,' she clarified, 'you are close to those who did. Give yourself a break.'

Jenny's shoulders relaxed.

'Thanks for that.'

Sergeant Mackenzie was the last to leave the aircraft carrying two more bags of forensic equipment. The rear of the plane opened slowly to reveal a police pilot, carrying a recovery board.

He nodded to the detective as he strolled past to place the orange plastic moulded board, loaded with a black body bag into the tray of the four-wheel-drive.

Al tied it down without a word, but his eyes studied everything going on around him.

'How you doing Williams?'

'I've had better days thanks Sarge.'

'Haven't we all.'

'Okay team. Let's get this body recovered and our investigation underway.'

Detective Grave opened the front passenger side door and slid in, leaving no doubt who was running this case.

Al double checked the stretcher, nodded to the police pilot and rounded the vehicle to open the driver's side door.

Penny placed her bags in the back, reached for the two from Sarge and secured them before joining Jenny and Sarge in the back seat.

Sarge's broad shoulders and Penny and Jenny's long legs made the rear seating area look like a circus act. Three big clowns trying to squeeze into a Morris Minor.

'How's Nick doing?' Penny whispered as she wiggled sideways to make space to clip her seatbelt on.

'He's a mess Pen, but I think he'll pull himself together. Sam was with Mick last night, at the William Creek Pub. Ed dropped Nick off so I haven't seen how Sam is doing.'

'At least now we can get stuck into this investigation. Cold cases don't get much of our time, but a double homicide will ramp up the man hours. We'll find out what happened to them Jen.'

Jenny peered through the front windscreen, her mind trying to forget the discoloured bones and matted hair of the body she was sure would turn out to be Patricia Johnston.

'I hope so.'

Chapter 3

The sound of car doors slamming echoed across the open space behind the William Creek Station Homestead.

Jenny rubbed her hand down her face, sucked in a slow, steady breath and forced her emotions into a little black box in the pit of her stomach. It ached in response.

'Okay McGregor, where do you want us?' Sarge's gruff voice startled Jenny back to reality.

Penny turned to Jenny. 'You can sit this one out Jen.' Her eyes returned to Sarge. 'I'll get you to bring the recovery board and body bag over. Lay out the bag on top of the stretcher, with the straps undone. We'll be here for a while, but I need to sift all this dirt…'

Jenny cut her off. 'I'll help or you'll be here more than a while. I've sifted with you before. I get your routine. I'll be fine.'

All eyes studied Jenny. Sarge sucked in a breath, ready to order her to stand down, Jenny could see it in his eyes.

'Okay Constable. Suit up.'

Detective Grave interrupted as Sarge's mouth opened, then slowly closed.

His eyebrows furrowed, but he remained silent. Sergeant Mackenzie was technically station sergeant and to an extent, in charge of his team, but Detective Sergeant Grave outranked him in the field.

Jenny didn't waste any time. Penny handed her gloves, a white disposable body suit and a pair of shoe covers.

'We'll start with this pile Nick dislodged first, then work our way back in to the main garden bed. Keep to a grid pattern so that anything you find in a sieve, we'll know where it came from.

Once we start on the main section, stop if you find bones. Don't touch it, I'll need to photograph it in situ.

Any loose bones we find I'll place on the inside of the body bag in an approximate location of where that body part would normally sit.'

'You're going to reconstruct the body here?' Jenny slipped shoe covers on and picked up the sieve.

'Yes, that way I'll know if I'm missing any bones.'

'Alright, you two carry on, Sarge, stand by in case they need anything. I'll interview the staff.' Grave said.

'We've got their statements on record.' Sarge didn't look happy to have the investigation out of his control.

Historically, her boss refused to bring in a detective from Adelaide. It was often a point of contention between the two of them.

'You do, but those statements are nearly ten years old, and we both know your Senior Constable wasn't exactly reliable.'

The investigating officer for Ron Johnston's death was Len Holmes, who was now in jail for covering up the murder his wife committed at Coober Pedy. The case was Jenny's first murder, and all in her first week in town. There was no doubt Len dropped the ball on Nick's dad's death and his mother's missing person report, but Jenny knew her boss accepted some of the blame on his broad shoulders.

His daughter died not long before and he was wallowing in grief, on a drunken bender. Len was covering a lot of ground, but mismanagement was just that. Now they were left to find the truth.

Sarge didn't respond.

'Al isn't it?' Grave turned to the old jackaroo, whose eyes followed the first bone Penny recovered as it made its way to the black body bag.

Penny placed the bone low on the left side of the recovery board.

Al made eye contact and nodded.

'You've been working here a while?' Grave's tone was calm, friendly, but focussed.

Al nodded.

'Don't say much do you Al?'

'No Miss.'

'Call me Dawn.'

Al nodded but didn't respond. He idly sucked on his unlit rollie, still hanging at the corner of his mouth. Jenny knew he'd relight it at some point, but it was extinguished more often than not.

'Al. Who else works here and was around back then?'

'Ed.' Al's shoulders lifted. 'No one else. The white fellas come and go for shearing, but…'

Detective Grave waited for more, but it didn't come. Jenny smiled. *But* on the end of a sentence wasn't uncommon out in the bush.

Had a good day but… I'd love one of those but… Jenny was familiar with the hung sentence and ignored it now.

'Can we talk to Ed too?'

Al nodded, turned and strolled toward the bunkhouse where Al and Ed lived.

Detective Grave frowned, turned to Jenny and Sarge, then watched Al's retreating back in confusion.

'He's going to get Ed. You can go with him. Or wait and he'll bring him out. If he's back from dropping Nick off to be with Sam.' Jenny sieved dark chocolate loam from the garden bed as she spoke, eyes fixed back on her work.

'I guess I can wait here.'

'I interviewed Ed and Al, when I was trying to find my cousin.' Jenny used a gloved finger to roll what looked like a rock over, but stopped as soon as her finger touched the solid object.

Detective Grave opened her mouth to ask a question, but Jenny cut her off.

'Hey Penny. I think this is one of the small finger bones.'

Penny peered over from her own sieve. 'Yep.' She reached for her camera. 'Where did you collect this sieve load from?'

'Here,' Jenny pointed.

'Okay, put the sieve down there. Grab me an evidence marker and I'll take photos.'

Sarge reached for a marker from the bag and handed it to Jenny.

'Don't think you're going to have enough markers McGregor, what are there, over two hundred bones in the human body?'

'Sarge. I'm impressed. Did you study anatomy?'

'Nah. Just Googled it.'

Penny chuckled. 'I'm expecting most of the bones to be found in one place, with the main skeleton. I'll carefully excavate them and should be able to get photos of the rest all in one spot. It's only the bones dislodged when Nick used the front-end loader that I need to photograph individually.'

'Makes sense.'

Jenny placed the sieve down with the marker and Penny shot a series of photos before collecting the bone and placing it on the body bag.

'You said you questioned Al and Ed, Constable?'

Grave picked up where she left off.

'I did. When I got the chance, I asked them if they ever saw Melanie here. Ed did, but Al couldn't recall. That was all before Melanie turned up.'

'Did either of them see your aunt?'

'Neither of them recalled her there.'

'I've read Melanie Williams' missing person report. Did your cousin ever tell you why she disappeared?'

'Not really.'

Jenny mulled the answer over. Melanie told her one of her teachers took advantage of her. She claimed her son Tristan was the teacher's boy, but Jenny now knew that wasn't the truth. Philip Treloar never stalked Melanie and it was unlikely Tristan was his son. The teacher *wasn't* the reason Melanie ran away.

But she had no intention of telling Grave her cousin lied to her.

Detective Grave's expression said she was ready to pursue a better explanation, but Jenny kept her head down and focussed on her work, hoping to deter her.

There was nothing to add. Melanie and her aunt ran off in her final year of school. Jenny spent nearly ten years trying to find them – even accepting the junior constable's job in Coober Pedy, but once Nick's dad's death was ruled a homicide, Melanie resurfaced. Only to walk out on Jenny again last month – apparently to return home, wherever *home* was.

Since then, Melanie hadn't called. Jenny recently asked her mum and dad where Melanie was living, but she was met with silence. The very same silence they offered her when Melanie disappeared back in high school.

There was nothing she could tell Detective Grave. She was not privy to the real reason Melanie left and she had no idea where to find her now.

Grave seemed to accept her silence. The team worked on, slowly sifted the loose dirt from Nick's tractor bucket and surrounding area and Grave waited for Al to return.

'What's happening?' Ed arrived, Al followed behind with his relit smoke dangling from his lip and his eyes downcast. 'Dad said you wanted to interview us.'

Sarge stepped forward. 'Hey Ed. This is Detective Grave. She's here from Adelaide Major Crimes department to handle this case.' Sarge nodded to the excavation site behind him. 'How are Nick and Sam doing?'

'I didn't see Sam. Dropped Nick off. Rebecca met us out front. We phoned ahead to let Mrs B. know we were coming and about this.' He waved at the few bones displayed on the black plastic.

Jenny stilled her stomach. Rebecca was the publican's daughter, childhood friend of Nick's and part time administrator for the station. For a time, Nick and Rebecca were expected to get married, but they didn't go ahead.

It wasn't an official arrangement, just an assumption and Nick told Jenny he had no feelings for Rebecca, but she wasn't sure Rebecca shared his opinion. Their first meeting was tense, the second not much better.

Now they seemed to get along, but still, Nick was upset, she should be with him for emotional support.

What if?

She forced the thought aside. The most important thing now was confirming if this was Patricia Johnston. Nick and Sam needed closure and she was going to give it to them.

'Ed. How old are you?' Grave steered him away from the excavation site as she spoke.

'Twenty-eight.'

'So you were how old when Ron Johnston died? Eighteen?'

'Nearly nineteen. Why?'

'Do you remember much about the weeks leading up to Ron's death and Patricia disappearing?'

'Do you think that's *her*?' Ed turned and pointed to the growing collection of bones – his face hard to read.

'We don't know yet, but it's possible. Can you answer the question?' Grave's tone was calm, methodical.

Ed scratched his head and screwed up his nose as he thought.

'I remember Jenny's cousin. Melanie was here around then.'

They both glanced at Jenny who quickly averted her gaze to return to sifting dirt. But not before noticing a curve of Detective Grave's lips.

Sprung!

'Any fights, domestic disturbances?'

'We live over there. They lived in there.' Ed pointed from the staff quarters two buildings over from the machinery shed, to the main homestead close to three hundred metres away. It was further than the average suburban houses would have been.

'So you didn't hear anything?'

Ed rubbed the stubble on his chin and Jenny wondered if he knew something – had known something all along and wasn't telling her or the detective.

'Nah.'

'What about visitors to the property? You said Constable Williams' cousin was here, anyone else out of the ordinary?'

'A few comings and goings. It was getting close to shearing time. The team hadn't turned up yet, but their boss called by to check the shearing quarters were ready.'

'You said a few comings and goings,' Grave coaxed.

Ed jiggled his shoulders as he bit his lip. Previously he mentioned Melanie stayed on the property and appeared to be sick. She likely was, with morning sickness.

Penny cleared her throat. Jenny realised she'd stopped sifting again and was staring at Ed. Refocussing on her work, she kept her eyes down, but her ears open.

'May I remind you this is now a *double* homicide investigation Ed. Anything you can recall, no matter how trivial, could help us.'

Ed sniffed, then drew a slow, steady breath.

'I feel bad.'

Jenny's pulse quickened at those three words.

'Why?' Grave asked the question Jenny desperately wanted to.

Her entire body stiffened, but she forced herself to keep working. Filling the sieve with another small trowel of dirt, she shook gently, hoping no bones would distract her from listening in.

'I should have said something back then, but old man Johnston shot himself. I didn't know he was murdered until recently. Back then it didn't seem important, but now...' Ed nodded to the excavation site.

'Now you know Mrs Johnston could have been killed around the same time.'

How could Detective Grave be so calm? Jenny's heart raced as she held her breath, waiting, desperately listening to what Ed was about to say.

'I didn't think of it at the time. It was only a car.'

Grave pursed her lips, but only nodded as she waited patiently for Ed to continue.

'I remember it because she was a beauty. A bloody classic car.'

Sarge crossed his arms and splayed his legs. Penny held a brush mid-air and Jenny's stomach churned with a mix of excitement and anxiety.

'Any day now Ed,' Grave coaxed, her patience obviously wearing thin.

'Sorry.' Ed looked coy. 'It must have been hard bringing a restored vintage car like that out on these roads, but the old Holden Sandman panel van seemed to handle the rough road pretty nicely.'

Jenny's heart leapt into her throat.

'Where did you see it?' Grave pulled a notepad from her shoulder bag.

'I saw it a couple of times. Once parked up outside the front gate. Looked like they might be lost.'

Did you see who was driving it?'

'No.' Ed shook his head.

Jenny opened her mouth but couldn't speak. Penny grabbed her by the elbow as she rose on unsteady legs.

'Are you okay?'

She must have been whiter than a sheet. Bright lights blinked at the edge of her vision and her mind grew foggy like she was mildly drunk.

'Jen?'

She was vaguely aware of everyone staring at her as she sank slowly to the ground.

'Williams?'

Sarge rushed to her side, but Jenny shook herself, willing the tunnel vision away. The rushing of blood in her ears subsided as Sarge's arm reached for hers.

'I think I might know who owns that car.' The words from her mouth were a whisper in her ears, but everyone waited on the rest of her reply.

'It could be a coincidence,' she mumbled to herself.

No one spoke for a few heartbeats, but eventually Sarge's usually gruff voice softly reached her ears.

'Take a breath Williams and let's have it.'

She did as she was instructed. The slow breath did nothing to ease the tightness in her chest. There was no way around it. The truth would come out one way or another. Ed saw him at William Creek Station, but why?

'My brother has a classic Holden panel van. Turquoise green, with a double pin-stripe down the sides.'

'That's the one.' Ed grinned, somehow not seeing how complicated this case had suddenly become.

Chapter 4

Jenny was numb, physically and emotionally as she sank to the ground on her haunches. Could Geoff be involved in Nick's parents' deaths or was he just visiting Melanie? If it were the latter, why on earth didn't he say something about it to her?

Did everyone except her know why and where her cousin disappeared to back in two-thousand and six?

'You okay?' Penny bent down next to Jenny.

Sarge hovered.

Jenny nodded, but inside her stomach clenched in a desperate effort to keep her morning coffee down.

'How am I going to tell Nick my *brother* was here when his parents died?'

'You're not.' Penny pulled Jenny to her feet as she rose.

'I can't keep this from him.'

'This is an ongoing investigation Constable. You'll keep *everything* to yourself. Do you understand me?' Detective Grave's earlier sympathetic tone evaporated.

'Yes Ma'am.'

'Don't *Ma'am* me. I'm barely a decade older than you.' Her expression softened.

'Yes Detective,' Jenny tried again.

Grave scrunched her lips together, seeming to consider if Detective was any better than Ma'am, but shook her head as though it suddenly didn't matter anymore.

'We'll need to speak with your brother, but for now, we can assume he was here for your cousin.'

'*We could.*'

'I hear a *but* in there Constable?'

Jenny was in no mood to be rehashing the entire story behind the last ten years, but it seemed as though there was no choice.

Detective Grave already said she'd read the case notes?

'You already know my cousin and aunt came to William Creek Station back in two-thousand and six and were never seen again. When I transferred here, I found out Ron and Patricia Johnston took in domestic violence victims and helped them relocate, but I still couldn't find out what happened to Melanie…

Until she turned up a few months ago after hearing we reopened Ron Johnston's death as a murder investigation. It's possible Geoff was visiting Melanie, but if he was, he was keeping it from me because, like I said, I've spent ten years looking for her.'

Jenny was breathless. Sharing her decade long obsession with hunting down her missing cousin came out in a rush. She calmed herself with a few measured breaths.

From becoming a cop straight out of school, to taking a job in the middle of nowhere – her whole adult life had revolved around finding Melanie.

'So you don't see why your brother would have been out here, since no one was supposed to know your cousin and aunt came here?'

'Exactly.'

Except Jenny knew her mum and dad knew more than they were telling her about Melanie's life. It was her dad who phoned her last month to tell her Tristan's dad was dangerous and might want to hurt Melanie or Tristan and somehow knew they were with Jenny.

Detective Grave rubbed the back of her neck as though a headache were looming. Jenny could relate.

‘So the next question is, do we call your brother and ask him why he was out here? Or do we assume he’s connected to our investigation and treat him as a suspect in the murders of Ron and Patricia Johnston?’

Jenny was stunned a detective would even consider keeping her in the loop, let alone asking *her* if *her* brother could have committed murder.

‘This is just bizarre.’ Jenny rubbed her hands over her eyes, hoping when she opened them, this would all be over. But as her vision cleared, five faces stared back at her for an answer.

Ed and Al watched silently. Penny seemed like she wanted to interject, and Sarge switched his weight from one foot to the other, arms gripping tightly over his chest.

‘I’m not a detective, Detective Grave but if I was, I’d have to treat everyone as a possible suspect until we can eliminate them. So I guess we get someone in Adelaide to pay my brother a visit.’

Detective Grave smiled. ‘I’ll make a call.’ She turned to Ed. ‘I’ll need a written statement from you.’

‘I’ll get that.’ Sarge stepped forward and Jenny couldn’t help but wonder when the last time he recorded a witness statement was, but said nothing.

‘Considering your connection to the victim and our possible suspects Williams, I think I need to ask you to step away from the investigation for now.’

‘But Ma…’ she stopped herself but didn’t get the chance to finish. It seemed getting her opinion and keeping her in the loop was short lived.

‘Not up for discussion Constable. Go see your boyfriend. Take a break. McGregor will recover our victim and collect any evidence on scene. If we need your help, we’ll let you know.’

'Is that really necessary?' Sarge was poised, pen in hand, but his focus was on Detective Grave.

'I'm afraid so. Williams just said it herself. We need to eliminate anyone close to her before she can re-join the investigation.'

'Well, you can eliminate Sam and Nick Johnston.' Sarge waved his pen in the air.

'And why is that?'

'Nick was at university in Adelaide and Sam was nine.'

'Well, the university alibi shouldn't be hard to substantiate, but I'm not writing off a nine-year-old just yet.'

'You're kidding?' Sarge's chest puffed out as he squared off to face Detective Grave. 'The kid wouldn't hurt a fly.'

'You'd be surprised what I've seen Sergeant Mackenzie, but either way, I've read the files on this investigation and it's less than stellar.'

Jenny tried not to consider exactly what Detective Grave must have been exposed to if she could think a nine-year-old boy would kill his parents.

'The whereabouts of the Johnston boys was not mentioned in the report. There are no witness statements, only a brief reference to Al here calling the Coober Pedy police station. The staff weren't subsequently questioned. No autopsy. Limited photos of the scene and you Sergeant. You haven't signed off on one report. Not one.

So I'm not sure your opinion on either of the Johnston boys can be taken without some scrutiny. Ron Johnston's death was ruled a suicide, even though his wife was unaccounted for at the time. Sloppy work at best. Deliberately negligent at worst.'

Sarge's gaze shifted to the ground a moment, then his eyes shot back to Grave.

'I'll accept that. I was suffering from grief and my personal issues at the time kept me from my work.'

'Is that what we call it these days?'

Sarge's eyebrows rose. There was no doubt Detective Dawn Grave was very familiar with exactly what Sarge's *personal issues* were. Jenny wanted to stand up for him, but the detective wasn't exactly wrong, and Sarge knew it.

Silence hung heavy in the air.

'None of this is relevant right now.' The words were out of Jenny's mouth before she could stop herself.

Detective Grave turned away from Sergeant McKenzie to face Jenny. Her mouth opened, then she closed it and nodded curtly.

'You're right. I'll call Adelaide and get them to track down Geoff Williams. Sergeant, you take Ed's statement. McGregor, get on with the recovery and get our victim off to Doc in Adelaide. I want a cause of death. Then keep digging in there for any additional evidence. I'll follow up with the Adelaide University and get a hold of Nick Johnston's attendance records.'

'And I'll go see how Nick is doing,' Jenny announced before Grave could tell her to leave again. Turning, she started toward her car.

'Williams.'

Jenny turned back.

'Detective?'

'Like I said. I've read your file. If you find anything, *anything* at all, I want to know about it. Don't go off on your own.'

Jenny pursed her lips.

'I'm serious. You're a candidate for a detective position in the future. Don't blow your career by stuffing up *my* investigation. Keep what you heard here today to yourself. All of it. And if you get even the slightest whiff of a lead, you bring it to me or your Sergeant.'

Grave's finger waggled in the air and pointed in her direction with every word.

'I've got it Detective. Can I go now?'

'Yes. Not a word.'

'I've got it!'

But all Jenny could think about as she strode to her car was how her brother visited Melanie at the William Creek Station and how her own family kept all this from her for the last decade. And how much she desperately needed to tell Nick *everything*. Her insides were burning up with suppressed emotions.

On face value it seemed everyone but her knew where Melanie was all this time. Everyone kept it from her, but why? And if she told Nick, would he understand? Or would he start to suspect her brother had something to do with his parents' deaths?

Her mind jumped to Sam as she dragged the heavy door of her Dodge truck open and slid behind the wheel.

Did Grave seriously suspect Sam? It was true no one got a statement from Al or even confirmed if he found Ron's body sprawled and bloody, hunched over the kitchen table in the William Creek kitchen with a rifle in his hand.

Maybe Sam found his dad dead. Or was it Ed or since Al called the station, did he discover the body?

Why was that piece of information missing from the police report? Was it on purpose? Was Senior Constable Len Holmes slack or just over worked? Or did he leave out *that* detail to protect someone?

Chapter 5

Jenny's stomach grumbled with hunger pangs despite the morning's trauma. Or maybe it was anxiety making her crave a medium-rare steak and chips.

A cloud of dust drifted in the air as she ignored the speed limit and rushed to the William Creek Pub to be with Nick.

Her mind raced as she considered if she should ask Nick who'd found his dad's body. Grave warned her off the investigation, but since when had that ever worked?

When she transferred to Coober Pedy, her first case was a dead woman at the bottom of an opal mine. She believed the woman was murdered. It was the source of many arguments between her and Sergeant Mackenzie, but now it seemed he was generally inclined to trust her instincts.

Would Grave be annoyed if she asked Nick? No doubt, but deep down she was desperate to know the truth. Deep down she needed to know if Melanie or her brother had anything to do with Nick's parents' murder.

The thought made her stomach growl again.

Pulling up outside the low set pub, she applied the handbrake, leant back and rested her head against the rear window. The last twenty-four hours were hectic. She was tired *before* hearing about Geoff's car. Now, she was anxious.

But Nick and Sam needed her. Breathing slow, calming breaths she waited for her emotions to settle, then she pulled the keys from the ignition and opened the door to step out.

A group of Japanese tourists hurried into an airconditioned coach with a twitter of unrecognised chatter.

The bus driver wore a cap resembling a boat captain's. He tipped the brim as she passed by, still in uniform. The burst of air-conditioning flooding from the open doorway reminded Jenny of her first visit to the pub.

That day was scorching. The flies relentless. Today was a dry and crisp upper twenty degrees. The sun shone brightly. Jenny adjusted her Akubra, thankful there were no flies crawling up her nose today.

Following the dust-covered concrete veranda, she reached the entrance. Taking a final steadying breath, she smoothed her features and entered.

The bar was the opposite of the sombre mood she was expecting.

What was she expecting?

The William Creek Pub was an Australian icon. People travelled from all over Australia and the world to stop in at the infamous location. It was the place where the rich flew in and taxied their light aircraft down the road like cars, stopping for a few pints at the pub.

A place where charity rally races pulled in for a pitstop or to sign caps and flags and banners and various memorabilia that lined the walls around the polished timber bar.

People queued three deep, waiting for the cool, bitter lager on tap. A hum rolled over the room and the smell of beer and fried food hung heavy in the air.

Jenny's stomach growled again. Only confirming it was hunger, not anxiety bringing it to life.

Approaching the bar, Jenny caught Mrs B.'s eye. The tall, lean woman waved her toward the kitchen end of the bar.

'Nick and Sam are out back. Tell Becca to get her butt back in here.'

'You're flat-out Mrs B., what's on?'

'This is just standard for a spring weekend.'

'I'll get Becca.'

'Thanks Luv.'

Jenny almost bumped into Mick, Mrs B.'s son and Sam's best mate as she ducked into the kitchen to head out back.

'Hey Constable. Sorry about that.'

'No Mick, my fault. You're mum's pretty busy.'

'I know. Just heading to help out now.' Mick shuffled past.

'How's Sam doing?'

Mick shrugged. 'He's been better.'

Mick didn't wait for an answer. Jenny hovered a moment, watching the crowd milling about – smiling, chatting, drinking and eating. The sight made her tense. How often did the world simply carry on oblivious to other people's troubles?

Her daydream was interrupted as a barmaid hurried past with two bowls of pasta on one arm two more plates on the other.

Jenny's stomach growled loud enough to make the waitress giggle.

'Where's the back door?'

The woman lifted one loaded arm and indicated the back of the kitchen.

'Thanks.'

Jenny dodged another waitress and a young man in checked pants with a white button up coat.

She should have gone around the back of the building and not cut through the kitchen, but it was too late now. Opening the back door, she stopped to get her bearings. A treated pine rail fence lined up on either side, corralled the yard. Garbage bins ran down one side, a bench seat along the other.

'Hey Jen.' Nick stood, leaving Rebecca's arm abandoned and hanging in the air.

'Nick. I'm so sorry I took so long.'

He wrapped his arms around her waist and pulled her close.

'You're here now.'

'Where's Sam?'

Jenny peered over his shoulder.

'He's gone for a walk. He needed some space.'

Jenny watched Rebecca watching them and remembered Mrs B. inside.

'Hi Bec. Sorry to break up this…' *Whatever this was!* 'Your mum said to tell you to get your, you know what back inside. It's bedlam in there.'

'Since I'm not needed out here, might as well.' Rebecca stalked past almost spinning Jenny aside.

'Did I interrupt something?'

Jenny studied Nick's eyes.

'We were just talking old times, when mum…' he choked on the word.

'I get it. I'm sorry. I wish I knew your mum. Sounds like she was pretty awesome.'

'She was.'

'Can we go for a walk too?'

'I'd like that.' Nick collected her hand in his and led her away from the back of the pub and out past the site where most of the fibro accommodation units were burnt down. The same arsonist who destroyed Nick's home, destroyed much of the pub's accommodation too.

'Are they going to rebuild?' Jenny nodded to the charred concrete slab.

'I think Mrs B.'s going to stick with renting tent and caravan space. The one set of units survived, but for the most part, travellers through here come towing vans, or in self-contained trucks these days.

'That makes sense. Less overheads with camping sites too.'

'Hmmm.'

Jenny could feel Nick's eyes on her.

'You okay?' he asked.

'Me? I should be asking you that question.'

'Maybe, but you look worried.'

Jenny sighed. Could she keep the truth from Nick? *Should she?*

'I'm just so sorry about your mum. *If* it's your mum.' She added the latter in a rush.

'It's her.'

'How can you be sure?'

Nick shrugged. 'I can't, but I always believed mum must have been dead. There is no other reason why she'd have left Sam here, at the age of nine, all alone.'

'I wish I could do something.'

'You can.' Nick's eyes held hers. She frowned. 'You can find whoever did this and throw them into a deep, dark cell for the rest of their lives.'

Jenny bit her lip. What if that someone was Geoff? Her own brother. But it couldn't be. Geoff was a surfer bum. He wore his hair long and curly and smoked too much dope and worked as little as possible, but he wasn't a murderer.

'Nick, did Al find your dad's body? He called the station, but there is no witness statement. Nothing to say how or when he found your dad.'

It was Nick's turn to bite his lip. Did he know Len left that detail out?

'Al was the first adult who found dad.'

'Adult?' Jenny coaxed.

'Sam found dad. Len didn't know. Al said he was the one to find dad.'

'Why?'

'Kids are kids in indigenous culture until they are thirteen and are initiated. I don't believe it was on purpose. Al wouldn't think to mention Sam.'

'But that means he was never interviewed, but he also never would have received counselling.'

'He bounced back pretty quickly.'

'Nick. I saw the crime scene photos. So did you. That's horrific for a nine-year-old. It would have been very confrontational.'

'Do you want to speak to him about it?'

Jenny wanted to do exactly that, but she wasn't on the case. She wasn't allowed to be on the case, but that was a whole new conversation she needed to have with Nick.

Would he understand?

Chapter 6

'You know how we worked on Melanie's case together? How we started working on your dad's?'

'Yes.' Nick studied her carefully.

'You know how I was worried someone at your place might have hurt Melanie, but we didn't dwell on it, we focussed on the evidence?'

'Jenny, what's going on?'

Jenny's stomach grumbled and Nick chuckled. The mood lifted.

'Let's get you some food before we go find Sam.'

'Hang on. I need to get this out. I'm not supposed to tell you anything because of our connection to the victim or possible victims.'

Nick cringed at the word, but then frowned. 'What do you mean *our* connection? You never met my mum or dad.'

'Well, I'm technically connected because of you.'

'But I'm not a suspect, surely. I was in Adelaide, at Uni.'

'Detective Grave is checking that out, but that's not the issue.'

'Detective Grave.'

'She's the lead detective, from Adelaide, but Nick, I'm not only connected because of you.'

Nick waited. Jenny reached for Nick's other hand, turning him to face her, holding his gaze and secretly begging him to understand.

'It's possible one of my relatives, not Melanie, not Aunt Carolyn, but another relative was seen at William Creek Station the day or the days before your dad died.'

'What?' Nick baulked, reflexively removing his hands from Jenny's.

The warmth drained from her body.

'Ed saw a car. The description he gave fits my brother Geoff's car. It could be a coincidence. Geoff might not have been driving. I don't know.' She shook her head, pin pricks stabbed at the back of her eyes, exploding into hot tears and cascading down her face, dripping from her chin.

'I don't know *anything* anymore. My family have kept me in the dark, fed me lies. Melanie has lied. Everyone has lied to me.'

Nick stepped closer once more, wrapping his arms around her.

'Don't….I should be the one consoling you.' Jenny tried to escape his embrace. 'You've lost your mum and your dad.' Her voice sounded nasally, tears dripped from her checks and pooled on Nick's shoulder as he held her close, not letting her go.

'But I found you, or you found me and if it wasn't for Melanie, for mum and dad's death, we might never have met.'

Jenny's head swam with the idiotic logic. But Nick was right. Out of all the mess, the chaos that was her family and his, they were together.

'For someone who wouldn't even say hello to me, you've certainly learnt how to put the positive spin in a story Nick Johnston. I'm sold.'

'So I'm guessing you're off the case because a car, matching your brother's was seen at the station before my dad was killed?'

Jenny nodded.

'That sucks!'

'I agree, but Detective Grave warned me not to share anything with you until your alibi was checked. And she explicitly told me not to go off on my own.'

Nick smiled. 'She's been speaking with Sarge then.'

'No. Apparently my record reflects my illustrious investigative career.' She smiled, pulled her sleeve over her palm and wiped the tears from her face.

'Let's find Sam, and Al and see if we can work out where to start. The police might be able to tell you what to do Constable Williams, but they can't tell me.'

'I can quiz Penny and I will still be able to view the information at work on Monday. I'm also going to ring home and see where Geoff is.'

'Is that wise?'

'What. You think Geoff could be involved?'

'And you don't?'

'I don't doubt his car was at the homestead, but he wouldn't *kill* anyone.'

'Would he cover up for someone?'

Jenny studied Nick's face a moment. It was entirely possible, but for who? Melanie? Aunt Carolyn? Whoever was chasing Mel?

'I think I need to find out who the hell Melanie was running from. I'll call her.'

'Is she taking your calls?'

'Not since she left a few weeks ago.'

'Don't you think that's strange?'

'Yes, but then again, not when you think about it. She went ten years without telling me where she was or if she was alive or dead.'

'But she turned up when Nellie shared the blog post about dad. Maybe she knew something?'

'Maybe she did! Maybe that's what she's running from?'

'I think trying to contact her is a bad idea, Jen.'

Jenny watched Nick's expression, trying to read it. He was uncomfortable with Melanie toward the end of her visit and wasn't exactly devastated when she left.

'I don't think I have a choice. Melanie is messed up big time, but I can't help thinking her past and your parents' deaths are connected. Especially now Geoff's car might have been seen around the time your dad was killed.'

'This new detective warned you off, so let's leave your family alone for now. We can start with Sam, then Al.'

'We can't go back to your place until Penny is finished, but I'll text her to call me as soon as she's done.'

'And until then. Let's eat.'

A thought popped into Jenny's head as Nick led her back toward the pub. 'You and Rebecca.'

'Don't even think about it. I told you, there was never any attraction between the two of us. It was always more like brother and sister. We grew up together. There aren't a lot of choices out this way and I think our parents just thought we'd make a nice match.'

Jenny let Nick kiss her cheek as he wrapped his arm around her shoulder and pulled her to him. But in the back of her mind, she was distracted by her concern Rebecca might have had feelings for Nick back then, and still did… and they weren't sisterly ones.

Chapter 7

As the sun began to dip over the horizon, the cool desert air settled in. Jenny and Nick waited on the veranda outside the William Creek Pub, not only for word Penny was finished at the homestead, but to hear from Sam.

'Did he take his car?'

Jenny asked calmly as Nick paced the front veranda, dust stirring around his feet with each step.

Jenny's mobile pinged. She dragged it from her top pocket, wondering why she stayed in her uniform all day when she was dismissed from active duty.

'It's a message from Penny. We are clear to head back to your place.'

'Ask her if Sam turned up.'

Jenny typed a quick text, unsure if the message would get through or not. Reception this far out was patchy. If it wasn't for the pub booster, there would be no signal at all. For all she knew Penny could be back in Coober Pedy sending that message.

Her phone buzzed in her hand. She almost dropped it but recovered and slid the answer bar across.

'Hey.'

'Hi. He didn't call in while I was there.'

'What time did you leave?' Jenny glanced at her watch.

'About an hour ago. I would have phoned you earlier, but there was no reception. Plane landed twenty minutes ago in town.'

'Guessed as much. Sam took off at lunch. Probably just wanted some space to clear his head, but Nick is worried about him.'

'For good reason.'

'You got anything to share?'

'I'm heading for a shower. I'll call you back later.'

Jenny considered Penny's carefully worded answer. She was either tired, unwilling to help or most likely still with Detective Grave and Sarge.

'I'll be on the road heading back to start work tomorrow. I might be off the case, but I still need to front up to the station tomorrow morning.'

Someone opened the pub door down the end of the veranda. A few chords of a Keith Urban song followed them out the door. Jenny blocked one ear so she could hear Penny.

'I'll see you at Niko's for coffee then?'

'Deal.' Jenny hung up. Her mouth watered at the thought of the Serbian café coffee.

What a day!

'What now?'

She turned to Nick. 'Can I help you look for Sam before I head back to town?'

'You shouldn't be driving on dusk. You'll hit a roo.'

'Should we look for Sam then?'

'It's too late to go looking for him tonight. You're probably right. He's likely just blowing off steam.'

'Would he decompress without Mick? I would have thought they'd be out shooting or something, but Mick's still here working.'

'It's not unusual for Sam to need some space. He might seem bright and happy on the outside, but he's got a bit of his big brother in there too.' Jenny could see the shy curve at the edge of Nick's lip.

'No. Really!'

She held her hand to her chest and faked a shocked expression.

'We both tend to vacate the universe occasionally.' Nick relaxed and reached for her hand. 'Why don't you stay with me tonight?' He lifted her arm by the fingertips and wound it around her head, making her twirl on the spot. 'We could head back in and do a little dancing.'

'I didn't think you were the dancing type.'

'I followed you to that B and S ball didn't I?'

'Yes, but I never saw you dance.'

'No. A murder kind of put an end to the night.'

Jenny remained silent a moment too long. Nick twirled her around once more, then held her to his chest.

'What's up?'

'Maybe *I am* a murder-magnet.'

'You're a magnet alright, but it has nothing to do with murder.'

Nick's lips brushed hers.

'I'm so sorry about your mum and dad.' Her words were soft.

'How about we ignore all of that tonight and head in for a dance? I'll ask Mrs B. if we can stay here tonight. You head to work in the morning. I'll head home and find Sam.

'I think that's the best idea I've heard all day.'

Chapter 8

The stereo system in her vintage Dodge truck consisted of an obsolete six stacker disc system which Jenny hadn't bothered to update. The same six CD's that came with the car rotated through a playlist she knew by heart.

Since working with Nick on their shared family mysteries, and then dating, she drove the two hours out and back to William Creek often over the past nine months. The mix of nineties hits and country rock was somehow comforting as she mulled over how she was going to stay in on the investigation, without getting into trouble with Detective Grave.

The city detective was right. Jenny had no intention of stuffing up her career chances but solving these two murders was at the top of her list, and the quicker she could sink her teeth in, the better.

But if she couldn't eliminate Geoff or Melanie from the suspect list, she'd remain benched.

Unless I convince Detective Grave that I can be impartial.

She pulled the handbrake on outside Niko's café, her mind made up. She was going to set the record straight. This was a small town. Everyone almost always knew someone involved in each investigation. Staying clear-headed and impartial was in the job description.

She slammed the heavy door, with the patchwork paint job of light blue, grey and mint green. The noise echoed through the quiet street.

'Gentlemen.' Jenny tipped her Akubra to the two old men who flanked the café entrance each morning.

'Constable,' they mumbled in unison.

Jenny smiled. It took a while, but they warmed to a female cop, eventually.

The screen door creaked as she entered the café.

'Constable.'

'You're supposed to call me Jenny, Niko.'

'Your friend has ordered already.'

Jenny glanced over to the table at the rear of the café where Penny sat hoovering down an apple turnover.

Jenny's stomach grumbled, quieter than usual.

'Can I grab one of those too thanks Niko?'

'Got one!' Penny held up a white paper bag and grinned – her lips rimmed with a light coating of icing sugar.

Jenny rolled her lips to suppress a laugh but failed as whipped cream squeezed from the sides of the turnover and Penny simultaneously tried to lick it up and catch it in her hand.

'Can't take me anywhere.' She licked cream from her fingertips one by one.

'That's the truth.' Jenny pulled a chair out and reached for the paper bag containing her treat.

'How did the excavation go in the end?'

'I'm not supposed to talk about it.' Penny spoke through another mouthful of cream.

'Yeah, but you and I know I'm not staying out of this. Right!'

Penny swallowed, reached for her coffee, sipped it calmly, appearing to ponder Jenny's statement.

'We are confident the body is likely to be Patricia's. Right size, time in the ground, but Doc will confirm with dental records this morning.'

'So, we have a double homicide at William Creek Station and my brother's car was last seen on the premises, along with my cousin, and maybe even my Aunt Carolyn.

Three of my family were near or around at the time of the murders.'

'That about sums it up.'

'Shit!'

'You got that right,' Penny sighed, reached for Jenny's arm, and patting the wrist lightly.

'I'm going to push to stay on this. What do you know about Grave?'

'Detective Dawn Grave, born in far North Queensland somewhere. Rose up through the ranks faster than normal, especially for a woman. Doesn't mince words. Doesn't take any crap from the boys either, but she's got a diplomatic streak.'

'Has she got a relative, high up in the force or something?'

Both women knew making Sergeant in your mid-thirties wasn't common for any female on the force.

'Nope, but she's received a few commendations. Not your average cop.'

'Impressive.'

'I don't think she wants to shut you out.'

'She certainly made it sound like she wanted to.'

Penny shrugged. 'She can't stop you listening in on what's going on and following up avenues that don't involve your family directly.'

'That was my thought.' Jenny sipped her coffee. A thought mulled around her head as she wondered if it was worth pursuing.

'Sam found his dad's body.'

'That's not in the report.' Penny's expression was hard to read.

'He was only nine.'

'You should tell Dawn.'

It felt odd to call the detective by her first name, so she didn't.

'I can't tell Grave. Nick will know it was me and she has it in her head a nine-year-old kid could do something like this. I don't want to give her any ammunition.'

'When you've seen what we've seen you might understand why she can believe that.'

'I don't want to see what you've seen if that's the case.'

'It could have been an accident.'

'Ron yes. Patricia? I don't think so. He certainly didn't bury her in the veggie patch on his own.'

'We don't know who died first?' Penny drained her coffee and put the remaining half of her turnover back into the paper bag. 'Ron could have killed and buried Patricia. Sam could have seen it and used the gun to kill his dad.'

'That is a horrible thought.' Jenny put her own turnover back in the bag, untouched, her appetite gone.

'Do me a favour and keep that hypothesis to yourself for now and that bit about Sam finding his dad's body.'

'I just find the evidence.'

'Tell me there is no evidence to indicate Sam had anything to do with either murder.'

'I can't tell you anything yet. I'm still processing what we recovered.'

Chapter 9

Jenny glazed over, her mind elsewhere as she wiggled the mouse, finger tapping to an unheard beat.

'You right there?' Philips handed her a cappuccino with the letter *J* inside a heart written on the top in black ink.

'Ah. Yeah. Thanks.' She reached for the coffee realising she hadn't even seen Philips leave the station to go to Niko's café for a morning tea run.

An eerie vibe filled the station. Jenny observed everything like she was hovering outside her body. Being excluded from the investigation was some form of brutal torture she wasn't sure she could endure much longer.

The sound of Sarge's office door opening made her snap out of her funk.

'Williams, Philips, O'Connell. In here.'

Philips passed O'Connell his coffee, then followed the Senior Constable into Sergeant McKenzie's office.

Jenny didn't know where to sit. Detective Grave occupied the chair opposite Sarge's desk. No one ever sat in Sergeant McKenzie's chair, so that left standing by the doorway, where Philips usually hovered. Or leaning against the side wall near the whiteboard.

She decided the other side of the room was her best option. It gave her a better view of the whiteboard.

Detective Grave nodded as Jenny found a space against the wall, leant with her shoulders against it and crossed her arms.

'Okay. Here is where we are so far.' Sarge didn't take his seat, instead, he collected the whiteboard marker and used it to point to the murder board.

Nick's dad's case occupied the back of the murder board for months. Usually, if they were all gathered in Sarge's office it was to view the front, with a new case. Finally having Nick's dad's death and now his mum's front and centre sent a chill down her spine.

'We've known Ron Johnston's death was murder for a few months. I've been digging through Nellie's notes from the hits she got on her blog when she featured Ron's case.' Sarge glanced at Jenny whose expression must have reflected her internal dialogue.

She discovered by accident, after talking with Nellie, that Sergeant McKenzie kept the tips he garnered from Nellie's cold case blog to himself.

'As you know, and for Grave's information, Williams' cousin Melanie came out of hiding when she discovered Ron was murdered, but so far,' he glanced at Jenny once more, 'we don't believe Melanie Williams has shed any light on Ron's death.'

All eyes turned to Jenny. Detective Grave's expression was hard to read. A mix of interest and pity was replaced with mild scepticism.

Jenny frowned and the detective's expression smoothed over.

Realising Sarge was waiting on her confirmation she drew herself up.

'Mel didn't shed any light on the case except…' she thought about it a moment. Maybe for the first time.

What was it Melanie said to Nick?

'Out with it Williams.'

'Mel did act pretty strange out at Nick's place before she left.'

'How so? Detective Grave turned in the chair to give Jenny her full attention.

Jenny shook her head slowly, trying to put her finger on why Nick's conversation with Melanie seemed strange. At the time, Nick was uncomfortable talking about it, but when she quizzed him, he said Melanie apologised for Nick's dad's death. It wasn't sympathy, more an apology, like it was her fault.

Did she feel responsible? Did she know more than she was sharing?

'It could be nothing, but Mel apologised to Nick about his dad. She was quite teary and when Nick said it wasn't her fault, he said she acted weird.'

'Why are we only just hearing about this now?' Grave turned to Sarge to read his expression, then back to Jenny.

'I guess the same reason I'm only just hearing about Sarge having a list of tips from Nellie's blog.' Jenny tried unsuccessfully not to sound snarky.

'Are you saying you believe there is a link between your cousin's time at the William Creek Station and the death of the Johnstons?'

'Do we have a positive ID on Patricia?' Jenny pushed off the wall and found herself leaning against Sergeant Mackenzie's desk, looming over Detective Grave before she knew it.

'We do.'

'Then why the hell wasn't I told!'

'Williams.' Sarge and O'Connell warned in unison.

Detective Grave said nothing, only sat back in her seat, fingers interlaced in her lap and a small curve at the corner of her lip.

'Well?' Jenny pushed.

'I like you Constable, and as I said when I got here, your reputation precedes you. But you need to remember one thing very clearly. You might have your commanding officer here eating out of your hand, but I've seen juniors like you come and go.'

'Hang on a minute,' Sarge protested. 'Williams and I definitely didn't hit it off on day one, but she's a good investigator with a nose for clues and a gut instinct for trouble.'

'I have no doubt,' Grave rose smoothly from the chair, 'but one thing a female officer *must* remember as she works her way up the ranks is that persuasion is far more productive than force.'

Jenny stepped back as Grave strolled to the whiteboard and plucked the whiteboard marker from Sergeant McKenzie's hand much like Jenny was often known to do.

Sarge frowned at his vacant hand a moment, then stepped aside to allow Detective Grave access to the board.

'Did you find anything in those tips from the blog Sergeant?'

Sarge chewed his cheek a moment. Jenny sat on the edge of his desk, arms crossed as she waited to see what Grave was planning.

'One woman, Madeline Temple stayed at William Creek the week before Ron's death. I spoke with her after Nellie organised a phone meeting. She advised she saw Melanie arrive a day or so before she left.'

'Was her mother with her?' Grave drew a line from the photo of Ron's body, splayed out on the farmhouse kitchen table covered in blood, to a photo of Melanie which Jenny had never seen on the board.

'Not according to Madeline.'

'Or Ed,' Grave added, then poised her pen on the whiteboard. 'What date did Madeline leave?'

'Tenth September.'

Grave wrote the date next to Melanie's photo.

'And when was Ron's body found?' She tapped the marker and waited.

'The twelfth.'

'By?' There was no doubt Grave knew the answer.

Was she asking Sarge or was she fishing?

Her eyes scanned Jenny's face.

Damn!

She stilled her jostling leg. Nick told her about Sam in confidence. But then again, she told Nick about her brother when she wasn't supposed to.

'Al.' Sarge answered from the file notes and Jenny let out a sigh as Grave noted Al's name on the board.

'Do we have any reason to suspect any of the farm hands,' she tapped Al's name on the board, 'would hurt the Johnstons?'

'There is no indication of any trouble. I've spoken to the neighbours. Murphy lives on the adjoining station, and he said Ron and Patricia were well respected by their staff, in particular Al and Ed who are the only permanent employees. Ron was very hands on, and Nick took over when his father died.'

'Is that the same Murphy who knew the Johnston's were relocating domestic violence victims and said nothing when Ron died?'

'He didn't think it was relevant. Patricia confided in him, and he saw no reason to share the information until we reopened Ron's case.' Sarge fought to keep the tension from his voice.

Jenny watched O'Connell sip the last of his coffee, unusually quiet. It was Senior Constable O'Connell who usually ran the day-to-day operations, but Sarge took the lead on major cases, or at least he had recently.

'None of this is news.' O'Connell finally broke his silent observations and stood, dropped his empty cup in the rubbish bin and joined Jenny sitting on Sergeant McKenzie's desk.

O'Connell was saying what Jenny was thinking. Where was Grave going with a recap? She knew the case notes. They all knew the case inside out.

Then it dawned on her. Grave was watching them all. Reading them. Reading their responses to each piece of information.

'Constable.' Grave turned to Jenny.

'Call me Jenny or Williams. There are two constables here and a senior constable and it will get very confusing otherwise.'

'Okay. Jenny. You say your cousin hasn't told you anything that ties to Ron and Patricia's murder.'

'I should be telling Nick we've ID's his mum is our victim.'

'He'll be informed through the usual channels.'

'It doesn't work like that out here.' Jenny was surprised she now understood the difference between the regional town she came from and the outback country she now occupied. There were no channels in the bush. News travelled like wildfire and the best way to tell someone their mother was dead, was face to face.

'You can call your partner after we've finished our briefing. Your cousin, Jenny. We now know she was staying at William Creek Station days before Ron died. She must know *something*. She must have seen something.'

'I've asked. She's not even told me the truth about why she ran away in the first place.' Jenny tried not to sound bitter.

'So she's been lying to you.'

Damn!

'She's been keeping things to herself. You said it yourself. William Creek was a place for domestic violence victims to find safety. She's been through a lot.'

Grave played with a curly tendril of hair that fell loose of her tight bun.

'Jenny. We've tried to get a hold of your brother Geoff.'

Jenny waited. Her stomach knotted.

'We've also tried to reach your cousin on the number you gave us.'

Sweat broke out under her arms.

'Your mother and father don't seem to know where Geoff is and according to them, your Aunt Carolyn thought Melanie was still staying with you.'

Jenny sensed O'Connell stiffen next to her. All eyes focussed her way as she tried to make sense of everything.

'Maybe she's back with Uncle Pete?'

'Adelaide based Detectives Cunningham and Fitzpatrick interviewed your father yesterday, when they tried to speak with your brother about his vehicle. They then visited your uncle, but he's not seen your cousin or brother recently.'

'How recently?' Her stomach knotted.

'Peter Williams claims he hasn't been in contact with Melanie since she went missing in September two-thousand-and-six.'

'That can't be right. Melanie said he visited her and her mother every month.'

'I think it's time we interviewed your aunt then.'

The pain in Jenny's stomach was matched by the instant headache sending electric shocks into her brain.

More lies from Melanie. She claimed Uncle Pete visited her and her mother every month since she ran away from the schoolteacher who raped her. But now Jenny knew the schoolteacher story was likely a complete and utter fabrication.

And what did Geoff have to do with any of this? He visited Melanie at William Creek Station and now he was missing along with her cousin.

Mel, what have you done?

Chapter 10

Jenny held her mobile in her hand, fingers hovering over the screen as she mulled over how she was going to tell Nick about his mum. She wanted to see him, hold him, to be the one to support him. But deep down, in the pit of her soul she knew he was already prepared for the worst.

Who else would have been buried in his backyard?

The dial tone sounded hollow. Jenny swallowed hard, her thoughts jumbling in her brain as the tone droned on.

'Hey.' Nick sounded cheerier than she expected.

'Hey yourself. Has Sam turned up yet?'

'No. I'm getting a bit worried now. Mick phoned around and no one's seen him since yesterday afternoon.'

Damn!

She desperately wanted Sam to be with Nick when she broke the news.

'He can't be far away. Is his car at the Station?'

'It is, but his bay mare Honey is gone. I think he's out riding. Swagging it. I'll go look for him if he's not back by tomorrow morning.'

'I wish I was there with you.'

'Me too.'

Silence hung in the air a moment. Jenny drew a slow, measured breath.

'Has anyone from the S.A. Police contacted you?'

On one hand she hoped they had, but on the other, she wanted to be the one to confirm Nick's suspicions.

'No. What's up Jen?'

'I've just heard news.'

'It's mum, isn't it?'

'I'm so sorry Nick. I should be there with you. Are you okay?' She held her breath with his silence, but a sound in the background made her wonder if Sam was home after all.

'Nick. What's up? Are you okay?' They were the words Jenny wanted to say, but it wasn't her saying them.

'Is that Rebecca?'

'Yeah. She didn't think it was a good idea for me to be alone.'

I bet she didn't!

'That's a good idea.'

'It's mum.' Nick confirmed and Jenny heard Becca's response but couldn't make out the words.

'I'm going to find out what happened Nick. I promise.' She kept the news about Melanie and Geoff to herself. Her gut was telling her they didn't do anything wrong. Her instincts never let her down.

'I know you are Jen. I have to go.'

'Let me know if Sam doesn't turn up.' The words rushed out. Anything to keep him on the phone. Anything to stop Becca from being the only one to catch him if he fell.

'I will.' She sensed he was going to hang up.

'Nick!'

A shuffling noise told her he was bringing the phone back to his ear.

'Yeah?'

'I haven't told you yet. I should have told you ages ago.'

'What?'

'I love you Nick Johnston.'

'I love you too Jenny Williams.'

She peered at the screen of her mobile phone, wishing with every fibre of her body to be with him right now.

The line went dead. Nick's picture popped up on her screen saver.

She should have told him about Melanie. About how Uncle Pete claimed he hadn't seen her since she ran away. She didn't know about the police in Adelaide, but Jenny needed to speak with her aunt. Now.

Opening her contacts, she found Aunt Carolyn's number. A noise made her jump.

'There you are.' Penny's hands were planted on her hips, her long hair pulled back in a low ponytail.

'Sorry. I was telling Nick the news.'

'Oh. That must have been hard.'

'Not as hard as knowing Becca is there to console him.'

'I thought you two had a bonding moment at the William Creek Pub fire?'

Jenny thought about the night Nick helped her pull two witnesses from a burning building. Rebecca and she didn't get off on the right foot by any means, but that night, Nick's childhood sweetheart finally warmed to Jenny.

Since then, while not exactly becoming firm friends, they were pleasant with one another. That didn't change the sinking feeling in Jenny's stomach warning her Rebecca still cared for Nick, whether Nick knew it or not.

'We did, but still. Nick's lonely and vulnerable.'

'Wait up there. There is nothing, and I mean nothing vulnerable about Nick Johnston.'

'You don't know him like I do.'

'Jenny. The guy is a hard rock around anyone else but you.'

'It's all show.'

'Maybe, but rest assured he *isn't* crying in Becca's arms.'

'Who?' Philips wandered out the front of the station as Jenny tried to go back inside.

'Nick. Jenny's worried Rebecca will have him in the sack with sad sex over his mum's murder.'

'Penny!' Jenny protested, but her partner was rubbing his chin in serious consideration of Penny's words.

'Nah. Not Nick. He's a one-woman kind of guy.'

'Can we go back to work now?' Jenny brushed past them.

'Actually, no. Detective Grave has tried to contact your aunt and she's not answering.'

'Oh my God, has everyone disappeared?'

'What do you mean?' Penny stopped Jenny with a gentle hand on her arm.

'Sam's gone walkabout since his mum's body was discovered. Melanie's gone. Geoff's gone.'

Penny frowned and Jenny realised Penny wasn't at the earlier briefing.

'Sorry, you missed that latest tidbit.'

'You sound like my grandmother,' Penny teased.

'It's this place. And Marj. They are rubbing off on me.'

'Grave wants you to leave your aunt a message to call as soon as she can.' Philips followed Jenny into the station. 'And we need to work with Nellie to go over the rest of her blog posts about Ron's murder.'

'And I need to finish sorting through evidence, catalogue it and send it off to the lab in Adelaide. I'll be done today and heading back in the morning.'

Jenny turned to face her friend. 'I'm not sure I can get through this one without you.'

'I'm more help to you working on evidence?'

'I'm not sure about that. There are loads of forensic techs in Adelaide and only one best friend.'

‘Hey, what am I?’ Philips teased.

Jenny ignored the comment and Philips carried on around the counter, returning to his position at the front desk.

Jenny’s eyes begged Penny, who bit her lip with obvious contemplation.

‘Melanie and my brother are mixed up in this whole mess Penny and I don’t know how I’m going to get to the bottom of it without losing my head.’

Penny sighed. ‘I’ll finish the evidence sorting and bagging, then I’ll request leave. How does that sound?’

Jenny wasn’t the hugging type, but her heart thudded like it was about to explode.

‘That would be awesome.’

‘Williams, McGregor. In here. Now!’ Sarge’s booming voice made them turn and hurry around the counter together.

Chapter 11

'What's up Sarge?' Jenny asked as she joined Senior Constable O'Connell and Sergeant Mackenzie at O'Connell's desk.

'This case is driving me nuts. We still don't have a solid motive for why anyone would want to kill Ron and Patricia Johnston.'

'The only one making any sense Sir is still the domestic violence rescue operation,' Jenny said.

'But I've gone over Nellie's blog records. I called everyone who was willing to give Nellie their details, including the witness who puts Melanie at the William Creek Station just before Ron was killed.'

Sarge strode toward his office and there was no doubt everyone was supposed to follow.

'I've reconciled each person with Ron and Patricia's records, from the ledger you and Nick found in his cellar, but there are at least three lots of initials around the same time I can't account for.'

'We could ask Gwen to put something in the paper and call for witnesses. And there's still Crime Stoppers.'

Jenny knew the Sergeant wasn't keen on asking for help, but this case was a double homicide, and Detective Grave was already involved. The quicker they got answers, the quicker Sarge would be cleared of any wrongdoing.

'Gwen and I aren't exactly on good terms.'

O'Connell scoffed and dropped heavily onto the corner of Sergeant Mackenzie's large desk.

'You want *me* to talk to her?' Jenny offered.

'Well I'm not going to.' O'Connell crossed his arms. 'I warned you about dating her.'

'Not now,' Jenny scowled. 'I'll talk to Gwen if you want her to run an article.'

'Make sure you give her only the basics.' O'Connell approached the whiteboard.

'The place will be crawling with press soon. I think we should just wait for a press conference?' Sergeant Mackenzie rounded his desk and dropped into his high-backed office chair.

'Grave is lead on this. Shouldn't she do that?' Jenny gazed around the room suddenly realising the detective was nowhere in sight. 'Where is she anyway?'

'She's relocating to the motel.'

A voice at the front counter made Philips turn to leave the room. He stopped and turned back, ducking his head inside the office door. 'It's Nellie.'

'Oh, yeah. Forgot to mention that.' Sarge sat back in his chair and steepled his fingertips. 'Show her in Philips.'

Philips frowned but did as he was told.

'What's going on Sarge?' Jenny searched her commanding officer's expression for a clue but found nothing.

'You'll find out.' He rose to greet Nellie.

Her wide smile and sparkling eyes lightened Jenny's dark mood.

'Hey!' Her grin widened.

'Hi.' Jenny said as Nellie confidently strolled into Sergeant Mackenzie's office like it was her loungeroom.

'Nellie will be joining our team.'

'You planning on becoming a cop?' The cold case blogger and investigative reporter was the last person Jenny expected her Sergeant to invite into the station during a major crime investigation.

'Not exactly.' Nellie's grin was mischievous.

'Nellie is going to be our admin assistant.'

'No offence Nel, but isn't that a conflict of interest, given you work on cold cases?'

'That's exactly why I've asked her. She's good at admin and proved it when you let her watch our front desk last month. She's got a nose for crime, much like you Williams, and she has extensive knowledge of this particular case.' Sarge crossed the room and reached for Nellie's hand.

'Welcome aboard Nellie.'

'Thanks for having me Sarge. Where do I start?'

'Watch the front for now. Then once we finish this briefing, you can help Philips and Williams track down contact information for the three bloggers on your site who match the initials in the ledger from the time of the murders. Maybe we'll get lucky.'

Nellie saluted casually and turned toward the front desk.

'I'm out of here too,' Penny waved. 'I've got evidence to sort.'

Jenny watched Penny leave.

'Grave wanted me to leave a message for my aunt. Should I do it now?'

'Let's recap what we know first. Motive people. Let's think.' Sarge turned to O'Connell who wiggled the whiteboard marker to indicate he was ready to go.

'Okay. Here's what we know.' O'Connell used the whiteboard marker as a pointer.

'Ron died September Two thousand and six. At this stage, we are assuming, based on witnesses at the station, that Patricia likely died the same day.

I spoke to McGregor earlier, and she said there is no way of knowing who died first.'

'That would have been handy.' Sarge's chair squeaked as he sat back down.

'There's no reason to believe Ron killed Patricia though, is there?' Jenny scanned faces, including Philips' as he returned from showing Nellie around the front office.

'None we've found.' O'Connell continued to wave the makeshift pointer.

Jenny's chest lightened.

'We know from those ledgers you and Nick found that Melanie was likely the last rescue staying at the homestead. Then she came back when she discovered Ron's death was a murder, according to you and Nick, all weird about it. Why?' O'Connell directed his question to Jenny.

'I still don't know, but just being around isn't a motive.'

'True. Did she do anything while she was staying out at the homestead that seemed odd?'

'Only the weird apology to Nick.'

'Nick said Melanie planted a lime tree in the garden.' Phillips' voice made Jenny turn toward the door where he hovered out of habit, one eye on the counter.

'What. And you think because she planted a lime tree, she knew Patricia's body was in there?'

'It's possible.' Grave re-joined the group as the temperature plummeted despite the warm spring weather.

'That Marj at the motel. She's a scream. Right!'

Grave's attempt to lighten the mood fell flat.

Jenny's heart pounded. They didn't seriously think Melanie could kill anyone.

Did they?

Jenny thought about her cousin's behaviour toward the end of her stay in Coober Pedy. She wondered over the sudden exit from town.

'She's definitely a bright spark.' O'Connell answered the detective to break the awkward silence.

'Have you called your aunt yet?' Grave's tone was casual, but Jenny could see the detective studying her carefully. 'And I thought I made it clear Williams wasn't investigating this case until all known suspects related to her were cleared?'

'I'm just listening to the briefing.' Jenny fought the urge to put her hands on her hips and tried unsuccessfully to lose the defensive tone.

'And doing a little grunt work on some old William Creek Station ledgers for me.' Sarge folded his arms and leant back in his chair in one smooth motion.

The detective rubbed her chin and nodded, seemingly deciding this wasn't a fight worth having.

'Williams, you get a hold of your aunt and encourage her to file a missing person's report. At least then we can get a warrant for Melanie's phone records. Then we might be able to work out where she is. Who she's been talking to.'

'So you want my help now?' Jenny suppressed a grin.

'I want your cooperation.'

'I'll see what I can do.' Jenny pulled her phone from her pocket and left the office with the distinct sensation of eyes drilling into her back.

Surely Grave didn't think *she* had anything to do with any of this?

Chapter 12

As Jenny dialled, all she could think about was what else her family were keeping from her and why?

She needed to call her mum and dad after trying to reach Aunt Carolyn.

The phone rang. Jenny paced a circle in the fine red dust, unable to remain still. Just as she prepared to hang up, the phone answered.

'Hello. Aunt…'

Then a recorded message told her she'd reached her aunt's voicemail.

The tone screeched in her ear, and for a moment, Jenny was silent, suddenly unable to articulate what she needed to say.

A quick breath gave her focus.

'Aunt Carolyn. It's Jenny. I need to speak with you about Melanie. It's important. Please, give me a call.'

She hung up and slid the phone into her pocket, turning back to the station doors, the glass nearly hit her in the face.

Penny appeared with an uncharacteristic frown.

'Whoops. Sorry.'

'What's up?'

'I've found something while I was going through the evidence collected out at Nick's.'

Jenny entered as Penny held the door open.

'And?'

'You better come back into Sarge's office.'

'That sounds ominous. Do I get a heads up?' Jenny's mind was racing. Surely there was nothing found in the grave site to link Melanie to Patricia's murder.

'You didn't hear this from me.'

'O…kay.'

'I found a Tamagotchi.'

'The toy?'

'Yeah.'

'What does that mean?'

'I don't know for sure.' Penny lifted the counter and stepped through. Jenny followed.

Nellie glanced up from the front desk, her expression bored. Jenny wondered how long until the blogger got over working admin in the station. Most days, the hours dragged on with mundane matters. If Nellie thought she was signing on for excitement city, she was in for a rude awakening.

'Bored yet?'

A wide grin split her lips. 'No way. Mrs Carson was on the phone earlier.'

'Oh, fun times then.'

Penny frowned, clearly having never met Mrs Carson, she was unaware of how cantankerous the old miner could be. Jenny had vivid memories of Mrs Carson shoving a shot gun in Phillips' face. Thankfully, her partner knew it was unlikely to be loaded. But still – the day was eventful.

'Anyway,' Penny continued as they dawdled their way to Sarge's office, 'I'm going to assume either she confiscated it from Nick's brother shortly before she died, or Sam was there the day his mum was murdered.'

Jenny remained silent. She knew Sam was. Now it was going to come out and she was going to be under the microscope for having not told anyone.

'Either way, it is a reason to question him, so I thought I better tell Grave, but wanted to let you know first.'

'Thanks for that. Not sure I can do much and Sam has been missing since his mum's body was recovered.'

'Not good.'

'What's not good?' Phillips' voice from beyond the office doorway startled them.

Stepping inside, Jenny noticed O'Connell still standing at the whiteboard, Sarge sitting and Grave hovering nearby. All eyes turned their way.

'Sir. I've got something that probably needs a follow up.'

'Go on McGregor.' Sarge turned his office chair away from the whiteboard to face Penny.

'The remains of Patricia are still being reviewed by Doc, but I've been sifting through the recovered evidence from around her body.'

Jenny studied Detective Grave's body language. She could have sworn they were talking about her when she walked in. Now, as the detective's eyes met hers, she was sure of it.

'It could be nothing, but buried with the body was a toy. They were popular around the time Patricia was killed, or died. We are still waiting on cause of death. Anyway, the toy was a Tamagotchi. I believe it was likely Sam's.'

'It could have belonged to one of the children escaping domestic violence.' Grave rested against the wall with her arms crossed.

'Possibly, but kids running away with distressed parents can't usually afford these toys. They weren't cheap.'

'Good point. Let's get Nick or Sam on the phone and see if we can organise an interview.'

Jenny sighed. Any minute now they were going to find out Sam was gone. Any minute they were going to haul her over the coals for not telling them.

'Sam's gone bush. When Patricia's body was found, he took off.'

'And you are only just telling us now?' Grave pushed off the wall, her body rigid.

'To be fair, it's only a toy, one that could have been confiscated by his mum before she died.'

'But he disappeared when the body was found. He didn't wait to find out if it was even his mum. He's likely hiding something.'

'Yes. He likely is. He was first on scene when his dad died. He could possibly have seen his father's killer, maybe he saw his mum's. Maybe he doesn't remember any of it. Maybe he ran off because he's only nineteen and it's all a lot to take in.' Jenny's cheeks burned hot. Her heart thudded in her chest, making her nauseous.

Grave's nostrils flared.

'And maybe you better start explaining a few things constable, before I remove you from this case permanently and reprimand your sorry arse.'

Chapter 13

'Okay ladies.' O'Connell still held the whiteboard marker in his right hand as he pressed between them.

'Williams. Spill.' Sarge rounded his desk.

'Sorry Sir. I wanted Sam to come back, and I could talk to him and then let you know what Nick told me about the missing information in the report.'

'You've been discussing the case with your *boyfriend*? That's beyond unprofessional Williams.'

'You. Sit!' Sarge pointed to what Jenny called Sarge's 'hot seat'. Grave opened her mouth. 'This is my station. Mine. You got that!'

Detective Grave rolled her lips, sniffed loudly and stormed toward the indicated seat. Spinning it around, she eyed Jenny with a firm expression.

Was it anger, or something else?

'Now you need to understand how it works out here Detective. Nick Johnston has been working with Williams on this case, before it became a case. I'm not defending Williams, but I understand why she'd discuss it with him.'

'And you,' Sarge rounded on her, 'you need to up the ante when it comes to discretion. This case has been in the news. Any sniff of information could leak out and impede our investigation.'

'Ah Sir,' Nellie stuck her head in the door, her usual smile absent, 'speaking of breaking stories.'

'What is it Nellie?'

'I just want you to know I had absolutely nothing to do with this. You know I wouldn't betray your trust.'

'Spit it out!' The vein at Sarge's temple throbbed at an unnaturally fast pace.

'This just hit the local paper, front page.'

Nellie held up a piece of black and white newspaper. The headline read:

Police debacle or deliberate cover up?

'There is stuff in here that isn't common knowledge.' Nellie passed the paper to Sarge's shaking hand.

'What's your bedside talk like Sarge?' O'Connell's expression told Jenny he wasn't poking fun. He knew who was behind the report, and it wasn't Nellie.

'Damn her.' Sarge cleared his throat. 'I'll deal with this. This is on me, but I assure you, there was no cover up by the police on this case. I'll pass the baton to you for now Grave but include Williams in this investigation. She's a damn blood hound when it comes to the truth.'

'She's related to, or dating most of the suspect pool,' Grave protested.

'Nick's been cleared, hasn't he?'

Grave reluctantly nodded. Jenny pursed her lips to keep from smiling. Nick was in the clear. Now she needed to clear Sam, Melanie and her brother and find out who killed the Johnstons.

'Then play nice, ladies. It's a small town. Everyone knows everyone. I'll leave you to it. I've got a reporter who needs a serious talking to.'

Sarge rolled the paper up under his arm and stormed out the office door. His muttering was still audible as he pulled his car keys from the peg on the wall and left the station.

Philips squirmed in the corner. O'Connell seemed to be contemplating murder and Grave adjusted the buttons on the front of her shirt.

'Okay. So Sam Johnston was likely with his mum when she died or not far away. Let's find him.' She pointed to Jenny.

'He's gone bush,' O'Connell interrupted. 'Give him a day to process things. He'll be back soon enough.' He casually wrote Sam's name on the whiteboard next to the photo of Patricia's remains.

'You head out to Nick's. You know him. He'll open up to you. Find out where Sam is. Bring him in.' Grave ignored O'Connell.

'He was nine. I know you think he could be capable of murder, but it's a theory I don't subscribe to, but even if he killed her, someone older and wiser must have helped him bury the body and stage Ron's death.'

'You're right.' Grave sat back in the chair.

'And Nick was in Adelaide,' Jenny reiterated.

'So while you are out there, interview Ed and Al again.'

Could Ed have been involved? He was quick to mention Geoff's car. Something he never mentioned to her, or Nick and they'd been investigating Ron's murder for months.

'There are too many suspects here, but I can't see a motive on the board.' Jenny crossed to the whiteboard and pulled the marker from O'Connell's hand. He stepped back with a grin.

'Here.' Jenny tapped the whiteboard marker on the pictures with the remains of Ron and Patricia. 'We know Ed and Al were on the property.' She tapped their names. 'It wasn't yet shearing time, so no other workmen where there. Rebecca….' Jenny turned to O'Connell 'Nick told me Rebecca was at school too, but we haven't confirmed her alibi yet.'

'Why would Rebecca be a suspect?' Philips stepped away from the door to the main office and Nellie hovered in her partner's usual spot, still listening despite not being a police officer.

'Rebecca worked at the station, helping Patricia do the books. She claimed to know nothing about the relocation of domestic violence victims, but I can't see how that would be possible since she worked closely with Nick's mum.'

'But Ed and Al knew nothing.' Philips sat on the corner of Sarge's desk.

'They are guys.'

'That's sexist.' Phillips wore a grin.

'They don't do admin. Rebecca did.'

'Fair point Jenny.' It seemed she was Jenny again. Not Constable, not Williams. Jenny. She was back in Grave's good books. 'Philips, run her alibi. Jenny, head out to the station, check Al and Ed's alibis again.'

'Al was at the station. The report shows he called Len out when he found Ron's body.'

'No statement was ever taken, and he didn't mention that when I questioned him the other day. He could have covered up for Sam.' Grave's eyes glinted with excitement.

'That's if Sam did anything and you've not met him. He wouldn't.'

'I hope you're right.' Grave turned to Penny.

'You get back to the evidence. If you find anything else, let me know immediately.'

Penny turned to leave.

'And McGregor.'

Penny spun back around.

'Call Doc. See what's happening. I could do with cause of death earlier rather than later. Then we can determine who our most likely suspect is. We still can't rule out Ron Johnston. If there's a bullet in our victim, see if we can match ballistics with the gun that killed Ron.'

'On it.' Penny hurried from the room.

'You, get out to the station and call in anything of interest. Get back in the morning.' Grave smiled mischievously. 'And don't stay up all night with that man of yours. You've got work to do.'

Jenny blushed. O'Connell snorted and Philips chuckled.

Puffing out her cheeks, she wondered if she could push one more boundary.

'Don't suppose I can take one of the police four-wheel drives.'

'Your assumption is correct.' Grave pointed to her partner. 'Phillips will need it. He's heading to the library to look up old newspaper records.'

'What for?' Phillips' expression said he couldn't think of anything worse.

'I want to find out what *wasn't* in Len Holmes official report on the death of Ron Johnston and the disappearance of Patricia Johnston. You'll be surprised what the local papers find.'

'Today's headline proves that.' O'Connell said.

'Can I do that?' Nellie almost put her hand up like she was in school.

'You hold no official rank here Nellie.'

'I'm good at digging up details and it's quiet out front today.'

'I've got no objection.' Phillips seemed relieved. 'I can watch the desk and make a few calls to confirm Rebecca's alibi.'

'Is it alright with you Senior Constable?'

'Call me O'Connell and yes. I think we can hold the fort here.'

'So, Williams will find Sam and interview Al and Ed. Nellie will research old papers. O'Connell, find out if we can pull up phone records based on the old missing person's file for Melanie Williams.'

'That would usually be a no.'

'Give it a shot.' She turned to Phillips. 'Looks like you're back on the front counter.'

'I'm okay with that.'

'Can I grab the four-wheel drive then?'

'No.' O'Connell and Grave spoke in unison then laughed.

The release of tension was welcome. Jenny wondered over whether she should head home to change or go in uniform. She wasn't sure but keeping her service weapon on her seemed overkill.

She crossed the main office to her locker, collected her backpack and keys, then locked the door.

'I'll walk you out.' Nellie circled Jenny's left arm with her right.

'Obviously Gwen wrote that article. Do you know anything about it?'

'Nothing. But Gwen is a hard task master.'

'She used to be married to O'Connell.' Jenny checked over her shoulder as she spoke.

'Yep. And then she started dating Sarge. Alarm bells should have been ringing.'

'They were, for O'Connell, but Sarge wasn't listening.'

Nellie sighed as she pushed the front door open. 'Live and learn I guess.'

A thought struck Jenny. 'You don't know why O'Connell and Gwen broke up do you?'

'None of my business really, but O'Connell is probably better off without her.'

She thought about his conversation with her last month. How he wouldn't take a promotion because of his partner. It puzzled her. Surely a partner would be willing to move for his career.

Then she thought about Nick. Could she ask him to move to the city if she applied for a detective position one day?

'Enjoy your treasure hunt.'

'I will. I love digging in the archives. All my cold cases require lots of research. I must admit, I never thought about dragging up old newspaper articles.' Nellie waved as she jumped on her scooter.

'Me neither.' Jenny spoke aloud, but Nellie was already firing up her scooter. As she reached to open her Dodge, a gold SUV drove past Nellie's scooter buzzing up the road. Jenny studied it a moment before recognising the driver.

Her stomach knotted when the car parked up outside the station and the tall, dark-haired woman in her fifties stepped out. The lines on her face were deeper than they were last time they saw each other.

'Jenny. Thank god.'

Jenny placed her keys back into her pocket and approached the woman.

'Aunt Carolyn. I'm glad you came.'

Chapter 14

Jenny knew she needed to take her aunt back into the station, but the expression on the woman's face told a story that Jenny wasn't sure Grave needed to hear right now.

Torn between finding Sam, seeing Nick, doing her duty and being there for her aunt, Jenny decided ultimately, there was no choice.

'You should come inside.'

'Oh Jenny. It's such a mess.'

'What's going on Aunt Carolyn?'

'I should have told you from the start. I should have told everyone, but…'

Jenny turned her aunt around and was moving toward the motel restaurant before she could stop herself.

'Let's grab you a coffee first. I need lunch in any case.'

'Oh Jenny. You've always had such a level head. So sensible. I'm so sorry we never told you the truth.'

Jenny was sorry they hadn't either. She lost nearly ten years with her cousin because they disappeared. The story about Melanie's teacher molesting her turned out to be a lie, so why did her aunt and cousin take off to William Creek Station? Why go to a place for domestic violence victims?

The comment Detective Grave made earlier about her uncle not seeing Melanie since she disappeared hit her like a blast of hot air. How had she missed it?

'You can tell me now Auntie.'

'Call me Carolyn, please. You're not a little girl anymore.'

Jenny pushed the door to the motel restaurant open. The smell of beer and fried food overloaded her senses and hunger pains ensued.

'Let's get you a drink. Coffee? Tea? Or something stronger? You look like you need it?'

Carolyn shook her head. 'I don't need anything.'

Jenny studied the woman's gaunt features and wanted to disagree but said nothing.

'I'll just order something.' She wondered if food was the right thing to be focussed on right now, but she wanted her aunt to relax. She needed to know everything. Something in the pit of her stomach was telling her Melanie's story and Nick's family murders were closely linked, she simply hadn't found the connection yet.

Ten minutes later they found a seat in the furthest corner of the large restaurant area. Squeezed up against the wall at a small table, Jenny willed her aunt to relax. Every fibre of her body was rigid.

'Take your time Au…Carolyn.' She smiled at the idea of using her aunt's first name. 'Did my mum and dad know you weren't missing since two-thousand and six?'

Her aunt reached for her hand across the table. 'I'm so sorry hun. We didn't think about the effect this would have on you.'

'I'm okay.'

'You became a cop and everything because of us.'

'I'm happy being a cop, but it would be good to know the truth about why you ran off, and why Uncle Pete never knew. Or did he lie to the police?'

The barmaid appeared with Jenny's order, including a non-alcoholic ginger beer.

'Thanks Cheryl.'

'Anytime. You coming to happy hour tonight?'

Jenny glanced at the bubbly barmaid who was now a good friend.

'Maybe. I'll let you know.'

Cheryl gazed from her to her aunt and realisation crossed her face. Squeezing Jenny's shoulder, Cheryl left without another word.

'You've made friends here.'

'I have.' She didn't mention Nick. Now didn't seem like the right time. 'You didn't answer my question earlier.'

Aunt Carolyn drew in a few calming breaths like she was preparing for a deep free dive. Her whole body shuddered.

'I didn't give your parents much information. They knew I left Peter, and they were aware it was a sore spot, so they never discussed it with your uncle. The boys were never emotionally close in any case, so it wasn't hard. They kept working together, keeping their private lives private and I stayed in touch with your mum.'

'Why did you leave?'

'Couples break up for all sorts of reasons.'

'That doesn't explain dad calling me worried Melanie was in danger or who Tristan's father is. I've totally investigated and debunked the cock and bull story you told about Melanie's school teacher.'

'You've embraced the bush lifestyle I see.' Her aunt pointed to her food. 'You should eat, before it gets cold.'

Jenny considered her aunt's words. The reference to her use of colloquial language was new but distracting her with food was an old habit everyone who knew her, knew usually worked.

'I'll eat, you talk. Who is the father of Melanie's child and why lie about it and disappear without telling anyone?'

'I think I should talk with the lead detective on your current murder case Jenny.'

Jenny held a forkful of food in front of her mouth, hovering as she digested her aunt's words.

'I got her message before yours as I came into reception in town. I know she wants to talk to me.'

'She does, but it can wait until you've told me Melanie's story.'

'I don't think it can Jen.'

Jenny watched her aunt closely. There was no doubt in her mind she was keeping something to herself. Why else would she suddenly not want to tell her the truth?

Chapter 15

Cold sweat covered Jenny's body as she watched her aunt through the one-way interview room glass.

The woman wrung her hands on the top of the interview room table as O'Connell pressed *Record* on the equipment and Detective Grave shuffled paperwork.

'Thanks for coming in today, Mrs Williams. We appreciate this is a difficult time for you.'

'When I found out Melanie wasn't with Jenny anymore, I got straight in the car.'

'Yes. About that. Can we lodge a new missing person report for Melanie? It could help us track her down.'

Jenny's aunt sat back. Her hands fell into her lap. There was something guarded about her expression that set Jenny's skin tingling. Viewing her from a distance, unseen, gave a totally different perspective than sitting opposite her in the restaurant not long before.

'She is missing, isn't she Mrs Williams?'

'Yes. She and my grandson.'

And my brother, thought Jenny. What was the connection between Geoff and Melanie?

'Then we have your permission? You can sign this form if you want us to try to trace Melanie.'

Detective Grave slid the completed paperwork across the table. Jenny's aunt studied it a moment, her fingers hovering over the pen Grave offered, but not quite ready to grasp it in her hand.

Finally, she retrieved it and signed. O'Connell took the paper and shuffled his chair back.

'Senior Constable O'Connell is leaving the interview room to lodge the missing person's paperwork.'

The door opened, Jenny was torn between meeting her boss in the hallway and watching her aunt's interview. There were so many unanswered questions she desperately needed the answer to.

Duty finally won out. She opened the door and stepped out.

'It's okay Williams. I'll give this to Philips and be right back.'

Jenny relaxed and stepped back into the adjoining room as O'Connell rushed down the hall.

'We have a few questions about your time at William Creek Station. Can you confirm the dates you were there please?'

'I was only there for a day, when Ron first picked us up from the William Creek Pub.'

'Yes. I understand the owner there…' Grave shuffled paperwork, 'Mrs B. was asked to lie to anyone who asked after you, including our own constable, your niece, nearly a decade after you disappeared?'

'Yes, well. It was standard I think, for Ron and Patricia to help people disappear. I guess the publican was aware of the situation.'

'It appears so.' Detective Grave picked up a pen to take notes. 'When did you arrive and leave and why did you go without your daughter?'

Aunt Carolyn chewed the inside of her cheek as the clock ticked loudly on the wall. Moments passed, then the door opened once more as O'Connell returned.

The sound of the chair legs scraping on lino echoed around the otherwise silent room.

'I left Melanie there because Ron found somewhere for me to go. I needed to check it out, attend a job interview and make the arrangements so Melanie could come a few weeks later.'

'So what date was that?'

'I don't recall exactly.'

'Come now Mrs Williams. You upended your entire world. Started a new life. I'm sure you recall the dates.'

The ticking clock echoed once more.

Why was her aunt being so vague, so evasive?

The stalemate broke as Aunt Carolyn puffed out her cheeks with a heavy sigh.

'I'm sure you have the dates for when we were at the William Creek Pub, but I left Melanie at the Station on the eleventh of September.'

'We have a witness placing Melanie at the Station on the eleventh, but not you Mrs Williams.'

Aunt Carolyn opened her mouth, then closed it with a frown on her forehead.

'They must have missed me. I was there.'

Grave's foot tapped on the floor under the table. Jenny watched, expecting the detective to rebut the comment.

'And when did you collect Melanie from the Station?'

'I didn't.'

'Can we ask who did?'

'Her cousin Geoff.'

'Do you have a date for that?'

'No. I'm sorry I don't. It was a hectic time. I was at Centrelink getting social services support and starting a new job, moving into a state housing trust home and it was manic.'

'Can you say how many days between you leaving William Creek Station and Melanie arriving, approximately?'

'Four, maybe five.' Aunt Carolyn shook her head. 'Maybe more. It was a chaotic time.'

'I understand.' Detective Grave rummaged with paperwork.

It was an interview technique Jenny used herself to give the interviewee time to compose themselves, but also to build tension for what might be coming next.

Aunt Carolyn's eyes scanned the room trying to look everywhere but at the paperwork in front of the detective.

'We are trying to piece together who might have information helpful in finding Ron Johnston's killer. It seems your daughter came forward once she heard Mr Johnston was murdered, but she never shed any light on the situation.'

Silence hung as Detective Grave studied Jenny's aunt, waiting.

'Is there a question in there somewhere detective?'

Grave smiled.

'Did your daughter tell you she saw anything strange at William Creek Station? Anything helpful to our enquires?'

'She didn't mention anything to me detective. I just want my daughter and grandson found. That's why I'm here. Nothing to do with any murder investigation.'

'Thank you for your time, Mrs Williams. We'll get a search on the go for Melanie and be in touch.'

As if they weren't already searching for Melanie.

Jenny watched the detective rise, cross the room and open the interview room door. Her aunt said she knew why Melanie was missing again, but she didn't reveal anything to Grave. Was it a ploy to stop her asking more questions?

'That's it?' Aunt Carolyn searched O'Connell's face as she rose, but he kept his eyes on the recording equipment as he switched it off.

'We'll do everything we can to find Melanie Mrs Williams. I assure you,' Grave spoke as she waited by the door.

Her aunt reached the doorway.

'Actually, Mrs Williams. I have to ask. It could be pertinent to our case.'

Aunt Carolyn stopped, turned to face Grave. An uneasy silence hung in the air. Jenny held her breath.

'Who is the father of Melanie's son?'

Chapter 16

Jenny waited for her aunt to disappear from the interview room before stepping out of the adjoining room into the hallway. O'Connell and Grave passed her as she waited, not wanting to let her aunt know she was listening in.

Her head swam and her stomach knotted as she considered her aunt's answer to the detective's questions.

Was she telling the truth? Did she genuinely have no idea who Tristan's father was?

Philips' head bobbed around the corner into the hallway. His eyes met hers.

'All clear.' He stepped around the corner. 'You okay? You look like you've seen a ghost.'

She shook her head, sucked in a quick breath and pasted a smile on her lips. 'I'm good. Thanks.'

'You're usually a bit more chipper on a full stomach.'

'Right now, that full stomach isn't helping.'

'Just don't throw up on me. Okay!' Philips stepped back with suspicion.

'I'm not a puker. I'll be okay.'

'Tommy was a projectile vomiter as a baby, so I'm trained to avoid spew at all costs.'

Jenny allowed herself a chuckle. Tommy was nearly five, already off to Kindy now, so imagining him as a baby was hard.

'Lucky he outgrew it.'

'Lucky is an understatement. Boss wants us in his office.'

'Guessed as much.'

'You okay?' Nellie stopped Jenny as she passed the front counter.

'I will be, thanks Nellie.'

'Drinks tonight, if you don't have to go bush.'

'You're on. You were quick. Did you get anything from the newspaper articles?'

Nellie pointed to a microfiche machine set up at the end of the counter. Jenny totally missed it when she brought her aunt in to see Grave.

'The library leant it to me, along with this.' Nellie pulled a wad of microfiche wrapped in dated paper out from under the counter. 'I'm going through it in between calls and counter enquires.'

'I don't envy you.'

'Williams!' Sarge leaned on the door frame to his office, toe tapping, eyes drilling. 'When you're ready.'

'Sorry Boss.' Philips scurried past.

Jenny studied Sarge's expression. His body language said annoyed, while his eyes told a different story. She lifted her chin and pulled back her shoulders as she passed him to join the others huddled around the whiteboard.

He nodded approval and followed her inside.

'Okay. Carolyn Williams claims to be unaware of her grandson's father. I find that hard to believe.' Grave used a whiteboard marker to update the board with Jenny's aunt's details.

She struggled to process the information.

'She told me she knew why Mel was missing again. But told you nothing.'

'Why would she do that?' Grave seemed to be asking anyone.

'Change of heart once she was in the interview room.' O'Connell was first to offer a scenario.

'She's worried about revealing too much?' Sarge sat down firmly in his chair.

'She's protecting Melanie.' Philips hovered by the door from habit.

'O'Connell. Run her story about a job interview. See if you can corroborate it with her employer and then see if any of her Centrelink references match up with meetings. I'm finding it hard to believe no one saw her at the William Creek Station unless she was never there.'

'Did you still want me to head out to Nick's? It's getting late now. I'm not sure I'll be able to do much.

'No. Leave it until tomorrow but give Nick a call and check in about Sam and I'd like you to call your parents.'

Jenny considered the detective's request. Aunt Carolyn didn't seem to be ready to share any insights. Would her parents be any different? Did they even know? Geoff sure as hell knew something, and Aunt Carolyn said her mum knew more than she ever shared with her.

'Yes Ma'am.'

'I told you not to call me that.' A shift of the detective's upper lip told Jenny the comment was meant to sooth her internal turmoil.

'Sorry. Detective.'

'We've requested Melanie Williams' bank records, mobile phone data, and we've issued a request on Crime Stoppers for any information about her.' A gush of air escaped as Sarge leant back into his leather chair.

'What about Gwen?' O'Connell's expression wasn't mocking.

'She wasn't apologetic. Some clap trap about the public having a right to know.'

'Point her in my direction Sergeant. I'll sic the media liaison officer from Adelaide on her to contain her or she'll face a charge of obstruction or interfering in a police investigation.'

'Good luck with that. She has a tendency to believe she's above the law,' O'Connell said.

'The fact she's had you two under the thumb could be the driving force behind her false sense of security.'

'Hey!' Both men crossed their arms in solidarity.

Detective Grave waved her hand dismissively.

'Let's focus. Have we interviewed the last three women on Nellie's list Sergeant? Anything come up?'

'Nothing. All of them provided information in relation to when they were at William Creek Station. Two were too far outside our timeline to be of any help or for their ex-spouses to be involved.'

'Two, what about the other one?'

'She was preparing to leave her boyfriend when she got word of Ron's death and her plans changed.'

'That's interesting. Who told her?'

'I'm not sure, but I think I have a sneaking suspicion.'

'And?'

'And Mrs B. might be able to shed a little more light on that.'

'The William Creek Pub owner?'

'The very same.'

'In that case Williams, you might like to call in on your way to Nick Johnston's place tomorrow.'

'I can do that, but Mrs B. said she had nothing to do with Ron and Patricia's relocation program except to help out with accommodation from time to time.'

'Well, that appears not to be the whole truth now doesn't it?'

The idea made Jenny's lunch threaten to projectile vomit after all.

Chapter 17

'Let's call it a day people.' Sarge pressed his palms down on his desk and rose stiffly. 'Williams, you head out first thing in the morning. Question Mrs B., interview Rebecca about her university so we can eliminate her and then check in on Sam.'

'Yes Sir.' Jenny turned to follow everyone from Sarge's office.

She noticed Detective Grave making straight for the front door. The woman was a stranger in town and Jenny knew what that was like more than most. But the detective worked all over the state. She was likely used to being in remote, rural towns where not everyone welcomed strangers. Still…

'Detective?'

Grave turned as she slipped her shoulder strap over her head.

'Did you want to join Penny and me at the pub for a drink or dinner?'

The detective looked ready to instantly dismiss the idea, but then something in her expression changed.

'Why not? What time?'

Penny joined Jenny.

'*Now*. No time like the present. I could use a drink about now.'

'Let's do it then.' Grave returned to the counter and waited while Jenny put her service weapon away and collected her backpack.

'Philips, Nellie, you coming too?' Jenny asked as she crossed the room.

Nellie's white teeth shone back at her.

'You betcha. Give me ten minutes to tidy this lot up and I'll meet you there.'

'Not me. Tommy's been at Kindy all day so he's going to be hyped up to the max and driving Deb crazy. But I'm on for Friday.'

'Say hi to Deb for me.' Jenny waved as the three women left the station foyer.

A buzzing in Detective Grave's pocket made them stop. The detective glanced at the screen and dismissed the call.

'Don't you want to take that?' Jenny asked as she opened her car door and threw her backpack inside.

'Not right now. It's not important. Just family stuff.'

Jenny noticed the pinched expression but said nothing. Whoever was phoning the detective was none of her business, but Jenny could see she didn't seem anxious to take the call. In fact, totally the opposite.

'You're from up north Queensland. Right?' Jenny chose a little light conversation to break the tension.

'That was a lifetime ago.'

Okay, maybe the wrong subject.

'How long have you been a detective?'

Try work. Everyone is always happy to talk about work.

'Six years. Started out at the Darlington station dealing mostly with shoplifters from the local shopping centre.'

'That would have been exhilarating,' Penny teased.

'It was boring as, but occasionally you got to set a kid on the straight and narrow.'

'I want to hear your story, but can you give me a sec? I'll just check in with Marj first.'

Jenny stopped outside reception and stuck her head in to find the motel owner sitting behind the counter, book in hand and a quiet rerun of *Days of our Lives* playing on the new flat screen TV on the wall.

'New colour Marj.'

Jenny noted the owner's burgundy highlights – a more subdued change from the usual dramatic colours of pink and orange.

She fluffed the ends of her new bob haircut and smiled a wide, red lipped grin.

The hair colour was subdued but the lipstick more than made up for it.

'Glad you like it.'

Jumping down from her stool, Marj scampered around the counter with a noticeable limp. It seemed the break from a few months back hadn't healed perfectly, but Marj was never one to complain.

'How are Nick and Sam doing? I heard about their mum.'

'How could you miss it? Gwen plastered it all over the front page of the paper!'

Marj leant in to whisper, noticing the detective and Penny waiting by the door.

'Yes. I saw, but I hate to say it. She's got a point.'

'We'll know more as we get the facts from the medical examiner. Until then, let's keep a lid on the speculation, for Nick and Sam's sake.'

Marj zipped her lips together and Jenny smiled. The gossip queen of Coober Pedy didn't know how to keep a lid on anything.

'Give the boys my love, will you?'

'Of course Marj.' She didn't mention Sam was walkabout. It would only fuel gossip, especially if someone decided the poor kid knew something important.

Marj peered over Jenny's shoulder, then leant in again with a hushed voice.

'Did I hear right?'

'What?' Jenny's heart skipped a beat.

'Is Sam a suspect?'

'How on earth did you hear that?'

Marj shrugged. 'So you're not denying it?'

'Marj, do you honestly think Sam could do something to his mum or dad?' Jenny was trying to sound mocking, but in saying the words aloud, her stomach ached. She didn't know Sam and Nick back then. More importantly, she didn't know Nick's parents at all.

Could Sam have something to do with his mother's death?

'I don't know luv. I hope you can find out what happened to Ron and Patricia. The town is buzzing with rumours. Ron's death was a suicide, now it's murder, and now Patricia's body has been found, people are talking Wolf Creek nonsense.'

Detective Grave stepped into the office.

'The Adelaide media liaison officer will be making a formal statement very soon, I'm sure.'

'Of course luv.'

Marj grinned widely, but her eyes weren't happy about the interruption to her gossip session.

'I've got to run Marj. I'll see you later.' Jenny hugged the woman quickly and rushed from the office.

The three women made their way down the covered veranda to the main dining room entrance in uneasy silence.

Jenny could see Grave wanted to say more. As they reached the door, Grave held her hand on the handle a moment, then turned to Jenny.

'Small towns are notorious for the rumour mill Jenny. Seriously, you need to pull them up when they start raving like that.'

'Marj is harmless enough and she can be useful. She's got her ear to the ground around here. I like to keep her onside.'

'Nothing wrong with that but try not to let her wild ideas run away from you next time.'

Jenny said nothing as Grave opened the door and held it for them.

What could she say? The detective was right. Marj was an asset when it came to gaining a sense of town sentiment in a case, and seemed to have an uncanny ability to know more than she should. But Jenny needed to set her straight quickly in the future.

'What will it be ladies? My shout.'

'No way. You're the guest in town. I'll get the first round.' Jenny squeezed her way up to the long wooden front bar where Cheryl and Stan pulled beer from two separate ends of the counter.

A short, wide high-vis vest to her left grumbled as she squeezed in but came to a sudden hush when he saw her uniform.

'Luv,' he nodded, then returned his gaze to his half empty beer and two more high-vis shirts.

'Be with you in a sec Jen.' Cheryl smiled as she rushed past, three frothy pots of beer squeezed together in her hands.

'You were saying, about kids and the straight and narrow.' Jenny half turned to face the detective as she waited for Cheryl.

'Yeah. The kids used to steal from the local department store and the security staff who caught them would bale them up in an interview room and call us in.'

Jenny could picture a terrified teen surrounded by security and cops.

'If they were first timers, we'd read them the riot act. Do the whole good cop, bad cop on them and basically try to scare them straight. Of course, there were plenty of serial offenders, but every one of them we scared straight was worth the time and effort.'

'When did you catch your first murder?'

The high-vis guy peered over his shoulder with eyebrows raised.

'What you having ladies?' Cheryl patted the beer brand logoed bar runner with one hand.

'You know my usual. Same for Penny. What will it be detective?'

'White wine thanks. I've never acquired the taste for beer.'

'That will be twenty-two smackaroos thanks.' Cheryl passed the credit card machine up to the polished timber bar and collected two empties while Jenny passed her credit card over.

'But you're from Far North Queensland. How does that happen?'

The credit card machine pinged approval and Jenny pocketed her card.

'Thanks Cheryl.'

'All part of the service.' She rushed away to pour the drinks.

'My dad was a heavy pub drinker. I was put off the smell of beer by the time I hit my teens.'

'Ah. I know the feeling.' Penny reached for the two glasses of wine Cheryl put on the counter and handed one to Grave.

'My dad was too busy milking cows to even set foot inside the pub.'

Jenny picked up her beer and the three women wove their way through the tables in the centre of the room, coming to a long table separating the bar and restaurant area.

'Speaking of your dad. Did you call your parents yet?' Grave pulled a chair out and sat.

'No. I'll do it after dinner. Dad won't be available during the day. He doesn't milk the cows anymore, but he does all the pasture and hay feeding.'

'When did you catch your first murder?' Penny picked up the earlier conversation.

'In two-thousand and nine. A murder, attempted suicide investigation.'

'Husband kills wife?'

'No. Mum killed her four-year-old, attempted to kill her nine-year-old and herself at the same time, but they both lived.'

'What the hell? Domestic murder of kids is nearly always the father, isn't it?' Jenny flipped cardboard coasters down the table.

'You've been studying for your detective badge then?' Grave smiled over her wine glass.

'No. But I did a few modules on criminology during my police academy days.'

'You should study to be a detective.'

'I have a boyfriend, in the middle of nowhere in case you've forgotten. Not much point in making detective and staying out here.'

'You're not staying out here Jen.' Penny said.

'I'm not going anywhere without Nick.'

'Don't let a man hold you back from your career.' Grave sipped her wine again.

Jenny frowned. She didn't want to be alone forever. She only became a cop to find Melanie, and her cousin was now found....well was, until recently.

She wanted kids, a family and a career. Being a local cop like Philips didn't look so bad now she was seeing Nick. She could live with that. Couldn't she?

'Do you have a partner?' The words slipped from Jenny's lips before she considered if they were the right words at the right time or not.

By the look on the detective's face, the timing and the words weren't right at all.

'I did. Now I don't.'

'I'm sorry. It's none of my business.'

'Hey! Who wants a top up?' Nellie's smiling face broke the tension.

A chorus in the affirmative followed.

Chapter 18

Jenny pushed the heavy wooden door open, entered and exhaled. A little tension eased, but not enough.

'Hey, where was *my* invite?' Her roommate Nev sat on the lounge, laptop open and a movie playing. The overhead light was off, making the screen glow across his dark features like a scene from a horror movie.

'Sorry Nev. It kind of ended up being a girls' session.'

She dropped her backpack on the kitchen counter and switched the light on.

'Even more reason to invite your wingman.'

'Nope. I'm not having you chat up my new boss.'

Nev closed the screen of his computer, shoved it aside and eyed her with interest.

'Do tell.'

'She's not actually my boss. She's a detective from Adelaide, helping, well overseeing really, Nick's parents' murder cases.'

'His mum was murdered too?'

Jenny threw herself down on the lounge as Nev shuffled over to make more room.

'Well, technically we don't have a cause of death yet, but she didn't accidentally bury herself in the family veggie garden.'

She knew she shouldn't be discussing an open investigation with Nev, but her housemate was well aware of the case surrounding Nick's dad's murder. She didn't see any real harm in it. He was a doctor and knew the importance of confidentiality.

'No way! That's got to have given Nick a kick in the guts.'

'You have no idea. He's taking it pretty well though. It's Sam I'm worried about.'

'Sam was only young when his mum disappeared, wasn't he?'

'Yes, but it looks like he might have been the one to find his dad's body and I think he could subconsciously know more about what happened to his mum.'

'Has he said anything?'

'No. He's been on Country since he found out. I'm going out there tomorrow morning to help Nick find him.'

'You look stuffed. Did you eat?'

'I did and I drank too much. I need to call my mum and dad and then hit the sack.'

'Let me know if I can help out.' Nev reached for her hand and squeezed it. 'Okay?'

'You got it.'

Jenny pushed up from the lounge, entered the kitchen, poured a glass of water and carried her phone out the front door.

Reception in the Dugout she rented with Nev and ambulance officer Tim was non-existent. The thick stone, semi-underground construction made the walls too thick for any signal to penetrate.

When she first arrived in town, living in a dugout was her dream. Now, she wasn't so sure it lived up to all the hype.

Holding the phone in the air, she watched the reception bars on her mobile flicker on and off until they finally settled on three.

Dialling, she blew out a breath and waited for someone to pick up.

'Bub. How's it going?'

'Hey Mum. It's been better. But Aunt Carolyn arrived today.'

Silence greeted her. Muffled voices told her that her mum's hand was over the receiver, and she was likely talking to her dad.

'Mum?'

'I'm here. How is Carolyn?'

Jenny's hair bristled at her mother's tone. It was a cross between forced boredom and suppressed anger. She knew it well. It was the same tone her mum used when she wanted to explode at her or her brothers but knew she should hold it together.

'Aunt Carolyn is worried. Melanie has gone missing again. The police told me Geoff is unreachable too.'

'Wait a second. I'll put you on to your father.'

A sure sign mum didn't know what to say about the whole situation. Jenny's stomach knotted. More lies were coming her way. She could sense it.

'Jenny.' Her dad's voice was even. No emotion. No nicknames.

'Dad. What's going on?'

It was time to get straight to the point.

'What do you mean?'

'No more bullshit dad.'

'Don't speak to me like that.'

'Okay. Maybe you'd rather speak with Detective Cunningham or Fitzpatrick then?'

Silence.

She hit a nerve. It was time to press on. She needed answers. She needed to know who was lying to her for all these years.

'This is what the police know. This is what *I* know.' She launched into her improvised spiel. Her inner turmoil – the theorising that was always at the back of her mind spilled out like a torrential downpour.

'Melanie is tied in with the death of Nick's parents. The police are sure of it. She was the last person to stay at the homestead before they died. Geoff's car was seen at the property the day before Nick's dad was found shot in the head. But the Adelaide cops told you the car was of interest.'

'I don't need to hear this Jenny.'

'Yes you do dad. You've all been lying to me since I was seventeen. You knew where Melanie was all that time. You knew she had a child. You knew Aunt Carolyn took her to William Creek to escape violence. Now spill.'

Muffled voices sounded again. Jenny's chest was heaving. Her eyes stung, and tears were forcing their way out and down her cheeks.

Get it together girl.

She was thankful this conversation wasn't happening in front of Detective Grave.

'Okay. This is all we know. We knew Carolyn took Melanie away. We were told she was pregnant to her teacher. He was dangerous and to keep her safe, they would stay away until they could prove he was guilty and get him locked up.'

'Well that's a load of crap. The teacher *isn't* Tristan's dad. I tried to get Mel to do a DNA paternity test to prove it, but she refused.'

'I don't know anything about that. We only know what we were told.'

'So why did Uncle Pete say he hasn't seen Melanie since she disappeared in two-thousand and six?'

'I guess because he hasn't. We don't talk about it Jenny.'

'Talk about what?'

'Carolyn was preparing to leave Pete before this all happened. The relationship was already strained. It's personal stuff. Not something adults talk to kids about and it should stay that way.'

But I'm not a kid anymore!

She kept her thoughts to herself. Taking a measured breath, she pushed on.

'So Uncle Pete lets Aunt Carolyn take Melanie away for nearly a decade and he doesn't ask to see her? Or her child?'

'He wanted to, but Carolyn said it was too risky to expose Melanie in case her teacher stalked her or followed Pete to see her.'

'Bullshit. I told you, the teacher isn't the father. He isn't the stalker dad. And Melanie told me Uncle Pete visited once a month. And what has Geoff got to do with this? Why is he missing and why was his car out at William Creek Station around the time of *two* murders?'

Silence hung heavy in the air. Her father sucked in a deep breath through his nostrils. She heard it, but she could see it in her mind. It was his go to when he wanted to hold back emotions, tears even.

'We saw Melanie's photo on Crime Stoppers on the news tonight, along with a story about Nick's brother and the police cocking up the investigation.'

'It made it to the Adelaide news! Damn!'

'Look. We are sorry to hear Nick lost both his parents. The police said they wanted to ask Geoff questions about his car because it was seen out there around the same time, but just because it was seen doesn't mean Geoff had anything to do with their deaths. Why would he? What's his motive?'

'You sound like me, talking to my boss. It's not me we need to convince dad. It's the Adelaide Major Crime detectives. One here, two there. If we don't find Geoff, and hopefully Melanie soon, the cops will be hunting them down as murder suspects. If you know how to get a hold of Geoff, tell me. Now!'

'I wish I knew Jenny. Geoff is Geoff. He can be vague, reckless, air-headed even. You know him as well as I do. He's probably off at Cactus or Elliston surfing or something.'

Jenny rolled her lips to keep her emotions in check. He was right. Geoff was a toker from way back. He could have gone bush with his buddies to go surfing in the middle of nowhere.

'Okay. You're right about Geoff. But why didn't you tell me you knew about Melanie and let me know she was safe, *before* I became a cop?'

She sensed more than heard her dad about to say something, but he didn't. Her gut twisted. There was still more to the story that he was unwilling to tell. Either he wasn't sure, or it was too horrible to share. Either way, it wasn't a good sign.

Chapter 19

The sun rose over the horizon, obscuring Jenny's view of the road. She pulled her visor down, donned her sunglasses and focussed as her old Dodge truck rumbled along the Coober Pedy to William Creek Road.

A road to most people meant two or more lanes of smooth bitumen, but this road was a dirt track – often rutted by big rig trucks and road trains hauling cattle from the local stations or delivering fuel and necessary supplies to the William Creek Hotel.

Tension rose in her shoulders as she gripped the oversized wheel. Without power steering, it was a constant juggle to keep the truck going in a straight line. Every muscle in her body ached as she pulled up outside the William Creek Pub.

The tightness in her muscles was exacerbated since this was not a conversation she was looking forward to. Mrs B. was welcoming from day one. Admittedly, she kept the truth about Melanie to herself at first, but for good reason.

Patricia Johnston rescued many women and children escaping domestic violence and each one who passed through the William Creek Pub was offered the same anonymous accommodation.

If anyone ever asked about them, anyone, no matter who they were, Mrs B. would deny ever seeing them or say they skipped out without paying their bill.

It was no exception when Jenny asked, even though she was dressed in her police uniform, Mrs B. kept the truth to herself until Ron's death was ruled homicide.

Did she keep more to herself even after that? Would she be willing to share it now they knew Patricia was likely killed by the same person?

Jenny slammed the heavy door with her foot. It creaked, then thudded home.

The moment she entered the pub, her stomach clenched at the smell of fried bacon. The dark wood and low ceiling should have been oppressive, but the signed caps, foreign currency hanging from the walls and photos of the rich and famous created a strange, eclectic atmosphere that tourists loved.

'Jenny. Goodness. What the hell are you doing out here so early?'

'Morning Mrs B.' Jenny couldn't help but grin at the tall, lean publican whose voice was deep and resonant and never seemed to match her stature.

'Can I get you a coffee, some breakie?'

'I'd love a bacon and egg burger if I'm not too early for the kitchen?'

'Of course not. We get cracking early out here. Already had a bus load of tourists in and a few guests in the campground have trundled through.'

'You do get going early.'

'Rebecca!' Mrs B. called over her shoulder.

A slim woman with her long straight brown hair pulled back in a low ponytail stuck her head out from the kitchen door.

'What's….' She stopped when she saw Jenny sitting at the front bar. 'Hey. What are you up and about so early for?'

'I'm on my way to Nick's.'

'It's a bit early in the week, isn't it?'

'You know Sam's gone off somewhere and he's not back yet. I'm heading out to go with Nick to find him.'

'So was his mum murdered?' Rebecca crossed to the bar.

'We are still waiting on cause of death.'

'Any suspects?' Rebecca's eyes sparkled with interest.

'We don't know it's murder until we get a cause of death, but I'm sorry I can't discuss details about the investigation, but since you raised the subject….' Jenny considered her words carefully.

'The lead detective asked me to make a few enquiries on the way to Nick's today.'

'So this isn't a social visit?' Rebecca stepped back and crossed her hands over her chest.

Jenny wondered why on earth Rebecca would think she came to say *Hi* to the publican and her daughter for the hell of it – but said nothing. Maybe Rebecca thought of her as a friend after all?

She considered fostering that idea, especially in light of how much time Nick spent with his former childhood sweetheart but dismissed it as a poor motive for friendship. Still, Rebecca was a likeable person once she warmed to you.

'Bit of both. I always love your coffee.'

Rebecca's hands dropped to her sides. 'In that case, I'll grab one for you.' She turned to the coffee machine and began sorting cups.

'Actually, I've got questions for you and your mum. Just routine ones.'

'You can ask them while we feed you. You need some meat on those bones luv.' Mrs B. squeezed Jenny's hand.

'I'm not sure Nick would agree.'

The coffee machine kicked into gear. The aroma of ground beans made Jenny's mouth water.

'Ask away luv.' Mrs B. wiped the bar down with a damp cloth, her eyes on Jenny.

'Bit of a list. You knew Ron and Patricia were relocating domestic violence victims Mrs B., you said you kept their details to yourself right? Was anyone in particular asking questions around the time of Ron's death?'

'To tell the truth, it was pretty rare for anyone to come here looking for any of those poor girls. I think most of the women did a good job of disappearing and who on earth would suspect they'd come all the way out here anyway?'

'Then that's a no?'

Mrs B. rubbed her chin and tapped her index finger on her lips.

'We did have someone hanging around the pub around that time. Didn't ask about anyone in particular. Never showed a photo or anything like that, but we don't get bar flies in here often. Not ones we don't know, that's for sure. This guy stayed here a few days and he didn't look like he was on a holiday.'

Rebecca put a coffee on the bar. Jenny reached for it as Mrs B.'s words sunk in.

'Can you describe him? Old, young, fit, tall, short, fat? Anything?' Her heart-rate quickened.

Mrs B. shrugged. 'Pretty non-descript. Older, maybe mid to late forties, average height, brownish hair. I didn't pay too much attention. He didn't harass anyone. Paid for his food and drink each time.'

'Order up!' A voice came from the kitchen.

'Could be nothing.' Rebecca turned to collect the food, disappearing inside the kitchen and reappearing a moment later, Jenny's breakfast in hand.

'What could be nothing?'

'I never saw the guy mum mentioned, but I did see a strange car.'

'So you weren't away at uni?'

'No. I was here, helping mum. I came home a few weeks early from Uni break because dad was sick with the flu, and it was spring, and mum was run off her feet.'

'Did you see Melanie?'

'Your cousin? No. Not that I was paying much attention to anything around that time. Nick and I agreed…' She glanced at her mum then smiled. 'We agreed we weren't in love, and we weren't going to get married like the entire family thought and I was on the lookout, if you get my drift?'

Jenny got it. She got more than Rebecca could know out of the conversation, but she kept her smile on the inside. Rebecca wasn't in love with Nick.

Is that your only takeaway?

'I was checking out the talent whenever I could, and a car rocked up that seriously got my attention.'

Jenny finally got her head back on track. Goosebumps covered her arms as Rebecca described the car.

'Teal colour, old school panel van. *Very* cool.'

'Who was driving?' Jenny's heart raced.

'I didn't get to see. Mum called me back into the pub. We were flat out.'

'Teal blue, panel van you say?' Jenny knew she was blubbering, but Rebecca was another witness placing Geoff in town around the time of Ron's murder.

Chapter 20

Jenny's mind mulled over Rebecca's information as she drove toward Nick's place. She took official statements from them about the car, and the lurker, but she was no closer to knowing who was driving Geoff's car. It just couldn't be him.

Could it?

She needed to find Geoff, but that was proving impossible. Was he with Mel? Would a trace on her phone find them together and if they were together…. Jenny shuddered.

Surely Tristan wasn't Geoff's son. That was all kinds of wrong. Would it be a good enough reason for Aunt Carolyn to take Melanie away?

Probably!

Would it be a plausible reason why her parents kept lying to her?

Absolutely!

She shook herself back to reality as her vehicle rumbled through the windbreak and down the track past the shearing shed. Ed and Al waved as she passed them sitting on the front step of their quarters. Ed smiled, Al nodded, his ever-present unlit smoke dangling from his lip.

Rounding the corner, she drove up to the yards. Wooden railing, faded from years of harsh sun blocked her view, but Nick said he'd be saddling horses ready to ride out after Sam.

She glanced at her watch as she parked the car. Thankful she ate a big breakfast at the pub because they'd be out looking for Sam most of the day.

Stepping out of the car, she reached for her backpack. Jogging, she slung it over one shoulder, then the next and jumped up to the railing. Nick's horse didn't flinch as she popped up over the top rail.

Maybe the gelding knew she was there?

'Sorry I took so long. The road is rough after the early spring rain, and I stopped at Mrs B.'s on the way.'

'I've got your swag, and I've packed provisions. Lucy is ready. Let's go.'

Nick didn't look up and made no comment about it being okay. Jenny was about to comment, when she saw the pinched lines around Nick's eyes.

He was worried.

'I'm ready.'

Nick stopped cinching the saddle on his gelding and finally glanced up. A soft smile crossed his lips. Jenny's heart skipped a beat.

'You look gorgeous in those buckskin jeans.'

'I wish we didn't have to rush off.' She flicked her leg over the railing.

'You're reading my mind, but I should find Sam.'

Jenny jumped down harder than intended inside the yard.

Nick's gelding shied away, but Nick pulled the rein gently and spoke softly.

'Whoops. Sorry about that. Out of practice around horses.'

She and Melanie used to ride every weekend. Pony club, around the dairy farm, over to friend's houses. Nothing like this stark, dry outback landscape, but she was familiar with horses and usually knew better than to make sudden movements.

'Prince is looking glossy.' She reached for his neck and rubbed gently. The horse nickered and dropped his head for a rub.

'He knows you're talking about him.'

'Bit like his owner. Your ears must have been burning yesterday.'

'Tell me as we ride.' Nick led Prince toward the gate.

Jenny stepped forward to open it. Lucy stomped her foot impatiently as Nick walked Prince out.

'Looks like Lucy is ready to go too. I just need to duck to the loo. Sorry. If only I could pee standing up, life would be perfect.'

'Use the shearers' loo. The team are due in next week, but it's still empty for now.'

Two minutes later, Jenny wriggled her foot into the stirrup and sprang up and over Lucy's wide back.

It was good to be back in the saddle, but Jenny wondered why they didn't take the Landcruiser. She said as much.

'I think I know where Sam will be, and it's tough going in the vehicle. We could take the chopper, but then we can't travel easily if it gets dark while we are still searching.'

'Yeah, sorry I'm late. You could have gotten out at first light if you didn't wait for me.'

'He'll be okay and you're worth waiting for.'

'Okay. What have you done with the real Nick Johnston?'

She signalled her mount into a slow canter with a gentle squeeze of her calves. Nick's horse matched hers.

'He was drowning, but you dragged him to the surface.'

Jenny slowed her mount. Nick matched her once more. Leaning over, she kissed his lips gently, wishing she had done so the moment she arrived.

'Did you mean what you said on the phone?' Jenny said.

'Which time?' Nick teased.

She thumped his arm softly.

'You know which time.'

'Did you?' Nick countered.

'What, mean it?'

'Yeah, or were you only saying it because Becca was here?'

'Am I that transparent?'

Nick's smile dropped away.

'So it was just jealousy talking?'

'It was jealouy, but not *just…*' She stopped riding. 'I admit, I blurted it out because Becca was here with you, but as soon as the words left my lips, I knew they were true.'

Nick reached for her hand and squeezed.

'I would have told you sooner, and first, but I didn't want to push you. So yes. I meant it.'

She reached for his jaw and gently pulled his lips to hers. When they separated, she wished she were back at the Homestead, in his bed, under the covers and none of the past few days ever happened.

'Come on then! The quicker we find Sam, the quicker I can get you into bed.'

Nick pushed his mount forward at a full canter.

Smiling to herself, she spoke softly.

'Let's go Lucy.'

The horse lunged forward without further encouragement.

Chapter 21

The late morning sun warmed Jenny's back as they cantered toward the escarpment Nick guided Jenny to on her first visit to the property.

It was the day she rode out, much like today, to ask Al and Ed if they ever saw Melanie at William Creek Station. It was the first real conversation she managed to drag out of Nick and when he took her on a detour to see the indigenous art gallery, he'd taken her breath away in more ways than one.

Jenny focussed back on riding. This terrain was no place to let your mind wander. Lucy was an experienced stock horse, but two sets of eyes were better than one when it came to the rough, rocky trails.

As if reading her mind, Lucy shifted position drastically mid-stride, nearly unmounting Jenny. If it wasn't for the stock saddle thigh braces, she would have landed hard on the ground and at this pace it could have caused a serious injury.

Scanning the ground, she spotted a brown snake slithering away into the salt bush at speed.

'That was a close call Lucy.'

The horses' ears twitched, but the animal didn't slow until Nick dropped his mount back to a fast trot, then a slow trot and turned in the saddle.

'I think he should be around here somewhere.'

'I've not seen this side of the escarpment.' Jenny drew up alongside as Nick's horse dropped back to a walk.

The sheer wall of rock rose high, shading out the hot sun. Small shrubs with tiny white flowers dotted the rocky slope leading to an opening, arched by overhanging sandstone.

'We used to come here when he was a kid, after mum and dad...'

'Then you're probably right. He would come out here after the news.'

Jenny wanted to reach out and grab Nick's hand, but he dismounted before she got the chance.

She followed, leading Lucy to a dead tree limb and looping the reins over a sturdy branch.

'Do you want me to wait here? He might want to be alone.'

Jenny's eyes scanned the trail. It appeared untouched, but the rocky ground wasn't conducive to leaving footprints.

Nick seemed to consider her a moment, then shook his head. 'No. You should come with me. I think he'll respond to you better than me anyway. He likes you.'

A rare Nick smile appeared, reaching his eyes and making Jenny's stomach toss, before Nick's eyes darted skyward. Jenny followed his gaze to find a large eagle circling effortlessly overhead. The large bird drifted over the rocky outcrop and circled once more.

She glanced back to Nick. His earlier smile gone. His brows knitted together.

'What's up?'

'Could be nothing.' He didn't wait to explain. Instead, he turned and jogged up the incline toward a break in the rock's face.

The ancient crevice was eroded smooth on the edges, but a large chunk of the escarpment must have fallen loose, creating an archway three times Jenny's height.

She followed Nick up the slope toward it. The scene lost its majesty as Nick's growing apprehension caused her to become tense.

'Sam! You up here?' Nick slowed as he passed under the stone arch. Sunlight filtered down the ravine, casting an orange glow over the mottled rockface inside.

‘Sam?’ He called again. At first Jenny heard no reply, then something made her stop and reach for Nick’s arm.

‘Did you hear that?’

They stepped closer, straining to hear anything. A muffled groan made Nick turn to look at Jenny as though he needed her confirmation he wasn’t imagining it.

‘Sam! Where are you?’ Nick rushed the rest of the way through the archway. Once into the opening, his eyes roved the looming rock face within, desperate to find the source of the noise.

Inside was like a waterless grotto. Trees struggled for light. Green undergrowth flourished.

Jenny turned in a slow circle, a mix of anxiety and marvel as the surroundings overwhelmed her a moment, before she heard another groan.

‘Over there!’ She pointed to a rocky incline ahead, where a tall, crooked gumtree struggled to gain purchase amongst the rugged, shale slope. ‘The sound came from over there!’

Nick scrambled up the slope, using the trunk of the gumtree as an anchor. Jenny followed to glimpse Sam, over the rise, sprawled out in a pool of blood.

‘Sam! What happened?’ Nick shuffled carefully down the slope, trying not to dislodge any rocks.

Jenny’s stomach knotted. Sweat instantly broke out on her back.

She knelt next to Sam as Nick began tearing open his brother’s blood-stained shirt. They gasped, as the wound in Sam’s stomach became obvious.

‘He’s been shot!’

Chapter 22

'Take your shirt off!'

Jenny pointed to Nick's press stud chequered long sleeve shirt.

'You need to go for help.' Nick handed her the shirt.

She rolled it into a ball, pressed it to Sam's abdomen then scanned the area, trying to find something to tie it in place.

'No, you do. The R.F.D.S. won't get close enough with that rough approach. You'll need to bring them in by chopper once the plane lands nearby.'

Nick wiped his hands down his face. 'How did this happen? He can't have shot himself.'

'Not now Nick. Hold this.' She pointed to the balled-up shirt. 'I need to take mine off and tie it around him. Give me a hand.'

Nick took over applying pressure to the wound. Sam moaned, but his eyes stayed closed, his colour white. His skin pasty.

'Hang in there Sam. We've got you now.'

She struggled out of her long-sleeved cotton shirt to reveal a sports bra. The scene instantly reminding her of the day she held Nick's life in her hands. Just like this, he was bleeding out on the polished wooden floor of Murphy's kitchen.

Shaking herself free of the memory, she reached under Sam to thread her shirt around his waist before tying it over the makeshift bandage.

'Go Nick.'

'Are you sure?'

'I'm sure. You are a better rider than me and you know the area. You must get back to the station and call for help and

The Royal Flying Doctor will need a lift here. They'll also need someone who knows the way after dark. Only you can fly a chopper back out of here after sunset. Only you know the terrain well enough.'

They both knew choppers flew by line of sight which was dangerous in unknown terrain at night.

'Hang in there Sam. You're in good hands mate. She saved my life. She's got you.' He squeezed his brother's shoulder, obviously reluctant to leave him.

'I'll do what I can.'

Nick nodded in understanding. They didn't know how much blood Sam had lost. They might already be too late.

'Grab two water canteens, then go.'

Nick sucked in a deep breath as he rose and turned to jog up the incline toward the archway.

Jenny knew he'd be back with water any moment. The horses weren't far away, but watching his back disappear over the rise made her heart rate increase. She scanned the area and hoped he could get help out here before nightfall.

It was a hot day, but it was only spring, and the night temperature would plummet.

A minute later, Nick returned breathless. A rock slid down the slope toward her. Jenny deflected it away from Sam's head with her hand.

'Sorry. This is heavy.' He rolled a swag down the rocky slope a metre from Jenny, then scurried down after it.

'Good thinking.' Jenny didn't move her hand from Sam's belly. She didn't dare.

'Here's water, a muesli bar and I thought you could use the sleeping bag and swag for shelter. It's going to get cool. I'll be as fast as I can.' He turned to rush off.

'Nick.'

His head spun back to her.

'Ride carefully. It will be no good if you break Prince's leg and get stuck out there.'

'I know.' He squeezed her shoulder and was gone – leaving Jenny alone, tired and scared that Sam might not make it.

She turned to Sam, checking his pulse with her free hand.

'Stay with us mate. You need to tell us what happened here.'

Sam's eyes fluttered open. He tried to speak. Jenny reached for the water canteen. Not wanting to take her hand from Sam's wound, she shoved the container between her knees, squeezed and undid the cap with her free hand but realised Sam couldn't drink lying flat on his back.

She didn't want to risk moving him. Instead, she reached for the swag, dragged it closer and eased it under his head. His eyes fluttered open as a groan left his lips.

'Here. You need to drink.'

She held the canteen to his lips, tipped it back and slowly let a little bit of moisture into his mouth. Reflexively he swallowed a few mouthfuls.

He'd lost a lot of blood. If she didn't keep up the fluids, he'd die of blood loss or dehydration.

'Why would anyone want to shoot you Sam?'

'Man.'

She didn't expect an answer. Pressing down on his wound, she leant forward, trying to hear what he was saying.

'What Sam? Who did this?'

A string of incoherent mumbles erupted, then two barely understandable words.

'Scary…..man.'

'It's okay Sam. You can tell me later. Save your strength.'

Sam began to shiver. Shock was setting in. That, or the blood loss was too much. Either way, she needed to keep him warm.

Nick already removed the sleeping bag from the swag. Unzipping it with one hand and her teeth, she maintained pressure on Sam's wound. Her arm ached. She knew it would go numb eventually.

Soon she'd have to swap sides, but for now, she snuggled up against Sam and pulled the sleeping bag over him. He needed to stay warm and hydrated. She needed to stem the blood loss as long as possible.

Or he *was* going to die.

Chapter 23

The sound of chopper blades broke the eerie silence. It was like all the critters of the bush knew Sam was bleeding out and were being reverent.

Jenny's adrenalin overrode her tiredness.

'They're here mate.'

She searched Sam's neck for a pulse. Fear hit her like a sucker punch when she couldn't find it.

'Come on Sam. Helps is here mate. Stay with me.' She leant forward, trying to see if his chest was rising, but it was impossible in the fading light. The ravine was too deep. The sun long set from this side of the escarpment.

Placing her cheek over his mouth, she hovered, praying for warmth to touch her face. Finally, a whisper of air brushed her cheek. It was so feather light, she could have sworn it only lifted the fine hairs on her face.

'Hurry up!' she called. The sound echoed around the rocks. Tears burnt their way forward, but she furiously wiped them away.

Seeing the blood on the back of her hand as she wiped her face made her shudder.

'Hold your shit together girl. He's going to be okay.'

'Jenny!' Nick's voice made her whole-body shake. 'We're coming. I've got the doc.'

'Hurry up. Please,' she begged, as tears exploded from her eyes like a rainstorm. 'I can't find a pulse. He's barely breathing.'

'We've got him now luv. You can let go.'

A hand pulled her arm away from Sam's stomach. She didn't realise they were even touching her. Her entire body was numb.

'Jenny.' Nick pulled her to her feet.

Her legs buckled. Pins and needles rushed down her calves and into her feet.

'I'm sorry. I'm sorry.'

'Got a pulse.'

The female paramedic's words flooded Jenny with instant relief. She collapsed into Nick's arms.

Silence unnerved Jenny as the team worked with practised precision.

'Systolic is sixty-four and dropping.'

The nurse took readings while the doctor cut Sam's shirt away from his arms.

Eerie silence reigned. Nick's hand caressed her back as she buried her face in his chest. Her heartbeat thudded in her ears.

'Okay. I've got a line Tammy. Grab me a bag of O neg. Then I'll need a bag of saline.'

'On it.'

'Give me another BP once this is in.'

'Okay.'

'Let's get him stable and ready to transport.'

'Can I help?' Nick spoke over Jenny's shoulder, her face still buried into his chest. Her heart rate slowing as the calm team worked on Sam.

'In a minute mate. We'll get him ready for a stretcher, then we'll need all hands to carry him out of here.'

'BP is sixty-five over forty-nine and rising.'

'Have you eaten?' Nick eased Jenny back so he could see her face in the fading light. She shook her head.

Nick reached down to collect a muesli bar from the ground where she left it untouched. Right next to Sam, where the R.F.D.S. team were now huddled over, working on him.

'Eat this, drink this. We need your help to carry him out.'

Jenny gazed around and realised he was right. There were only two R.F.D.S. staff and no C.F.S. to help.

Nodding, she opened the muesli bar and drank a few mouthfuls of water from the canteen. The cool liquid soothed her throat. Realising how dehydrated she was, she continued to drink deeply.

As her mind focussed, she recalled Sam's words.

'He said something, not much, but he mentioned something about a scary man?'

Nick bit his lip. 'He was probably delirious. He used to have nightmares, after mum disappeared. Took years for them to go away.'

'What sort of nightmares?' Jenny's fogginess faded with each mouthful of food. She was useless when she was hungry and grumbled at herself for ignoring the food while Nick was gone.

'He could never fully explain. He was only nine. I put it down to dad's death and mum not being there. I did the best I could.'

'I know you did.'

She wrapped her arm in his, realising he was taking responsibility, even now. He was only nineteen, nearly twenty when his dad died and being left alone to run the cattle property and look after his brother was a huge responsibility.

'You said he was there when your dad died. Maybe he was there when your mum died too?'

'You think he saw something?'

Jenny's focus was fixed on the R.F.D.S. team as they worked methodically on Sam. Their headtorch lights flicked around in the faded light, resting on Sam's expressionless face intermittently. His words echoed in her mind. *Scary...man.*

'I don't know Nick, but someone shot your brother. We'll check his weapon to see if it was fired. If it was one of his bullets. But I don't think he could have accidentally shot himself in the stomach.'

'Okay you two. Let's get him out of here.' The doctor glanced up, his headtorch light illuminating them. All thought of shooting and past murder faded away.

****

Jenny's head dropped forward, waking her from a power nap. Sitting back, she rested her head against the rear window of her car. Her stomach knotted at the memory of watching the Royal Flying Doctors' plane take off. She would have given anything to be with Nick and Sam. But someone needed to wait for the forensic team – for Penny.

Her jaw clenched as hot tears threatened to spill free.

'He'll be alright,' she told herself aloud, but her stomach wouldn't stop churning.

Who would shoot Sam? And why?

The sound of an aircraft overhead woke her from another doze she never noticed coming on. The early, eerie light of pre-dawn saw the last few stars blink out, as the aircraft circled around to land into the light morning breeze.

The wheels of the plane skipped and skidded on the dusty airstrip. The prop noise echoed across the open, barren landscape. Jenny stepped out of her vehicle, into the crisp morning air.

Rubbing her arms, she waited for the plane to taxi toward her. The engines wound down as the side door opened. Jenny expected the detective to lead the exit, but it was Penny who appeared in the doorway. Leaping down the steps, she jogged to Jenny – all decorum forgotten. Flinging her arms around her, she hugged Jenny in a *no escape* bear hug.

'Don't Pen. I'll fall to pieces.'

Penny pulled back, holding her friend at arm's length.

'He'll make it. He's young and tough and you got to him in time Jen.'

'Is that optimism or professionalism speaking?'

'Sorry to be all business ladies, but we need to get on site as soon as possible.' Detective Grave hovered behind Penny, two bags of forensic equipment in hand.

Philips wandered behind, another load of gear in his grasp. Penny suddenly recalled the reason for the visit and jumped to assist.

'Sorry Phillips, got side tracked.'

As soon as Penny relieved him of his baggage, he joined Jenny and wrapped a brotherly hug around her shoulder with one arm.

'Nick's still waiting on news. Sam's in surgery. Nev went with him to Adelaide.'

Jenny sighed, letting hours of tension ease from her shoulders. She knew Nev would make sure Sam got the best surgeon Adelaide could offer, but her heart still ached. Nick was now in Adelaide, miles away from her and there was nothing she could do to make sure Sam was okay.

Nothing except find out who the hell shot him.

Chapter 24

As Jenny drove toward the newly rebuilt homestead, she recognised Rebecca's car parked out front.

The administrator of the William Creek Station waited with Al on the long, covered veranda – her eyes fixed on Jenny as she stepped out of the car.

'Jenny.' She jumped down from the concrete. Red dust billowed at her feet. 'I've got some food ready for you to take with you.'

'Ah. Thanks.' Jenny's stomach grumbled to signify how hungry she was.

'Just in time by the sound of that.' Rebecca's smile was forced, but under the circumstances, she didn't read too much into it.

'Thanks. But I don't think we have…'

'Food sounds good.' Philips strode past Jenny. 'Can we eat before we go?' He glanced over his shoulder at the detective.

'Grab a quick snack, then pack the rest.' Detective Grave breezed past Jenny.

'Looks like you've been out voted.' Rebecca put her hand on Jenny's arm and squeezed gently. 'Seriously. You need to eat. Nick's told me how hungry you can get.' Her lips turned up into a grin.

'Did he?'

'Al and Ed are out getting the Troopy ready, so you've got a few minutes to refuel. Take it Jenny. It's been a long night and it's going to be an even longer day.' Rebecca grabbed her arm and dragged her toward the homestead. Then stopped and turned around. 'How is Sam going?'

'I don't know for sure. Only that he's in Adelaide, with Nick and Nev.'

Rebecca bit her lip. 'He'll be okay.'

She turned and continued dragging Jenny through the distressed timber front doors and down past the freshly polished timber staircase. A hum of activity greeted them. Jenny spotted the food spread out over the kitchen table.

Her tastebuds ignited, colliding with saliva to signal her stomach to announce once again, just how hungry she was.

'Here. Eat this.' Penny spoke through a mouthful of food as she handed an egg and bacon burger to Jenny.

'How long to get out to the site?' Grave said before taking a large bite of her own burger.

'A couple of hours to the escarpment. It's rough territory. Then we'll need to go on foot a few kilometres.'

'Fun times. Okay, finish up, load up and let's get going.'

'Should I test to see if Sam's gun was fired first?' Penny shoved the last of her food in her mouth and washed it down with a tall glass of orange juice.

'I left it on scene. Didn't want to disturb anything. Besides, there's no point. Sam will definitely have fired his rifle. He was out there to hunt and escape, so we'll need to check ballistics once the bullet is recovered.' Jenny nibbled at her burger, her appetite fading as visions of Sam's pale, grimacing face invaded her thoughts.

'Even if they match, Sam couldn't have shot himself. Even by accident,' she added, then forced herself to take another bite.

'How can you be so sure?' Grave reached for a napkin and wiped her hands, her eyes, fixed on Jenny were full of concern.

'Because his arms wouldn't have been long enough to pull the trigger and get the weapon into the right spot on his stomach. He'd have to be a contortionist and even then, it wouldn't be accidental.'

'And no one tries to off themselves with a bullet to the guts.' Penny began packing food into a backpack.

Rebecca stepped forward to help, her eyes fixed on Jenny as she spoke. 'Sam's been around guns all his life. There is no way he accidentally shot himself.'

'I agree. Farm kids know how to handle guns.'

Grave rose from the long bench seat and crossed toward the front door.

'Let's get going team.'

Jenny wondered how Detective Grave knew about farm kids. The thought made her want to ask more, but now wasn't the right time.

Al appeared in the hallway. 'Ready?'

'Ready,' Grave assured him.

'Ah.' Philips shoved food in his mouth as his hands worked furiously trying to pour himself a drink.

'Come on Philips.' Grave picked up the backpack Penny packed and waved it in front of the hungry constable. 'We've got more food and drinks in here.'

Philips followed as ordered. Jenny and Penny joined the end of the line.

'Let me know if you need anything,' Rebecca called after them.

Jenny sat in the middle of the front bench seat. Grave on her left, Al in the driver's seat.

Penny and Philips sat either side of the rear cargo area on the long bench seats with a pile of equipment at their feet.

'You come from a farm Detective?' Jenny didn't want to go over Sam's shooting just yet and the scenery was too beautiful, too serene to want to think about it right now.

'It's in the past.'

'I grew up on a dairy farm. Never expected to become a cop. What about you?'

Grave bit her lip. Jenny opened her mouth to change the subject, but Grave carried on.

'Everything in Far North Queensland is a bit isolated, a bit countrified.'

'You know about farm kids and rifles? Did you shoot?'

'Not much, but my brother used to go wild pig shooting with my dad until…' The detective trailed off as her vision misted over like a memory was playing in front of her eyes. She shook her head abruptly.

'My brothers did a bit of shooting, but it wasn't their thing. I went shooting with my uncle more than any of them.'

'What about Geoff?' Grave's interest was piqued, and Jenny realised she just put a firearm in her brother's hands. The same brother who was now a person of interest in Ron Johnston's murder.

'Geoff was the least interested in guns.'

Was she saying that because of the circumstances? She let her mind drift back to her days on the family dairy farm. It seemed so long ago now. She used to go shooting with her uncle Pete. Geoff never went with them.

'He doesn't have a gun licence.' Grave stated the fact.

Jenny wasn't surprised she checked.

'He was into saving the ocean and surfing.'

'He also has a record for possession.' Grave spoke, then turned to study the vast, rugged terrain from the window.

Tinges of green native grasses worked their way from the shale rock. Spent wildflowers hung, drooping and drying.

All signs spring was in the wind and summer was right around the corner.

Jenny pondered her brother's police record. It wasn't a surprise to her. But any black mark could give fuel to the fire when it came to a police investigation.

'I ran my family through the database when I became a cop. It's not strictly kosher, but considering I was trying to find my cousin, I didn't feel guilty over it.'

'So you know about his drug charge.'

Jenny nodded.

'I asked him about it.'

'And?'

'He was seventeen. Got caught with a joint at an Eagles' concert.

Grave laughed aloud.

'Why on earth was he at an Eagles' concert? They were a band of my parents' era.'

'He was a long-time fan. Maybe because our parents listened to them all the time. I don't know.'

'Where do you think your brother is?'

'I have no idea.'

'Would you tell me if you did?'

Jenny turned to face the detective.

'I'd probably want to talk with him first.'

Grave smiled. 'Are you close with your family?'

Jenny shrugged. *Was she?*

'I thought I was. We don't talk all the time or anything, but we were close when I was growing up. But Mel's disappearance changed things.'

'Losing a family member can do that.'

The way Grave said those few words made Jenny want to ask questions, but she realised now wasn't the time to be digging into the detective's private life. She needed to update Grave on her interview with Mrs B. and Rebecca.

'I got some information from Rebecca and her mum that might put Geoff in the clear in any case.'

'Oh.'

'Mrs B. said there was a guy hanging out at the pub around the time Ron died, but he never asked any questions about Ron, William Creek Station or any missing family.'

'That's interesting. Did you get a description?'

'It was ten years ago. Mrs B. didn't exactly recall details, but Rebecca did see Geoff's car.'

'And.'

Al slowed the vehicle to a full stop below the escarpment.

'We go by foot now.' Al pulled the handbrake on and turned the motor off.

Grave didn't move. Her eyes were fixed on Jenny's.

'She never saw Geoff.'

'She knows this how?'

Al opened the door to get out, but Jenny could tell he was listening in on their conversation. The old man never said much, but he was a tracker – always watching and paying attention to his surroundings.

'Because she didn't see the driver. She was keeping an eye out, hoping to see a young, hot guy driving, but she needed to get back to the bar.'

'So she can't confirm if your brother was or wasn't there?'

'No, but she served in the bar all afternoon and never saw Geoff in the pub. I showed her a photo.'

'Would he lend his car to someone?'

Jenny shrugged. 'Maybe one of his surfing mates or...' Jenny stopped as Penny opened the rear doors of the Landcruiser.

'We won't know for sure until we find Geoff.' Jenny shuffled from the front seat out Al's side of the vehicle, suddenly not wanting to contemplate who else could have been driving Geoff's car and if they could be connected to what happened to Nick's parents.

Chapter 25

Sweat dripped down the middle of Jenny's back as she approached the escarpment. The rock formation rose in front of them, shielding out the sun and offering welcoming shade.

In the shadow of the rugged rocky face, the events of the previous night hit home.

Detective Grave's warm hand patted her shoulder. The woman's words echoing the sentiment of Jenny's inner turmoil.

'You can't change what happens to Sam. You can only make sure whoever put him in the hospital goes to jail for it.'

'Here. Everyone put these on.' Penny handed out shoe covers.

Al's unlit rollie jostled on his lip as he studied the item thrust into his hand.

'They are so your footprints and trace on your shoes don't mess up any possible evidence collection.'

Al appeared on the verge of saying something, but a grin split his lips instead.

'Something funny Al?' Detective Grave pulled a shoe cover on, balancing expertly on one foot upon the rugged rocky ground.

'Nah. All good.'

'She's not having a go at your tracking Al. It's police procedure.' Jenny said.

Al nodded, put the covers on, then bent down to study the ground as Penny pulled her digital camera from an old worn leather doctor's style bag.

'Interesting bag.'

Grave nodded toward the soft light brown bag, with worn wrinkles resembling Hooch's soft, flappy cheeks, from the movie. Jenny wasn't sure if the detective was being polite or was genuinely interested.

'A gift maybe? A family heirloom?'

'A thrift shop find.' Penny hung the camera around her neck and grinned.

Philips laughed.

Al wandered up the escarpment, ignoring the conversation. Jenny watched him study the ground as he picked his way over the rocky terrain.

He glanced back at her feet, then studied the ground some more.

'You found something Al?' She stepped forward to follow him.

'Tracks.'

All conversation stopped as everyone studied the old bow-legged jackaroo ambling his way along the trail toward the natural arched opening in the rock face.

Jenny's skin tingled as visions of Sam lying in a pool of blood swamped her memory.

'Sam came up here, fast.'

Detective Grave approached Al, studying the ground with a frown as she carefully picked her way toward him.

'How do you know?'

'Scuffs here. This mark.' He pointed to the ground to the left of the entrance. 'This one's Jenny. This one's Nick. Slow, steady.'

Jenny followed the detective, the hairs on her arms standing on end.

'This one, panicked.' He pointed to the ground. 'And this one.'

'Can you see any other tracks but mine and Nick's?'

The whites of Al's eyes contrasted against his dark skin. The still unlit smoke hung from his lip, then lifted up and down as he continued to study the area.

'Nah.'

'So Sam runs up the hill here, in a panic. Why?' Jenny asked the question to anyone willing to offer a plausible reason.

Philips shrugged. Penny snapped photos of every spot Al pointed out.

'He needed a place to hide.' Grave offered.

Al grunted he agreed.

'So he was running from the shooter and it wasn't a random accidental shot. Who would do that?' Jenny's pulse quickened.

Someone was hunting Sam.

'Look at this.' Penny fingered a mark in the rock face, around head high. 'And this.' She put an evidence marker on the ground and snapped a series of photos.

The rock face was scarred by an impact that left a white, chalk like residue behind.

'High velocity round. We should be able to find where it landed.' Penny focussed on the ground around the entrance to the rock formation.

'Where was the shooter?'

Penny nodded over Jenny's shoulder and down the escarpment to where the Landcruiser troop carrier was parked.

'From down there, I'd say.'

'Okay. Fan out everyone. Philips, you need to get back down to the vehicle and check for shell casings, vehicle tracks.' Grave pointed down the hill, Philips turned to leave but waited as Penny spoke.

'Blood.' She crouched down to study a dark spot on the ground.

'So the shot struck him out here, before he got inside the ravine.' Jenny joined Penny.

'That might explain why he bled out slowly. A ricochet, not a clean shot.' Penny adjusted the lens on her camera and shot another series of photos of the blood trail.

'So the shooter never followed Sam inside?' Grave turned to Al for clarification.

He remained silent, only a nod of his head told her she was correct.

'He was confident his shot was good. Otherwise why didn't he follow Sam inside to finish the job?' Grave continued surmising.

'Sam was armed, maybe they decided he was setting up a defensive position and didn't want to risk climbing inside the ravine after him. This is familiar territory to Sam and maybe not to the shooter.

'Good point Williams.'

Jenny's adrenalin kicked in as she put their findings together in her head.

'If they know we got to him in time and he's still alive, he could still be at risk.'

'But why would anyone want to kill Sam?' Philips frowned, bit his lip and scanned everyone's face for an answer.

Jenny mulled over the question. Sam's only audible words, as he lay in a pool of blood came back to her.

'When I was with Sam last night, he could barely make a sound, but he desperately struggled to tell me something. When he finally got the words out, they didn't make a lot of sense. All he said was *scary man.* I told Nick and he said Sam used to have nightmares, after his dad's death. Apparently, he grew out of them, but…'

'But.' Grave waited for Jenny to continue.

'But last night, his words sounded like they were coming from a scared little boy.'

'And you think he was reliving those nightmares?'

'I think he might have been carrying around the identity of his dad's killer all these years but never recalled.'

'So why remember now?'

'Maybe he saw the person responsible again. Maybe us finding his mum's body brought back the nightmares?'

'And you think the perpetrator followed him all the way out here to silence him?'

'It sounds far-fetched when you say it like that, but if Sam did see his dad's killer, and that killer tried to silence him out here, then he could still be in danger.'

'Does that radio work out here Al?' The detective pointed to the tall aerial on the bullbar of the Landcruiser.

Al shrugged, pulled the unlit smoke from his lip, studied the end and rummaged in his pocket for a light.

'Give it a go Philips.' Grave pointed to the vehicle.

Philips nodded, then scurried back down the rise, loose stones rolled down after him.

'Let's finish with this scene and get back to Coober Pedy.' Grave skirted around Penny's evidence marker on the ground and entered the ravine.

Jenny was rooted to the spot as she watched her disappear. Turning, she waited anxiously as Philips tried to contact the station.

Who killed Nick's dad and mum and why go after Sam? There must to be a connection between the murders and the domestic violence rescue efforts, but the only recent rescue at the time of Ron's death was Melanie.

She was back at square one. Whoever Tristan's father was, he was likely connected to the murders of Patricia and Ron Johnston.

Now she needed to do two things. Find out who he was, and hope to heaven he wasn’t her brother.

Chapter 26

Hot water eased tired muscles as Jenny watched the day's dust turn the white tiled shower floor rusty red.

Her eyes were gritty, despite the water running down her face. A serious lack of sleep, adrenalin overload and hurried eating were mounting up with the tension in every fibre of her body.

The water turned cold.

Shutting off the shower, she leaned against the cool tile, trying to get her head straight.

O'Connell's request to track Melanie's phone was granted, but the phone wasn't switched on, so they still had no idea where her cousin was now.

Geoff was not answering and without a warrant, they couldn't trace his phone. His car being out at the William Creek Station around the time of Ron's death wasn't grounds for any sort of evidence hunt and Jenny was thankful for that.

Visions of her childhood bounced around her head. There was no indication to her that Geoff was even remotely interested in Melanie back then.

Did she miss something?

And why did her aunt take Melanie away? Her dad told her Uncle Pete and Aunt Carolyn's relationship was shaky, but still, to take Melanie away because of her pregnancy and to keep her away from her family all that time.

It just didn't make sense.

Jenny squeezed her long auburn hair into a ponytail and wrung out the excess water. Washing her hair in the evening was always a nightmare, but there was too much dust in it. Gritty bits of sand were caked to her scalp, giving her no other choice.

Stepping out of the shower, she dried off, dressed and opened the bathroom door.

Eerie silence greeted her. The living room light illuminated the machinery marked stone walls of the dugout, creating a creepy vibe.

Her housemates, Tim and Nev were doing night duty this week. Nick was still in Adelaide, waiting to see how Sam was recovering and she was overwhelmed with the need not to be alone.

Penny was always good company, but she didn't want to talk work tonight.

She collected her keys from the kitchen counter, grabbed her backpack and stepped outside into the cool night air.

Stars flickered in a blanket overhead. Stopping, she peered up to study them a moment, her heart heavy, her mind buzzing. As her eyes focussed on each tiny dot of light, a little bit of tension eased away.

The buzzing of her phone in her pocket made her jump. Retrieving it, she checked the caller ID. Her heart skipped a beat as she slid the answer bar across.

'Nick!'

Silence greeted her. Her stomach knotted as she scanned the screen to be sure she had a connection. She did, but it wasn't great.

'Nick. Are you there?'

'Yep. Sorry, someone came into the room just as the call connected. I need to ring you back.'

She didn't get the chance to say okay before the line went dead.

Was Sam alright?

Visions of a casket and funeral flowers swam in front of her vision. She dismissed them. Sam was okay. He had to be.

Taking a deep, steadying breath, Jenny strode to her car. She should have been dead tired. Instead, she was wired tighter than a ball of string.

She needed a drink. She needed noise, company, people around her. She needed Nick, but he was a thousand ks away.

Ten minutes later, as she stepped out of her car at the Opal Motel car park, her phone buzzed again.

'Hello. Nick. Is everything okay?'

'Sorry about that Jen. The doctor came in right as I called you. I'd been waiting for hours and I…'

'It's okay Nick.' She could hear the tension in his voice. She wanted him to tell her what the hell was going on, but she knew she needed to give him a minute.

'Sam's…' His voice choked.

Oh my God no. He's not dead. Please…

'He's still unconscious. He lost a lot of blood Jen.'

She waited, not knowing what to say. At least he was alive.

'He's going to be okay Jen.'

She let the breath she'd be holding go with a rush.

'Oh Nick.'

'You've saved us both now. In more ways than you can imagine.'

Warm tears stung the back of her eyes and spilled down her cheeks.

'That is so good.'

'The surgeon said the bullet was spent when it hit Sam. It missed all the vital organs, hit his spleen and fragmented into little pieces.'

All Jenny could think about was ballistics and how difficult their job was going to be now. She shoved the thought away.

'They removed his spleen and all the shrapnel. He'll be able to come home in one or two days.'

'That is such a relief. Are they sure he can come home so soon?'

'He has to take it easy for four to six weeks but yeah. I'll fly home tomorrow sometime. He'll likely get transported with Careflight the day after.'

'How are you getting home?'

'Nev's pulled a few strings and got me on standby for a return R.F.D.S. flight.'

'Not what you know, but who you know, as they say.'

'For sure.' Silence hung in the air a moment.

'There is a police officer outside the room Jen. What's that about?'

'The detectives from Adelaide haven't spoken to you?'

'They have, but they aren't telling me much.'

'We believe the bullet that hit Sam was intentional.'

'No doubt about it. Other than a few indigenous locals, no one goes out to the escarpment. But why Jen? No one is telling me why.'

She hesitated. Was this outside her scope? Was she going to get in trouble with Grave? If the Adelaide detectives were being vague, it was likely for a reason.

'You said Sam used to have nightmares and I told you what he told me in the ravine, right?'

'Aha.'

'We think Sam saw whoever killed your dad, or, maybe your mum, or both. He must not have known he did, or never remembered or blocked it out.'

'And you think they tried to kill Sam? But why? And how would they know about his nightmares? How would they know he might recall who they are and why now?'

'All very good questions and ones I've been trying to work out all day.'

Sounds of music and loud voices greeted Jenny as she opened the glass doors to the restaurant and bar.

'Where are you Jen?'

'At the motel. The dugout was empty and I'm missing you and I didn't feel like cooking after spending the whole day…'

She didn't say where. She didn't need to.

'Be careful Jen. If someone is desperate enough to try and shoot Sam, they might try and stop you too. And I'm not there to get shot trying to protect you.'

She could hear the smile in his words, but there was tension too. Nick had a habit of stepping up to protect her, but it didn't always go to plan.

'I'm okay Nick. Penny is here still. She'll make sure no one hurts anyone.'

Nick chuckled. 'Between her and Detective Grave, I think girl power has your back.'

'You can bank on it.' The noise grew louder. 'I'll call you back in the morning and see when your flight is coming in.'

'Okay. Like I said. Be careful. It wouldn't be the first time the police have been a target during a murder investigation.'

'I'll be careful.'

'Love you.'

Jenny smiled at his words. There they were, up front and freely given.

'And I love you right back.'

She hung up before she said anything soppy and stupid to ruin the moment.

Glancing up, she saw the very woman she wanted to catch up with sitting at the bar, beer in hand.

Chapter 27

Nellie's dark wavy hair hung down her back. The scrunched top of her peasant blouse stretched over her chest, creating a distraction for two locals trying to look like they weren't looking.

'I was already here when I got your text.' Nellie patted the worn vinyl stool next to her. 'It was manic today hey.'

'For us or for you?' Jenny sat as Stan plonked a frothy brew in front of her with a broad smile.

'How's Sam?' The barman's dark eyes studied her.

'He's gonna be okay. Just got off the phone to Nick. They should let him come home in a day or two.'

'Wow. That quick.' Stan didn't have time to wait for more details. A holler from the end of the bar sent him running.

'That's great news.' Nellie squeezed her hand. 'He's been through enough.'

'Yeah, losing his mum and dad has been hard.'

'And witnessing it all.' Nellie sipped her beer.

Jenny gaped open-mouthed a moment. Nellie was working in the station, sure, but she wasn't in the briefing when they talked about Sam discovering his dad's body, but even if she was…no one said he saw the murder.

'Ah…what makes you say Sam saw his dad die?'

Nellie pressed up on the stool rung, peered down the bar, reached over and ripped a newspaper out from under a miner's elbow. He started, eyes wide and disoriented as he was awakened from his bar snooze.

'Hey!'

'Sorry Bruce. Can I borrow this?' She waved the paper in the air.

The miner frowned, pulled back as though he needed to focus on it, then shook his head.

'Not mine luv. Do what you want with it.' And promptly returned to leaning on his elbow, eyes glazed over staring into his half empty beer.

Nellie opened the paper to page three, placed it on the bar and tapped the rest of the article from the front page that Jenny never bothered to read.

She wondered if Sarge or anyone else had.

As she scanned the words, her blood ran cold. She didn't want to talk about the Johnston murders tonight. She hoped to ignore the mounting suspicion that Melanie's disappearance and stay at Nick's family property was linked, but now, as she considered each word on the black and white paper before her, she realised that was going to be impossible.

'How on earth did Gwen find this out?'

Nellie bit her cheek and averted her eyes.

'You didn't.'

Nellie's eyes grew wide.

'No way, not me. I never knew anything about this.' Nellie tapped the paper firmly with her pointer finger, sat back on her stool and sculled the last of her beer.

'Then who? And why do you look guilty?'

Nellie reached for the paper, closed it then proceeded to curl it up like a baton.

'Uncle.'

'Who?'

'Al, but we all call him Uncle.'

'Why on earth would Al tell a reporter Sam saw his dad die?'

'He told me about it a while back. I honestly thought Gwen was doing the right thing, not exposing Sam, but when

Patricia's body turned up, all sense of community and care must have gone out the window.'

'When did Al tell Gwen about Sam?'

'It wasn't exactly like she wrote in the article. Al got a little hammered. He's on the wagon now, has been for years but he was blubbering at the bar one night and Gwen must have overheard. When Patricia's body came to light, she put two and two together and made one hundred out of it.'

'So Al doesn't know if Sam saw either of his parents murdered, only that he found his dad's body?'

Nellie shrugged. 'I haven't had a chance to ask him.'

'Did Sarge see the full article, or just the headline before he confronted Gwen?'

'Don't know that either.'

Jenny hoped he did. She hoped he told her to print a retraction pronto, especially in light of the attack on Sam.

'She's probably the reason Sam was shot. I should…' Jenny snapped to her feet.

Nellie reached for her arm.

'Don't cross Gwen. Believe me. That woman has no scruples. She'll sell her own grandmother for a headline. Don't give her any ammunition.'

Jenny sat back down, drew a deep breath, puffed out her cheeks and drank a long swig of beer which went straight to her head.

'You said you needed a night out, no work, no bodies, no gunshot victims. So… let's go girl. You can strangle Gwen tomorrow, but I don't advise it. The woman has her finger in every pie around town.'

'You mean her claws into every eligible bachelor with any clout.'

'That too.' Nellie smiled her white, bright, toothy grin and Jenny laughed aloud.

'So how is your first week in the cop shop going?'

'Great. Sarge and O'Connell have been awesome. Showing me the ropes and all.'

'Interesting.'

'What?' Nellie waved her hand in the air and signalled with her fingers for two more beers. Stan waved and gave her the thumbs up.

'He made my life a living hell for the first month or more.'

'That's because you're a cop and a little headstrong.'

Jenny pouted as a fresh beer arrived on the bar runner, froth rolling over the rim.

'In a good kind of way, but I'm a blogger, a reporter. I need to gently ease information from the source.'

'So what you're saying is you've got tact and I don't.'

'Your words, not mine.' Nellie put her beer to her lips.

Jenny shoved Nellie gently. Froth spilled over the rim of her glass. They giggled.

'It's Karaoke tonight. I hear you sing up a storm.' Nellie's wicked grin grew wider.

'Why does bad news always travel so far and wide?'

As if on cue, a tapping on the mic was followed by the town's regular ice breaking karaoke miner massacring the first few lines of Keith Urban's most recent hit *John Cougar, John Deere, John 3:16.*

****

It was nearly midnight when Nellie, rightfully suggested Jenny not drive home and she should walk to her place instead to crash.

'I just need to grab my backpack from the car and make sure it's locked.'

'Good idea.' Nellie wavered, then leant against a veranda post to right herself. 'You can certainly sing you know.'

Jenny waved her hand dismissively. 'Marj keeps going on about following in her footsteps with her annual birthday bash.'

'That's big boots to fill, but I reckon you could do it.' Nellie pushed off the post to follow Jenny down the well-lit veranda, past the motel reception and into the carpark.

'Absolutely. And I'm not wearing that Liza Minnelli outfit she wears. Top hat, low cut front with sequins. Never going to happen.'

'I don't know, Nick might like it.'

Jenny snorted. A sure sign she drank *way* too much. The two women held each other up as they rocked and rolled toward Jenny's car.

In the dim carpark lighting, something caught Jenny's eye. A light breeze fluttered a piece of paper shoved under her windscreen wiper.

Leaning against the hood, she reached for the large sheet of paper and pulled it out from under the wiper.

Fully expecting some religious flyer about the evils of drink and gambling, she was surprised to see no pictures, no bold lettering, just a few lines typed neatly, all in capitals.

Focussing, she struggled to read it in the dim carpark lighting. Pulling out her mobile phone, she fumbled around, finally opening her torch app after the third attempt.

'What you got?' Nellie leant around her to get a better look.

'Don't know.' Jenny held her torch aloft.

Seeing the words sent a chill down her spine.

'What the!' Nellie's words echoed Jenny's thoughts.

'Who?' Was all Jenny could say as she read each word slowly again out loud.

'LEAVE... THE... PAST... ALONE...
OR ELSE!'

Chapter 28

Everyone huddled around the letter, now in a plastic bag lying on Jenny's desk in the front office of the police station. Not that she expected Penny to find anything useful on it, but keeping it protected was instinctive.

'Take a photo, put it on our board and then let's see what McGregor can find.' Sarge tapped the plastic cover with his plump, stubby pointer finger.

'Someone doesn't want us digging into the Johnston's murders.' O'Connell returned to his desk and sat down heavily.

'Why put the message on Williams' windscreen? They aren't going to put a halt to a police investigation into a double homicide by harassing a constable.' Detective Grave wasn't saying anything Jenny hadn't already thought about.

Once she sobered up.

Sipping a glass of water, she swore to herself. She thought Nev and Tim could drink like fish. Nellie put them both to shame.

What was she thinking, trying to keep up with her?

'This seems personal.' Philips frowned as he studied the typed words.

'That's my take too constable.' Grave's nostrils flared as she pulled her mobile from her pocket, snapped a photo, then handed the plastic covered letter to Penny.

Penny absently accepted the letter, her gaze on her friend.

'Why Jenny?'

'Because of Sam and Nick maybe?' Jenny knew her answer was flawed. Her instincts were telling her this was linked to Melanie.

'Where's your aunt?' Grave was obviously on the same wavelength. 'We need to find her, bring her in and see what she has to say about this.'

Grave turned to Philips. He nodded and stepped away from the group toward the front counter.

'Okay team. We couldn't trace Melanie's phone signal, but let's get her phone records for the past three months. I want to know where she was before she turned back up in Coober Pedy.'

'What about Williams' brother?' Sarge said.

'Him too, if we can wrangle a warrant. Are they together now? Have they been in contact recently? Geoff Williams' car was seen at the William Creek Station and the Pub. Maybe he was simply picking Melanie up, but I think there is something more to this.'

'Sam should be home in a day or two. We'll be able to ask him more about what he recalls of the events leading up to his dad's body being found.' Jenny didn't want to put Sam through the trauma, but they had no choice.

Someone was trying to silence him. Someone thought he knew something, even if he didn't know what he knew.

'Found Carolyn Williams. She's been staying at the Opal Motel.' Philips waited for further instructions.

'Williams, Philips. You two head over and ask her politely to come in for a few more questions. I'll get this photo printed and go stare at a whiteboard. We are missing something. I can feel it in my bones.' Detective Grave's eyes were on her phone, sending the photo to the Wi-fi printer before Jenny could complain.

The order had been given. There was no getting around it. Sarge focussed on her, nodded he understood, but his eyes told her she had to follow the order.

Sighing, she turned and followed Philips from the station.

They remained silent during the short walk to the motel reception. As Jenny poked her head around the corner, her anxiety abated. Sitting in her usual spot, on a stool, behind the reception desk was Marj.

The motel owner's earlier burgundy rinse was now dark purple. The colour was nice, but the brighter red or orange she favoured last month suited her better.

'Marj. Sorry to bother you.'

The busty woman jumped from her seat, rounded the counter and wrapped her arms around Jenny before she could protest.

'Never a bother luv. How's Sam doing?'

'Better than expected.' Jenny didn't try to pull back from the firm embrace. There was no point. Marj was a force to be reckoned with. A one woman show – she managed the Opal Motel on her own after her partner died.

The former opal miner was one tough nugget and everyone in town loved her.

'I read that article in the paper. Is it true?' Marj whispered in her usual conspiratorial tone when she wanted to gossip.

Jenny bit her lip. Marj was a compulsive busy body. The last person Jenny should share sensitive information with, but in that moment, it took every ounce of self-control not to let her turmoil and anxiety loose.

'It's exaggerated Marj, like all newspaper articles and I've not had a chance to speak with Sam yet. He went missing when his mum's body was discovered, then the shooting.'

Marj smiled. Patted her shoulder and nodded.

'So it *is* true.'

Philips coughed and cleared his throat, stepping forward to gallantly offer his perspective.

'Sarge has put a gag order on Gwen. She's gone off on another tangent and this one might finally see her in trouble.'

'The press is never gagged for long Danny.' Marj crossed her arms.

Philips grinned cheekily.

'What room is my aunt staying in?'

'Ah, she checked out just after Danny rang me Luv.'

Jenny turned to Philips, then back to Marj.

'Did she say where she was going?'

'No luv. Sorry. I didn't ask and she didn't say.'

'Can I grab her registration details then thanks Marj.'

'Is this an official police request?'

'It is.' Philips answered for Jenny. 'We don't need a warrant, do we Marj?'

'I don't see why.'

Marj scurried around her desk, flipped open a green ledger and ran her finger down the page.

'I'm sure you can get registration numbers from the registration office in a flash in any case.'

She scribbled the number on a piece of paper, slammed the ledger closed and hurried back around the raised counter.

'Is this about your cousin luv, or Nick's parents' murders?'

Jenny bit her lip. What was she going to say to Marj?

'It's just an old case we're working on Marj,' Philips interceded.

Marj handed the paper to Jenny. 'I know when to keep my mouth shut luv. You need to talk, you know where to find me.' She held the paper, not letting Jenny take it until she made eye contact.

Nodding, she wordlessly agreed. Marj let the paper go, a genuine smile touched her lips.

'When is Nick due back?'

'Today sometime, not sure when.'

Marj's eyes rose over Jenny's shoulder. 'I think I might.'

Jenny spun around. Standing in the reception doorway was the only person in the world she desperately needed to see today.

A curve of his lip told her he was glad to see her too.

Philips stepped aside as Nick wasted no time reaching her. Every fibre in her body screamed as tears prickled at the back of her eyes.

There was no need to be so emotional. She tried to tell herself to get it together. Sam was going to be okay, and Nick was home.

But the letter last night had her on edge. The past few days of stress were taking their toll as her memory revisited the scene out at the escarpment.

'It's okay.' Nick wrapped his strong arms around her.

She hated the fact she needed his strength right now. It should have been her being strong for him. It was his parents who were murdered, but the thought Melanie or Aunt Carolyn or maybe her brother might be involved ripped at her heart.

'I'm back.' Nick tightened his grip.

Marj trotted back to the reception desk. Philips disappeared outside. Jenny hung in Nick's arms like a limp rag, tears rolling down her face.

Chapter 29

Jenny wiped the tears from her face.

'I'm so sorry. I'm such a wuss.'

'You are definitely not a wuss. You took charge when we found Sam. You're badass Jen. Everyone needs to let the tension go occasionally.' He hugged her again, wrapped his arm around her shoulder, nodded to Marj and led the way from reception.

'Nick, there's something we need to talk about.'

Philips overheard them talking.

'I'll go back to the station, run this plate and update the boss.'

'Which one,' Jenny quipped.

'All of them.' Philips patted her shoulder. 'You okay?'

'I'm good. Thanks Danny.'

They rarely used first names on the job, but her partner was a softy at heart. She needed him to know she valued his support, personally. Not professionally.

'What did you need to talk about?' Nick spoke as Philips jogged back down the veranda toward the station.

Jenny sighed. She wanted coffee, but the motel brew wasn't going to cut it.

'Let's go to Niko's, grab coffees for the team and I'll explain.'

A few minutes later they parked outside Niko's café. Two locals, one with a pipe, one hanging on to an unlit hand rolled cigarette watched them from the front veranda.

'Can we talk in here?'

Nick turned the motor off but left the keys in the ignition.

'Sure.' He studied her face carefully.

She tried to collect her thoughts. She already told him about her brother's car being seen at William Creek Station. But he didn't know about Melanie, Geoff and Aunt Carolyn being missing.

'Nick. I don't know how, or why, but I think my family mystery, my missing cousin, Geoff's car...' She choked on her own words.

Nick squeezed her hand. 'Jen. No matter what, I'm not going to blame you for anything. I've been thinking the same thing. Melanie being at the station around the same time can't be a coincidence. When she was here, talking about mum and dad, apologising like it was her fault….'

'I don't think Mel killed your dad.'

'I don't think she did either, but I think she knows who did.'

'Then the next big question is, does my aunt know?'

'Your aunt?'

'She came to town, but now she's disappeared, just like Mel and Geoff.'

'Jenny, if they all know who killed my dad and maybe my mum, they could be in real danger.'

'I know Nick. Believe me. That's all I've been thinking about, but last night I was out with Nellie at the motel bar.'

He lifted an eyebrow.

'Big night?'

She tried to read his expression.

'More a late one and when I got to my car, there was a note under the windscreen wiper warning me to back off.'

'You, not the police?'

'That's exactly what Detective Grave said.'

'Jen. Someone is making this personal.'

'That's not what I'm worried about Nick. First someone shoots Sam. Now the note. Then Aunt Carolyn goes missing, and Mel and Geoff are still off the grid.'

'You think your aunt's disappearance isn't by choice?'

The same thought was already mulling around in her head. She needed to find out how her aunt was when she checked out. Was she calm, or did she appear upset?

'We need to go back to Marj's.'

'Can we grab coffee first. The R.F.D.S. I dead headed on didn't exactly serve breakfast.'

****

'Hi Jenny.' Nellie didn't appear to have the same hangover Jenny did.

'Hi Nellie. Can't stop.'

Jenny hurried past the front counter toward Sarge's office.

'Sir?' She tapped the door frame.

Detective Grave sat in the Sarge's spare chair.

'What's up Williams?' Sarge waved her in. Grave spun in her chair, a notepad on the desk forgotten.

'Philips told you my aunt checked out right?'

'He did. He's running her vehicle registration now to see if it comes up on any city traffic cameras.'

'Sir, I don't think she's gone back home.'

Grave rose from the chair and leant on Sarge's desk, waving for Jenny to enter the office.

'What's going on Jenny?'

'I was talking with Nick and I got an idea.'

'About the case.'

'Not now Grave,' Sarge interrupted. 'We've been over this.'

'Yes, about the case. About how my family being at his property when his parents died isn't a coincidence and how we both think Melanie likely knows who killed his dad.'

'What makes you say that?' Sarge couldn't remain seated. Standing, he paced toward her.

'It was the things she said. The way she acted. Nick said she put the lime tree in the garden bed. I thought nothing of it at first, but then he said she tended the garden every day.'

'She was out in the middle of nowhere, likely bored to tears,' Grave offered.

'Melanie hated gardening when we were kids. She hated farming. The bikes, the horses, yes, but not the tractors, the cow shit, the dirt.'

'She did come back when she heard about Ron's death.' Sarge sat on the edge of his desk and crossed his arms.

'You think she killed Ron Johnston?' Grave studied Jenny closely.

'No. I think she might know who did. We've eliminated all the other domestic violence victims. She's the only one who was there around the time Ron died. I think Tristan's father, whoever caused her to run, is likely the murderer.

'And Geoff's car? Does he know who the murderer is too, or is he the boy's father?' Grave sat back down on the edge of her seat.

'I don't know. I don't think so, but now Aunt Carolyn has gone missing too, and did you read the whole article Gwen wrote?'

Sarge pursed his lips. 'I've told her to print a retraction. That crap about Sam nearly got him killed.'

'But that's just it Sir. Nick said Sam found his dad and Al kept it quiet. Gwen's source was Al. He apparently spilled the story one night in the bar after too many drinks.'

'But we already know Sam found his dad.'

'Yes, but did he see who killed his mum? Is that why he was targeted? Gwen's article alludes to as much.'

'Possibly. But how does that connect with your cousin?'

'I think Mel was there too. I think Geoff came and got her, after the murders. That's why his car was seen there.'

'That could make sense.'

'Then why do you think your aunt has gone missing?'

'I spoke with Marj. Aunt Carolyn didn't look relaxed. Marj didn't think anything of it, and I wouldn't have either. Her daughter is missing again, but if my aunt knows Melanie knows who killed the Johnstons then someone might be using her to find Melanie.'

'But your aunt said she doesn't know where your cousin is.'

'We know that, but they might not.'

'So what happens to your aunt when she can't lead them to Melanie?'

'Exactly Sir. We need to find Aunt Carolyn and I think finding Melanie is the key.'

'I've been going over past phone records. Maybe you can help me identify some of these numbers faster, so we can eliminate them.'

Grave handed Jenny the report from Sarge's desk. 'Mark every phone number you recognise, then circle the ones you don't.'

'Do we have any forensics back on the letter, or the scene where Sam was shot?'

'We have tyre tracks with a distinctive gouge out of the tread. McGregor is running a check on make and model now to see if we can get an idea of the vehicle they were on.

We scoured the area and found no bullet casings, and the bullet pulled out of Sam was a ricochet fragment, as we expected.

Forensics in Adelaide are working on it, but they won't be able to match any rifling striations. Calibre maybe.'

'Do we have a cause of death for Patricia yet?' Jenny scanned the phone numbers on the printout.

'Doc couldn't find anything on the remains. No obvious bullet holes or broken bones.'

'This is Geoff's number.' Jenny tapped the list.

'So your brother was in contact with your cousin recently?'

'It's dated the day after Patricia's body was found. When Gwen's article ran in the paper.'

'Anything before that?'

Jenny flipped through the past few months, right back to the beginning of the report period, shortly after Melanie turned up back in Coober Pedy.

'No. Nothing.'

'We should go back further.' Grave turned to Sarge.

'You think back to when Ron died?' Sarge said.

'Exactly. If Jenny's theory is correct, and Geoff picked Melanie up from William Creek Station and took her to hide with her mum, then we'll find a link there. A call to Geoff from the William Creek landline maybe.'

Another number caught Jenny's eye, but she didn't have time to consider it.

'We've found Carolyn Williams' car.' Philips disappeared as soon as the words left his lips.

Jenny's heart skipped a beat.

'What are you waiting for Williams? Get out there with Philips.'

'Yes Sir.'

Chapter 30

Jenny gripped the handle above the passenger's side door. Her knuckles were white, but it wasn't the rough terrain making her hold on so tightly.

Her adrenalin was pumping from Philips' announcement about her aunt's car being found.

'This is a long way out of town.' She glanced at her partner, whose eyes were fixed on the rutted road.

'Yep.'

'She must have been picked up out here, or…'

She didn't want to think about it but struggled to suppress her imagination. There were too many ominous scenarios.

'She might have broken down.'

'If she broke down out here, that's not good. It's an impossible walk back in this late spring heat.'

'We don't know anything Jenny. Don't work yourself up yet.'

'Yet!'

For nearly ten years she thought her aunt and cousin could be dead. She spent all of her early adult years trying to find them.

Now they were missing again.

Jenny's stomach did summersaults. She forced the nausea away. But each time she thought about Nick's parents' brutal murders, the anxiety returned.

'There it is.' Jenny pointed to the gold SUV parked at an odd angle, up on the side of the road, amongst small shrubs and rocks.

'How did she get it up there? It's not four-wheel drive.' Philips pulled up alongside the vehicle but didn't mount the rugged roadside.

'Let's find out.' Jenny opened the door and jumped out in one smooth motion.

Philips carefully scanned the ground as he followed.

'There's no one in here.'

Jenny let a little of her anxiety abate. But it was quickly replaced with the realisation that just because her aunt wasn't hurt and dying in the vehicle, didn't mean she wasn't still in trouble.

Philips circled around the vehicle carefully, eyes scanning every inch of the ground.

Jenny pulled on her leather gloves and opened the driver's side door carefully.

'It can't have been here long.'

'Why?' Philips didn't look up.

'The keys are still in it. No one has stolen it or set it alight.'

'The last bit I agree. But it could be out of fuel.'

Jenny flicked the key to light up the dash. The fuel gauge rose.

'It's not empty,' she called over her shoulder.

Philips glanced up. His brow creased.

Jenny returned her gaze to scan the interior thoroughly for her aunt's handbag or personal belongings.

'Come and check this out.'

Jenny turned to see Philips hovering over something on the ground.

'What is it?'

Her stomach knotted again. Philips' expression made her second guess if she wanted to take a look.

'This looks like the vehicle slid up over the embankment. I think your aunt might have been forced off the road and check this out.'

Jenny peered where Philips pointed. The tyre tracks were difficult to make out, but the gouge out of the tread was unmistakable.

'The same tyre as the tracks left out where Sam was shot.'

'Exactly.'

'That means we are on the right track. There is a connection between Sam's shooting and my cousin.'

'Looks like it.' Philips approached the front of the car and put his hand on the bonnet.

Jenny knew what he was thinking, but the sun was belting down so hot, the bonnet was going to be roasting without a motor running.

A rumble in the distance caused them to glance up the road.

'We need to put some markers up to preserve the site, then get Penny out here.' She rushed toward the police Landcruiser.

'I'll radio it in, you grab the star droppers and tape.'

Philips didn't wait for her reply. The dust cloud closed in on them. Jenny ran to the rear cargo area, flung the doors open and dragged out a roll of tape and an armful of star pickets. Shoving them under her arm, she rummaged around trying to find the hammer to drive them in.

The rumbling grew louder. As the ground vibrated, she glanced up to see a wide shiny grill and bullbar with huge spotlights bearing down on her at full speed.

'Damn!' She dropped the star pickets and ran for the tyre tracks, frantically trying to pull her phone from her pocket.

Philips gazed up. His eyes grew wide. Slamming the driver's door shut, he scooted around the vehicle toward the roadside.

'He's not slowing down!'

Jenny reached the tyre tracks, snapped a quick series of photos between frantic glances over her shoulder, then scurried up the embankment as the road train charged by leaving a cloud of red dust in its wake.

They grabbed their Akubras to shield their faces as the cloud closed in on them.

'Bastard didn't give a hoot.' Jenny coughed, then sneezed. Adrenalin fired up, but the truck was long gone.

'We should have put the lights on.'

'If we didn't have a crime scene to preserve, I'd put the lights on alright and chase his arse down.'

Philips grinned, then turned and jogged back to the Landcruiser and opened the door. Within a few seconds red and blue lights began to strobe on top of the vehicle.

Jenny followed him down the embankment.

'Let's get this tape up, take some more photos and then I'll finish searching the car.' She collected the star pickets from the ground where she abandoned them and continued to search for the hammer.

****

Nearly thirty minutes later, a Police Landcruiser pulled up in front of the first. Penny stepped out of the passenger's side. The rear passenger side door opened to reveal Detective Grave. They joined Jenny beside her aunt's SUV.

'What've we found so far?' Detective Grave picked her way up the embankment, being careful not to disturb the ground.

'It's Carolyn Williams' vehicle. There was no sign of her when we arrived, but it appears the car was forced off the road,' Philips said.

'What makes you say that?' Grave circled the vehicle to the driver's side, then leant inside.

'Philips found skid marks up the embankment, to where the vehicle sits now. We found tyre tracks close by, but they are impossible to cast because the ground is too rough out here, but at the top of a rut there,' she pointed, 'there's a track with the same missing chunk as the tread from Sam's shooting.'

Penny arrived with two bags. O'Connell followed with another.

'Who called in the car?' Penny opened the first bag, pulled out gloves and a set of disposable overalls.

'We don't know. It was anonymous,' Grave answered the question.

'There aren't many people living out this way.' O'Connell gazed off over the gently undulating desert.

Occasional salt bush and low growing shrubs scattered the red earth. A heat haze rose off in the distance.

'That's Tallaringa Conservation Park out that way.' O'Connell pointed northwest. 'The highway is back that way.' He hoicked his thumb over his shoulder to the southeast. 'Over there is a series of salt pans.' He pointed south.

'Any settlements? The road train we saw must have been heading somewhere.'

Jenny was still fuming over the jerk driving the truck. If she could get her hands on him, she'd write him up for sure.

'Was he a cattle truck or carrying goods?' O'Connell rubbed his chin.

'He went past in a cloud of dust, so fast I didn't see if it was full or empty, but the last dog trailer was a cattle crate.'

'Then it's likely Carl Jamison.'

'How on earth do you know that?' Grave put her hands on her hips like she thought O'Connell was making the story up.

He chuckled. 'Twenty odd years and you get to know a few people.'

'He's right,' Philips nodded. 'There are only two cattle stations out this way. Most of the area is conservation park and cattle haven't been allowed to graze in them for years. Carl Jamison is the only cattle carrier to service this area because the roads are so crappy.'

'And you know this how?' The detective was still unconvinced.

'I've lived here all my life. You get to know a few things.'

Grave puffed out her cheeks. 'Small towns.' Shrugging, she pointed to the abandoned vehicle. 'McGregor, you process the scene. O'Connell will stay here with you. Philips and Williams. You two are with me.'

'Where are we going?'

'To find Carl Jamison of course. He probably saw the car on his way into the cattle property. Then he loaded up and passed you on the way out.'

'Or maybe the person who ran my aunt off the road called it in.'

'Why would they?'

'Maybe if it was an accident?'

Grave shook her head.

'Either your aunt staged this to look like she was run off the road and arranged a lift, or someone ran her off the road and kidnapped her. If it was a regular accident, they would have stayed here, and your aunt wouldn't be missing.'

'Let's go then. The quicker we find a witness, the quicker we might be able to find my aunt.'

And cousin. And brother. Damn where the hell are you Geoff?

Chapter 31

As Philips turned the Landcruiser left on to Malliotis Boulevard, heading for the station, Jenny heard Detective Grave gasp.

'Well I'll be. Seems it might be our lucky day people.'

Peering between the two front seats, Jenny spotted a cattle crate parked up on the side of the road between the police station and the Opal Motel.

'Do you think he came into the station to check on his report?' Philips glanced at Grave as he pulled up outside.

'Possibly. Let's go and see.'

Jenny was first out of the vehicle, not bothering to wait for anyone else before charging through the glass front door.

Nellie glanced up from the front counter.

'You look like you've seen a ghost. What's up?'

'Did a truck driver come in here to make a report?' Jenny's eyes darted around the office.

Sergeant Mackenzie's door was open, Nellie appeared to be on her own.

'No.'

Jenny spun around to leave, just in time to catch Grave entering.

'He's not in here.'

Walking past Philips and the detective, she pushed the front door open and strode outside.

'Where are you going?'

She heard Grave's voice behind her but ignored it. The truck driver could only be one other place and she was in a hurry to catch up with him.

'I'll check out the restaurant.'

'I'll come with you.' Detective Grave jogged to catch up. 'You're too close to this Williams. I told you. You could have a very promising career. In fact, I'll be recommending you for detective training when this is done, but you need to slow down.'

A hand hauled Jenny to stop.

'Now Williams.'

'I'm not interested in a career right now Detective. I need to find my aunt. I need to find my cousin. I have to know what the hell is going on.'

Jenny's pulse quickened. Nausea threatened to swamp her.

Was she too close?

She turned to carry on down the dirt path toward the motel reception.

'Jenny.'

The tone in Grave's voice sent a chill down her spine. It wasn't malicious. It wasn't threatening. It was the worst possible tone she could hope for.

It was sympathy.

She halted. A shuddering breath vibrated in her chest as she realised she was on the verge of a complete meltdown. Tears burned behind her eyes. Her heart raced. Her entire body was rigid with tension.

'This is hard. I get it.'

'I don't think you do.' Jenny spread the red dirt around with her boot, her eyes focussed on the ground so the detective couldn't see how close she was to losing control.

'Believe me. I do.'

Jenny glanced up at the sincerity in Grave's words. Their eyes met and Jenny suddenly realised there was so much about the detective she didn't know.

'I know my cousin and aunt running away has something to do with Nick's family's murders. I'm sure of it.'

'We'll figure it out. I agree, your cousin being the last to stay on the property before Ron Johnston was killed isn't a coincidence, and the tyre tracks, if they check out, link the cases, but try to follow the evidence, not your heart.'

'What about my gut?'

'Your gut instinct is telling you something is off. I get it. But you can't trust your gut to be logical and clear. That's a lesson you *have to* learn if you want to make detective.'

'I'm not sure I want to.'

Grave squeezed Jenny's shoulder.

'Maybe not today, but you do want it. I can see it in you. You remind me of myself a decade ago.'

'Only a decade?' Jenny smiled.

Grave patted her shoulder with a 'don't push it' sentiment, but her lips were curled at the corners.

'Come on. Take a breath. I know I said your aunt could be kidnapped or somehow involved in something sinister, but that's only a working theory. I probably shouldn't have said it out aloud.'

'Yes you should have. I need to learn to keep my shit together under pressure.'

Grave nodded.

'Don't beat yourself up. Let's see if we can get to the truth, but we'll do this *my* way.'

Detective Grave didn't wait for a reply, turning, she led the way down the covered veranda into the main restaurant.

Jenny followed, her pulse finally returning to normal.

The smell of sweat and beer greeted her as she stepped into the air-conditioning. It wasn't full summer heat yet, but the day reminded her a lot of the first week she arrived in Coober Pedy.

The bush wildflowers were gone. The daily temperatures were rising. The scorching heat was just around the corner.

'Ah.' Grave exhaled, lifted her arms and plucked at the front of her button up shirt.

'That is glorious.'

'There's an air vent over there.' Jenny pointed to the ceiling. 'I've been known to hover there for an extended period.'

'Good idea, but I think it will have to wait because *that* might be our man.'

Grave pointed to a rugged middle-aged man with a rounder girth than Nick's gelding. His grey beard was closely cropped, as was his hair. Half a schooner of beer sat on the bar, a partially devoured counter meal of steak and chips alongside.

Cheryl wiped the counter around him, offering to top up his beer as they approached.

'I hope you're not planning on getting back behind the wheel Mr Jamison.'

Grave approached the truck driver, blocking Jenny's view. Probably a good thing because she was still pissed off over him tearing past them on the roadside.

The big man pulled back his shoulder as he rose and puffed out his chest, shoulders back. Snorting like a bull, his nostrils flared a moment – until he spotted Jenny's uniform.

'You're in charge of the road train out there, right?' Grave pointed in the general direction of the road, missing it by at least twenty degrees.

Mr Jamison bit the side of his cheek, no doubt wondering if lying was an option.

'You know you're required to have a zero-blood alcohol level when in charge of a commercial vehicle. Right?'

The big man slumped down onto the worn vinyl stool and sighed.

'Look. Stop there, give yourself an extra half an hour and I'll turn the other way….'

His face brightened.

'If you answer a few questions for me.'

The smile turned to a grimace.

'You called in an abandoned vehicle out off the Clarence Station road this morning. Right?'

Jenny was impressed Grave knew the name of the station Jamison was picking up from. She must have missed Philips telling the detective.

Jamison grunted something inaudible.

'I'll take that as a yes. Did you see another vehicle out that way? It's very important you think carefully.'

Jamison reached for his half empty beer, then stopped himself. Looking up, he waved Cheryl over.

'Can I grab a cola thanks luv?'

Cheryl nodded and stepped away. Jamison turned back to Grave, a crease between his brow joining his thick eyebrows together.

The cola arrived, he reached for it. Jenny's stomach tightened. He knew something. She could see it in his eyes. What was he waiting for?

'What's it worth to you?'

'What kind of question is that?' Jenny's patience was wearing thin.

Grave glanced at her, gently shook her head and turned her gaze on Jamison.

'I take it you have an unpaid fine Mr Jamison. I've already offered not to breathalyse you the moment you leave this establishment, let's not push our luck hey!'

'I'm just trying to make a living Luv.'

'Detective to you Mr Jamison.' She pulled her phone out of her pocket. Her finger hovered over the screen. 'Should I call the duty constable now? I'm sure I can have him sit outside your truck and wait for you.'

'I've got a crate load of cattle. You want them left standing around all day in the heat? I'll have the R.S.P.C.A. onto me in no time. The world's gone to the bloody dogs as it is. A man can't have a crap these days without some goody two shoes having a go at him.'

'Take a breath Mr Jamison.' Grave's tone was icy.

Wiping his hand over his head, the big man drew a ragged breath.

For a moment, Jenny felt sorry for him. Grave continued her penetrating gaze.

Jamison scratched the back of his head roughly, no doubt realising he pushed the detective to the limit.

'Okay. You win. I saw an older model Navara, dark blue or black. Hard to tell with all the dust.'

'Did you get a registration number?'

'What the.... Why the hell would I take a rego number from a moving vehicle on a narrow dirt road while I'm travelling at...'

'Speed.' Grave sighed with obvious frustration. 'That's another charge the young constable here would be happy to write up for you. I think it's Dangerous Driving under the Road Traffic Act, isn't it Constable?'

Grave turned and glanced over her shoulder at Jenny.

'It is. Saw it with my own eyes.'

The driver's shoulders pulled back, but Grave interrupted him before he could fire up.

'I get it. You've got a job to do. So have I. Did you see the driver of the Nissan? Was there a passenger?'

The truck driver's eyes searched Grave's, then Jenny's. Seeing no give in either, he sighed.

'I saw two people in the front, no idea if anyone was in the back.'

'Male, female?'

'What is this? Twenty questions? I don't bloody know.'

Grave seemed to be considering how much more she might be able to get out of the truck driver. Finally, she nodded.

'At least half an hour.' Grave reached for the beer, removed it from the bar and passed it to Jenny. 'Get rid of this constable.'

'Yes Ma'am.'

Grave rolled her eyes.

'Detective,' she corrected.

The tone, the manner, the efficiency Grave used to handle Jamison made calling her Ma'am automatic.

'Maybe you should think about having lunch *before* you load up the crates next time Mr Jamison, or maybe, just maybe the R.S.P.C.A. will get a call from an anonymous source.'

Jamison nearly spit his cola out. Coughing, he eyed the detective maliciously but wisely said nothing.

Jenny passed the half-drunk beer over the counter. Cheryl grinned, took it from her and rolled her lips in an attempt to stifle a laugh.

Leaning over the bar she whispered. 'I like her.'

'Me too,' Jenny whispered back.

Chapter 32

'We need an APB out on that vehicle, and a description of your aunt circulated.'

'On it.' Jenny hurried to her workstation.

'Philips. Do you know anyone who drives a late model Navara, dark, likely black or navy?'

'No. Sorry.'

'See if there are any dark coloured Navara utes registered in the area.' Grave tapped on Sarge's office door and disappeared inside as Philips answered into thin air.

'Will do.'

A noise made everyone stop what they were doing and turn to the front of the station.

Penny strode inside, talking behind her to O'Connell who followed like an obedient puppy, his arms full of a large box of evidence.

'Did you find anything?' Nellie asked before Jenny could say a word.

Penny grinned. 'Lots, not sure any of it will help, but I'll use the back break room and see what we've got.'

Grave strolled back out from Sergeant Mackenzie's office with Sarge two steps behind.

'Williams. Finish lodging the APB, then go with McGregor. See if anything she's collected looks out of place.'

'Yes Detective.'

'Philips. Sarge has just told me Sam Johnston flew back into town on a CareFlight about half an hour ago. Meet him at the hospital and see if he's up to answering a few questions.'

Jenny wanted to swap tasks, but knew the detective was running the show and no doubt didn't want Jenny questioning

Sam. There was no point arguing. She knew it never worked with Sarge, it was even less likely to work with Grave.

'Sergeant Mackenzie and I'll pay the reporter a little visit. It seems she might still be keeping evidence to herself.'

'No surprise there,' O'Connell muttered loud enough for everyone to hear.

The Senior Constable's history with Gwen was well known. Jenny wondered if the reporter was still seeing Sarge after betraying his trust. She doubted the woman would get another chance.

Still, Gwen was linked to three people in the police station now. Nellie freelanced for the paper, and O'Connell and the Sergeant shared a personal relationship with the woman.

What else could she be hiding?

'Gwen will do anything to sell a paper,' Nellie offered. O'Connell grunted in agreement.

'Anyone would think she's editor of the Advertiser or Sunday Mail the way she carries on,' Grave added as she led the way out the front door.

'Let's do this.' O'Connell jiggled the box in his hands.

'Yes Sir. I'll be with you in a minute.'

Jenny lodged the APB and joined O'Connell and Penny down the hallway in the break room.

Kitchen benches lined three of the walls. A fridge hummed loudly at the end of the right-hand bench. A large table occupied too much space in the middle.

O'Connell and Penny were finishing up emptying the contents onto the table when she arrived.

The senior constable turned to leave.

'Where do you think you're going?' Penny thrust her hands on her hips.

'I've got work to do McGregor. I'm sure you two can cope.'

Penny huffed as O'Connell left, then turned to see Jenny's frown.

'What?'

'Why so keen to have O'Connell stay and help?'

Penny sighed. 'He was in the middle of telling me something, but for whatever reason, he doesn't seem to want to share it with anyone else.'

'What was the subject?'

Jenny's interest was piqued. Getting anything personal out of O'Connell was next to impossible. She knew, she tried often enough. Other than a very basic knowledge about his divorce and new partner, Jenny knew very little about the Senior Constable – who'd put his own career on hold to stay in Coober Pedy.

'Now, how well do you know your aunt?' Penny changed the subject.

Jenny was going to argue, then decided her missing aunt should be her focus right now. Joining Penny at the table, she pulled on a pair of gloves and began spacing items out over the worn fake-marble dining table.

'Pretty well. Not as well as Uncle Pete, but I spent a gazillion hours in their old farmhouse, eating home-made scones and helping with odd jobs around the place.'

'Let's start with this then.' Penny held up a cherry red shoulder bag and tipped out the contents. 'Recognise it?'

'The bag no, but that is Aunt Carolyn's foundation compact.' Jenny lifted a round, tortoise shell object, and flicked the button on the front to reveal a tiny round mirror, aged at the edges. 'It was her mother's.'

'Okay, so we know she was in the vehicle.'

'Yes, but where is she now? Did you find a phone, her wallet?'

'No.'

'So she could have gone with someone willingly?'

'She's your aunt, what do you think?'

Jenny's stomach rolled and tossed.

'I honestly don't know Pen. None of this is making any sense. Where has Mel been the past month if she didn't go back to Aunt Carolyn's and *why* didn't she go back?'

'I work with evidence. I leave the theorising to you guys.'

Penny continued to spread items over the table. Most were mundane like pieces of clothing, tissues, more makeup.

Something shiny caught Jenny's attention.

'Hey, what's that?'

Penny lifted a plum-coloured scarf aside to reveal a silver cigarette lighter.

'Aunt Carolyn never smoked.'

Penny carefully lifted the intricately embossed object with forefinger and thumb, being careful not to touch any printable surface.

'Okay then. I'll start with this.'

The forensic scientist mode kicked in as Penny placed the item on a clean sheet of paper. Removing a long-handled brush that was more like a makeup brush than a forensic implement from her bag, she carefully skimmed the surface to loosen any debris onto the paper.

Pulling a pair of strange looking glasses from her bag, Penny slipped them on and rubbed a cotton tip over the flint wheel. The tip touched every surface before she placed the lighter down, took out a soft plastic vial and cut the tip off the swab inside the vial. Sealing the top, she labelled it and popped it into an evidence bag.

Finally, she placed the lighter on another sheet of paper and dusted it with dark pink powder.

'Got prints. I'll scan these and prepare to send this lot to the lab. You carry on and let me know if anything else seems out of place so I can send it at the same time.'

Jenny returned her focus to the table as Penny rummaged through her bag for something.

Two piles of clothes later, Jenny was about to finish. Her heart leapt into her throat when she spotted a reminder of her childhood. The item threw her mind back to summer days walking the paddocks of irrigated lucerne. Back to whittling birds out of discarded wood she found around the farm.

But why would her aunt have something like that in her car? It made no sense.

'What's up?' Penny's voice didn't penetrate the first time.

It took her friend's hand on her shoulder to jar her from her memories.

'What's up?' Penny repeated. 'You okay?'

'Not really. I just found something.' Jenny pointed.

Penny reached for the item, turned it over in her gloved hands and frowned at Jenny.

'It's just a pocketknife.'

But it wasn't just any pocketknife. It belonged to someone else. Not her aunt, not Melanie, not anyone who by all accounts should have been in a car owned and driven by her aunt.

'It's not Aunt Carolyn's knife Penny.'

'Whose is it?' Her friend's eyes focussed on Jenny's, drilling into her for answers.

'It's my brother's.'

Chapter 33

'Oh shit Jen.'

'Exactly. Any chance we can keep this to ourselves?'

She knew the answer to that question before it even left her lips.

'Scratch that. Damn!'

'I was going to say yes, for you, anything, but just because your brother's knife is in your aunt's car, doesn't mean your brother had anything to do with her disappearance.'

'Or it does, and he picked her up after she got run off the road.'

'We'll go with that.'

'Then where is she now!'

The voice made them spin around. Jenny knew her cheeks were flushing. How long had Detective Grave been standing there? Did she hear Jenny consider keeping evidence under wraps?

'We found a lighter too. Jenny says her aunt doesn't smoke. I've taken samples and I'll get them away shortly, just finishing up here first.'

'Good work McGregor.' Grave turned to Jenny. 'Your brother smokes though, right?'

'Not cigarettes.' Jenny wanted to defend Geoff, but what was the point. His car was seen at the William Creek Homestead. He disappeared from home shortly after Patricia's body was found and when the police started asking about his car, his pocketknife was found in his aunt's vehicle, after it was run off the road.

Her theory about Geoff simply picking her cousin up from the William Creek Station was withering.

A thought hit her. The words were out of her mouth before she could think about it.

'But he doesn't own or drive a dark coloured Nissan Navara.'

A tiny smile crept across Grave's lips.

'No, he doesn't.'

'What did Gwen have to say?' Penny changed the subject.

Grave's smile widened.

'You two are a pigeon pair.'

She shook her head.

'Seems Nellie wasn't the only one keeping tabs on this case. Gwen told us she's been storing up information, trying to break the case wide open and finally land herself a shot at a *real* reporting job.'

Penny laughed. 'She's way too old for anyone to take her seriously this late in her career.'

Grave's eyebrows lifted but she said nothing.

'What did she say?'

Jenny wondered which case Grave was referring to. Nick's parents, the rescue operation they ran or something else.

'She said she was out at William Creek Pub, covering an event around the time Ron died. She's been going through photos, since we discovered Patricia's body.'

'Did she have anything?' Jenny's heart-rate quickened.

'Gwen backs up the William Creek Pub owner's account. She also recalls a stranger hanging around the pub the week before Ron Johnston died. Took some convincing, but she admitted to trying to go back through her photos to see if she snapped a shot of him.'

'And did she?'

'She's still looking.'

'I'll get this evidence off to Adelaide.' Penny packed labelled bags, fastened with evidence tape and dated, into the cardboard box and taped it shut.

'You do that.' Grave turned to Jenny. 'Williams, go with Philips and interview Sam Johnston. He's heading home in the morning and his brother won't let anyone except you do the interview.'

'On it.'

Jenny pushed away from the kitchen bench and left quickly, before Grave could change her mind.

Her own mind wandered as she dawdled down the hallways. The lighter wasn't Geoff's, but something about it seemed familiar. Retrieving her phone, she dialled Geoff's number, hopeful he might finally take her call.

What was he doing?

As she rounded the corner into the office, she noticed Nellie working her way through print outs.

'What you got there?' She peered over the new receptionist's shoulder.

'I hate printing out stuff, but Sarge made me print off all my blog information on the Johnston case.'

'What is he hoping to find?'

Her call went to voicemail. She hung up and shoved her phone in her pocket.

'Not sure, but when you see it like this.' Nellie held up a wad of paper.

'It's kind of daunting. I had no idea so many people made so many comments on this blog post. Imagine how many I've received all up, across all the cold cases I've posted about.'

Jenny gawked at the piles, neatly spaced out around Nellie's spot at the front counter.

'This is all for Ron Johnston's murder?'

'Yes and no. It's all posts relating to William Creek Station. This pile is old stuff, relating to Nick's grandfather. When I first posted about Ron's death, and how I wasn't buying the suicide verdict, I got a trickle of opinions about the William Creek Station history, more so than Ron himself.'

'Really. I'd like to take a look at those when I'm not so busy.'

Nellie screwed up her nose. 'You probably wouldn't. They are pretty derogatory.'

Jenny's skin tingled, not in a good way.

'Why?'

Nellie pursed her lips. 'Nick is good, his dad was pretty good, but his grandfather… Let's just say a lot has changed in the way the Johnston's treat my people since old man Johnston carked it.'

'I read Nick's grandmother's diary a while ago. We found it in the cellar, before the fire.'

'Oooh. That would be a great read.'

'It was. I think Nick's grandmother, on his mum's side might have been embroiled in an affair with one of your mob.'

'No way!'

'Williams!' Jenny jumped and spun round to find Sergeant Mackenzie standing by his office door, foot tapping impatiently.

'Don't you have somewhere you're supposed to be?'

'Yes Sir. On it Sir.' Jenny crossed the office, opened her locker and retrieved her utility vest and Taser. Checking the weapon, she closed the door and rushed to the gun safe.

Philips joined her to sign out his own service weapon. 'You okay interviewing Sam? It's not too raw, is it?'

Was that why she let Nellie side track her over history?

'I'm good thanks Philips. Be good to check up on him. Besides, I'm the one he told about the scary man. It would be good to know if it was a memory recall from his childhood due to the trauma, or if he saw the person who shot him.'

'Let's hope he saw something. It would make our life a whole lot easier.'

Chapter 34

The smell of bleach and antiseptic assaulted Jenny's nostrils. While the cool air-conditioning welcomed her into the hospital.

Nurse Pat was busy doing his usual juggling job of taking a call, while filing paperwork and fielding reception inquires all at the same time. The Coober Pedy hospital was small. With only a handful of beds, and staff were always stretched to the limit.

He glanced up from taking notes, the receiver jammed between ear and shoulder. Seeing her, he smiled and pointed, lifting four fingers up to indicate Sam was in room four.

'Thanks Pat,' she mouthed and waved.

Walking down the hallway reminded her of her first visit to the hospital. Sam and his mate Mick stayed overnight after a car accident. It was the day she met Nick. Not the day he practically ignored her. They weren't exactly enemies from day one, but she certainly never expected to become lovers.

So much had changed since then.

Poking her head around the corner into the ward, she noticed Sam in the second bed on the right. Nick sitting at the edge.

'Hey you two.'

Nick glanced her way, rose and crossed the room.

'Hey.'

He met her halfway, his eyes studying hers. He was relieved, but not relaxed. She could sense his anxiety. She couldn't blame him. Someone shot his brother, and he was lucky to be alive.

'Here on official duty. Sorry mate.' She spoke to Sam but squeezed Nick's hand before letting go to focus on her interview.

'How are you mate?' Philips rounded the other side of the bed from Jenny and Nick.

Sam appeared tired, a little pale, but otherwise in good health.

Jenny let the worry of the past few days seep away.

'I've been better Danny.'

'I bet. Jenny said you were in a bad way when they found you.'

Sam's eyes met hers. Understanding passed between them.

'I'm sorry to do this to you Sam, but we need to go over your statement.'

'I don't remember much. Like I told the Adelaide detectives.'

'It's okay. Let's start with the day we found the body at your place and go from there. Anything you can remember could help. Even if you don't think it's important.'

Sam nodded, then laid back in the wall of soft pillows behind his head.

'I was upset about the body. Pretty sure it would turn out to be mum.'

Jenny wanted to ask about *scary man* but instead she let Sam talk. Philips took notes with pen and paper. Jenny pressed record on her phone and sat down next to Sam with Nick hovering alongside.

'Just needed some time alone, so I saddled Honey and went for a ride. I did a bit of shooting, stopped off at the water hole and jumped in for a swim.'

'I know it's unlikely, but did you see anyone out there?'

Sam studied his hands a moment. A strange expression crossed his face.

'Some locals were out that way, having an initiation ceremony. I didn't want to disturb them, so never stopped to catch up.'

'How's the patient?' Jenny turned at the sound of Nev's voice. 'Sorry to bother you guys, but I need to check Sam's wound and sign off on his release paperwork. Can this wait?'

'Actually. I've only got one more question, well, actually two.'

Nev nodded for her to go on.

'Do you have the names of any of the locals at the ceremony? One of them might have seen something.'

Sam frowned at Nev, then Nick.

'I think it was Eric.'

Nev grunted. Jenny studied her housemate's face.

'They were probably out there drinking. I doubt you'll get anything useful out of Eric.'

'Who's Eric? What's his last name?' Jenny scanned each face, one by one.

'Newman.' Nick nodded toward Nev.

'Your brother?'

'Half, but yep, he's part of my mob, or I'm part of his. He's older than me.'

'You have his contact details?' Jenny nodded toward Philips to get ready to take a number.

'He won't be any help.'

'Let's give it a go in any case. Someone shot Sam. We need all the help we can get. Maybe Eric saw something, a car maybe.'

Nev sighed in defeat.

'Okay. I'll give it to you, but don't expect much.'

'Thanks Nev.'

Philips scribbled the number down.

'You had another question, then you need to let me check my patient officer.' Nev grinned.

'Yes Doctor.'

Nick fidgeted uncomfortably – his eyes watching her closely.

Was he jealous? Of Nev?

'Sam. You told me, when you were semi-conscious, that a *scary man* shot you. Or at least you mentioned a scary man.'

Sam studied his hands once more. Seemingly in no hurry to elaborate.

'Sam. You used to have nightmares, when mum first went missing. Do you remember those?' Nick encouraged his brother to think back.

'I don't remember. Most of my friends can remember from the age of three or four and I can remember a few things from back then, but the year mum went missing, and dad died – it's a blur.

All I remember is when Nick came home. Even then, I don't recall him actually arriving home, just that he was home and running the property.'

'It's okay mate.' Nick patted his brother's arm. 'It was a tough time. It's probably not important.'

Jenny knew it was, but let Nick change the subject.

'I studied a semester of hypnosis at uni. I can call a friend, brush up on my technique and give it a go.' Nev peered from Nick to Sam. 'If you want to, of course.'

Nick glanced at Jenny. They'd discussed how Sam may have witnessed his father's death, or maybe even his mother's. This could be the break she needed to finally put their family mystery to bed.

'I don't think so.'

As the words left Nick's mouth, Jenny deflated.

'It's alright Nick. I can do it.' Sam wriggled himself upright in bed.

'No.'

Every fibre of his body told Jenny he wasn't about to change his mind. Sam might be an adult now, but Nick wasn't letting anyone hurt his little brother.

'Really. It's safe, you don't actually go off into a trance like they do on the Vegas television shows. It's medically based.'

Nick puffed out his chest and crossed his arms.

'I said no. And that's final. Let's get out and leave Nev to check Sam.'

Nick strode from the room. Jenny watched his narrow hips and broad shoulders make a beeline for the door.

There was no give in his rigid back, squarely set shoulders and purposeful stride.

Chapter 35

'Nick stop.' Jenny jogged to catch up with him.

'It's not up for debate Jenny.'

He hardly ever called her Jenny anymore.

'Someone tried to kill Sam. Nick, we are now absolutely sure it wasn't an accident.'

Nick stopped, then turned to face her, a frown creased his brow. He assumed as much but hearing it must have hit a nerve.

'Penny assessed the scene, but you don't need her to tell you there is no way he accidentally shot himself. The bullet casings were removed. The shooter lined up his shot. Sam was a target. He must know something, even if he doesn't know he knows and he won't necessarily be safe until he tells us.'

Nick chewed his bottom lip.

'Then put a guard on him or something. You had one on him in Adelaide.'

'We don't have enough manpower here. The quicker we work out who tried to kill him and why, the quicker we make him safe.'

Jenny stepped forward and put a hand on his arm.

'Nick, you told me yourself, Sam was first on scene when your dad died. We agreed he could have seen the killer.'

'And you think after ten years they've come back to kill him. Why now?'

'Gwen printed that story in the paper the other day. It might have tipped them off.'

'Bloody reporters.'

'I agree, but the cat is out of the bag now. We need to protect Sam, but we also need his cooperation to find who did this. Maybe he saw something, maybe he didn't, but Nick –

you weren't there, waiting, hoping while he was lying in a pool of blood.'

Jenny's stomach knotted. Her whole body buzzed with tension.

Nick's square jaw softened. His crystal blue eyes focussed on hers.

'I'm sorry you went through that again. I know, when you saved me, it was rough.'

'You know I'd do anything for you two. Right?'

Nick wrapped his arms around her shoulders and pulled her close.

'I know you would.' He drew a slow, measured breath and exhaled into her hair.

'I'll tell Nev to give it a go and I should probably stay with Sam tonight, if you genuinely think he's still in danger.'

'I don't know for sure Nick, but I wouldn't take a chance. I'll stay with you here tonight, just in case.'

'He's good to go.' Nev caught them in the hallway.

'Now?' Nick said.

'Yep. He's young, strong and the wound is recovering well. No infection. You need to make sure he doesn't do anything too strenuous for another few weeks at least.'

Nick dropped his arm away from Jenny's shoulder and stepped toward Nev, hand extended.

'Thanks Nev.'

They shook hands, Nick held on longer than necessary. Nev searched Nick's eyes, his brow creased.

'I was thinking about your offer to try hypnosis with Sam.'

He let Nev's hand go and glanced over his shoulder at Jenny. She nodded for him to go on.

'It won't traumatise him or anything?'

'I'll go easy. He can stop whenever he wants. Like I said, he isn't in a trance. Hypnosis is just a relaxed state, where your mind is freed up to recall things better or visualise being in a different place. It's been used extensively and very effectively for pain control.'

'What about if he recalls something too traumatic?'

'Keeping stuff buried isn't good either Nick. If we reveal something, then we'll bring in a professional counsellor to help.'

Jenny watched Nick breathe in and out slowly. His lips pursed, then relaxed as he gave Nev a curt nod.

'I'll call my friend, go over a few things and come back to you later today for a session time tomorrow morning.'

'Can we record it?' Jenny interrupted.

'I have no objections, what about you Nick?'

Nick studied Jenny, then Nev, then his feet as he considered the question.

'If Sam says something he only recalls under hypnosis, it would be good to have it on record.'

Jenny stepped closer to Nick, hoping he understood but knowing it was hard for him.

'Alright. I'll book into the motel tonight with Sam. If we can get in to see you as early as possible, that would be great. I've got work to do and I'd like to get Sam home.'

'You got it.' Nev turned and hurried down the hallway.

'You okay with this?' Jenny slipped her arm around Nick's waist.

'The quicker we find whoever did this, the quicker Sam can safely go back to normal life.'

'Exactly. I'll grab Philips, you sign Sam out. See you in the motel for dinner?'

Nick leaned in and kissed her on the cheek.

'We'll be there.'

****

'You coming to the motel restaurant for dinner tonight detective?' Jenny opened the safe to stow her weapon.

Grave's phone buzzed in her pocket. She pulled it out and glanced at the screen, a frown knitted her brow.

'I don't think so. I need an early night. This dry heat out here is starting to get to me.'

'It's nothing compared to December or January.'

Jenny collected her backpack from her locker.

'You should come and grab a drink. You have to eat something anyway.'

'I'll call it a day, but thanks for the offer.'

'If you're sure.'

The detective didn't answer as she headed for the front door, head down, focussed on her phone.

Penny appeared from the hallway.

'She keeps to herself.' Jenny nodded toward the retreating detective.

'I've worked with her a bit in Adelaide, but not seen much of her at the gym or bars frequented by the cops.

'Is she based in the Adelaide office?'

Penny shrugged. 'Maybe not. My forensic reports get uploaded to the system. I see the detectives on site or in the morgue, but not in their office.'

'Oh well. She came out the other night. Maybe she's got a lot on her mind.'

Jenny turned the key on her locker and strode toward the front entrance.

'You coming to dinner?'

'Of course.'

'I've called Nev and Tim. Everyone should be there. Be good to celebrate Sam's recovery.'

'Is he coming?'

'I think so. Nick is.'

'I am too.' Nellie called from the front counter as she stacked a pile of paperwork and carried it to Jenny's desk.

'You okay if I leave this here?'

Jenny nodded.

'Great. Thanks. I need to find out what you were on about with that diary too.'

'I'll ask Nick if it's okay and then let you read it yourself if you like. Maybe you recognise some of the names, or maybe someone in the family does.'

'What's this all about?' Penny's eyes scanned Jenny and Nellie's.

'You know how I found paperwork out at the William Creek Station when I was searching for Melanie?'

Penny nodded.

'Well, I found an old diary from Nick's grandma.'

'And it sounds like she had a fling with one of our mob.' Nellie's eyes sparkled.

'You love a good mystery, don't you.' Penny led the way from the building.

'I do, but this one is particularly interesting. This one could be about my people, my mob. Nick could be related.'

'Speaking of relations. Nev's brother Eric. What's his story?'

Chapter 36

A low hum greeted the three women as Jenny flung open the glass door to the restaurant. Philips waved from a long table in the centre of the main dining area.

Jenny wound her way through the tables to join her partner.

'Are Nick and Sam coming?'

'For a little while, just to eat. Sam needs all the rest he can get, and Nick won't leave him alone after…you know.'

Philips nodded understanding.

'Couldn't convince the detective to join you ladies?' O'Connell lifted the jug of beer and frosty glass.

'Can I grab anyone a drink?'

'I'm good. I'll grab a wine thanks.' Penny headed straight to the bar.

Jenny accepted the beer offered.

'Detective Dawn Grave is an aloof lady. Seems nice enough, but I couldn't convince her to come to dinner.'

'Wonder why?' O'Connell handed a full glass to Nellie, who accepted it with her signature smile.

O'Connell's expression darkened. Jenny sipped her beer as she turned to see the cause of the Senior Constable's expression.

She nearly choked. Coughed, then took another sip of beer hoping it would help. It didn't.

'Is that…' she squeaked out but stopped herself. Of course it was. There was no mistaking the woman's unsteady high-heeled totter.

'What's *she* doing here?' Nellie whispered.

'I don't know. She's your former boss,' Jenny whispered back, then coughed once more to clear her throat.

'I thought he'd learnt his lesson,' O'Connell grumbled, then sculled his beer and topped it up in one smooth motion.

'Before you start.' Sarge put up his hand. 'She's not here for a drink.'

'What's she here for then?' O'Connell's jaw clenched.

'I can speak for myself Mac.' Gwen's tone was sweet, too sweet.

Jenny stifled a shudder.

'I just wanted to give you this photo. Thought it might be helpful.'

Gwen held out a grainy photo and waved it toward Jenny who stood up to receive it.

'Why me?'

'Hey. What's up?'

Nick stepped up to Jenny and placed his arm around her. Peering over her shoulder, his eyes scanned the picture, then Gwen.

The glint in the woman's eye set Jenny's nerves on edge.

'Look at the photo Constable,' Gwen coaxed, the smile in her eyes now curving her lips.

What was she up to?

Jenny hesitated, then drew her eyes to the image. The background was unmistakably the William Creek Pub. Caps hung from the roofline, with foreign currency notes pinned to the wall beyond.

Sucking in a breath, she held it, then released it as stars began to appear in front of her eyes.

'What's going on?' Nick's tone changed from pleasant to agitated in a heartbeat.

'Jen, sit down. You look like you're about to pass out.'

There was no doubt Jenny was dizzy, but she still made out Gwen's sneer.

What was she playing at?

'Williams! Sarge!' A frantic yell came from across the room.

Jenny glanced sideways to see Detective Grave steaming across the restaurant like a train.

'Your cousin's mobile signal has gone live again, along with your brother's.'

Jenny's head began to clear.

'What about the photo?' Gwen's voice was an octave higher than usual.

'What photo?' Grave scanned faces.

'Nothing. Let's go. I need to find Mel.' Jenny shoved the photo in her pocket and turned to see Nick kneeling alongside the chair she'd dropped into.

Gently standing, she coaxed him to his feet again.

'I'm fine. You stay with Sam. I'll go find my cousin and brother.'

'We need everyone for this. We've been looking for this pair for days and Carolyn Williams is possibly with them.' Grave was moving for the door before anyone could reply.

Penny returned to the table, wine in hand in time to see Grave retreating.

'What's going on?'

'Nick can you fill Penny in. We have to rush.'

'Not another body at least,' Penny deduced.

'O'Connell, you head back to the station. Philips, with Williams and Grave. I'll finish up here and wait on standby in case you need another unit.'

'Okay Sarge.'

The table vacated in a flurry, causing all eyes in the bar to follow the commotion.

'But I want my picture back,' Gwen called out.

Jenny ignored the reporter. The photo surprised her. It was the last person she was expecting to see in town.

What worried her more was why Gwen didn't tell her Sergeant.

Or did she? Was that why he was staying back?

Philips pressed *unlock* on the police Landcruiser he usually drove home.

Jenny jumped in the backseat, leaving the passenger seat for the detective. She was thankful to grab a moment to herself. In the darkness of the rear seating, she retrieved her mobile phone as Philips discussed which direction they were heading.

Grave studied her own phone screen a moment, then cleared it to give directions.

Jenny typed out a quick text to Nick.

Sorry to rush off. Got something important to tell you. See you when I get back.

The reply came within seconds.

Okay. Text me when you're back. I'll be here.

Jenny's heart thumped frantically as she studied the screen. When it rang, she nearly dropped the phone onto the Landcruiser floor.

She juggled the phone back upright and stared at the screen.

'Are you going to answer that?' Grave turned around to look at her as she spoke.

Jenny was frozen a moment, trying to get her thoughts together.

'It's Geoff.'

'Well don't gawk at it. Answer it!'

Grave shimmied around so she could overhear the conversation.

'Put it on speaker.'

That was the last thing Jenny wanted to do, but Grave gave her an order.

'Geoff! Where the hell are you?'

Static crackled down the line. 'Jen…sor…be…cha'd…'

The sound of glass breaking made Jenny's entire body shake.

'Geoff!'

A loud banging echoed down the line.

'Geoff!'

Her heart was beating so hard she was sure everyone in the car could hear it.

'Geoff, is Mel with you?'

Another loud bang, the sound of twisting metal, then another bang, and another, then silence…

Jenny held the phone aloft, trying to see if it was her signal or his that was lost. It wasn't her.

A sound echoed from the silence. It resonated inside her like a beating drum, but it wasn't her heart.

The wailing started deep and low, then turned into a shrill, high-pitched scream.

'That's Mel.'

'You can't know for sure.' Grave's voice was calm. 'Put your foot into it Philips.'

The car surged forward.

No!

Let her go.

Three buzzing sounds echoed down the line before it went silent.

'That was Geoff's voice,' Jenny whispered. 'And Mel's scream…'

Chapter 37

Inside the vehicle was silence. Jenny gaped at the mobile phone screen, willing it to reconnect with her brother.

'Down this road.' Grave pointed.

Philips steered the vehicle sideways, taking the corner at speed.

Jenny clung to the handle above the door, her phone still in one hand. Hot tears threatened to spill free. She swallowed hard and focussed on looking out the window for the crash site she knew was coming.

'There!' She thrust her arm between the passenger and driver seat.

'Headlights.'

'We see them.' Grave's voice was cool and calm.

How can she be so steadfast given the circumstances?

Because it isn't her brother and cousin in a mangled mess.

Jenny's stomach tossed as the scene came into full view.

Dust hung in the air in front of the headlight beam. Philips parked the Landcruiser with spotlights and headlights facing the wreck. Red and blue police lights strobed over the scene.

'Unit two requesting ambulance and back up.'

Philips' voiced droned on, but Jenny wasn't listening. All she could focus on was the arm hanging limply from the driver's side window, covered in blood.

'Let's go Williams.'

Grave flung the car door open, jumped out and opened Jenny's door.

'Now!'

The detective's order jarred her, bringing her focus back to her work.

'Yes Ma'am.'

'I'll let that slide given the circumstances.'

They jogged to the vehicle. Jenny hunched down and peered into the window. Geoff's face was covered in blood, but she could see it was him. His long, curly blonde hair hung over his cheek, matted with blood, but she'd recognise him anywhere.

'Geoff. Talk to me.' She wiped the hair from his eyes.

A low moan was all the response she got, but it was something. He wasn't dead.

'Where's Melanie?'

Another moan.

'Not in the vehicle,' Grave answered from the passenger's side.

'Where are you hurt?'

Jenny pulled on the driver's side door, trying to get to her brother to assess his injuries. It wouldn't budge.

'Philips, give me a hand.' Jenny called out as Philips exited the Police vehicle.

'Help is on the way. C.F.S. and S.E.S. are bringing the jaws of life.'

'I don't know how long we've got Danny. We need to get Geoff out now.'

'Jen.' Her partner used her first name too. This was all too personal, too close to home now.

'Best we leave him be.'

He focussed a flashlight on Geoff's midriff and Jenny gagged.

The steering wheel was caved in, like it was designed to do in order to minimise injury, but a piece was wedged in Geoff's chest.

'If we move him, he might bleed to death.'

'Ta…ken.'

'It's okay Geoff. Don't speak. Save your energy.'

Jenny glanced at Philips. He tried to keep his expression smooth.

'Stay with me Geoff. I've got you. I might only be your little sister, but I've got this. Trust me.'

The hand hanging from the broken window drifted toward her. Then flopped back down with a thud.

'Geoff?'

Jenny frantically searched his neck for a pulse.

Nothing.

The wail of sirens in the distance told her help was on the way, but they were going to be too late.

Her heart thudded in her chest.

'Any sign of Tristan?' Philips shook Jenny by the shoulder.

'Ah. I don't know?'

'Come on Jenny. We need to search the area for Melanie and Tristan.'

'No.' She resisted his gentle pull with a flick of her shoulder.

'I need to stay with Geoff.'

Jenny was vaguely aware the sirens were now silent. More lights flashed over the scene.

'Come on Jenny. We've got work to do.'

Hands guided her away from the vehicle.

A strange thought struck in that moment.

'It's not a dark Navara.'

'No.' There was an unusual tone to Philips' voice.

A shiny silver emergency blanket appeared around her shoulders.

'Someone took them.' Jenny's words sounded muffled to her own ears.

'Over here!' A voice called out.

It sounded like O'Connell's.

'Jen.' A soft voice spoke into her ear as a warm arm squeezed her close.

'Nick.'

A thumb wiped away a tear she didn't even know she shed.

'Geoff. That's Geoff.'

'Get her home.'

Yes, it was O'Connell's voice again.

'I'll take Sam as well.'

'Do that. Keep an eye on them. This case has gotten too personal.'

Sarge's gruff voice seemed unusually firm.

'Jen. I'll take you home.' A firm grip steered her away from the flashing lights.

'But Geoff needs me.'

She resisted, but there was no strength in her.

'We'll talk about it tomorrow.'

Another figure appeared, but Jenny didn't know who it was in the darkness.

'Give her one of these. I'll check in on you when I'm done here.'

'Thanks Nev.'

Nick's voice sounded distant. Like he was talking down a bad phone line or from the toilet. Jenny chuckled under her breath.

'It's a shock Jen. We'll get you tucked up warm in bed. You'll be good after some sleep.'

Why did Nick sound so unsure. She'd never heard Nick sound like that. Always so cocky, so aloof.

The warmth of his arm eased the tightness in her chest.

Why did she feel like she'd been run over?

The touch of cloth trim seat touched her cheek as she gazed out the window at the strobing lights.

The mangled wreck seemed so far away, so distant…. like it belonged on the set of a Mad Max movie.

A hand squeezed hers. The scene blurred. She craned her neck to glimpse the bright, flashing blue and red lights as they disappeared in the distance.

Chapter 38

The darkness closed in on her. The room spun, even though she couldn't see it moving, her eyes rolled in her head, making her stomach lurch like she was drunk.

Movement next to her told her she wasn't alone in the darkness.

Her whole body ached like someone used it as a punching bag. Why? Was she in an accident? She recalled the lights, the sirens, the ambulance.

Then realisation struck.

Rolling over, she glanced at the time on her phone charging clock radio. A gift. From Geoff.

A tear rolled down her cheek.

'Jen. You should get some more rest.' Nick's voice was soft in the shadows.

'No. I need to get up. To get moving.'

She was late for work already.

'O'Connell and Sarge gave me strict instructions to keep you away from work and safe. After Sam sees Nev this morning, we are heading out to the farm.'

Jenny sat up, switched on the lamp, aware the dugout gave her no real sense of time and thankful no one turned her clock off during the night.

'You should all know better than to make plans for me.'

Yesterday's uniform was laid out over the chair in the corner of her room. Standing, she reached for the shirt and noticed blood on the sleeve. Dropping it back down, she crossed the room to her wardrobe and retrieved a clean shirt.

Nick shuffled into his moleskin jeans, his chest still bare. Given any other day, any other time she would have revelled in every ridge, every muscle of his chest, but not today.

Today she had work to do.

'What time is Sam's appointment?'

'Ten.'

Jenny scanned the clock once more.

'Any word on Melanie or Tristan?'

'Jenny, you need time, and rest.'

'What I need are answers.'

She recalled the photo Gwen gave her. Crossing back to the chair, she held her breath as she searched the pants of her uniform for the photo.

Retrieving it, she exhaled. Pulling back her shoulders, she psyched herself up for what needed to come next.

'I'll meet you at Nev's to record Sam's session. In the meantime, I've got things to do.'

'What things?' Nick turned her to face him, one hand on each shoulder. 'What aren't you telling me?'

She shook her head. 'I'm not sure yet. I need to get to the station, check on a few things.'

'I'm coming with you then.'

'You need to be with Sam. He could be in danger.'

'Sam's in the lounge room, here.'

'Here?'

Jenny opened her bedroom door and peeked down the short hallway to the main living area.

No sunlight streamed through windows in the dugout. Nothing to mark the start of a new day. At first, she found living in the iconic opal mining dugout quaint, but today she craved the fresh air and sunshine.

The sound of dishes and water filtered down the hallway.

Turning back, she watched Nick pull on a white T-shirt. She reached for her backpack and tossed it over one shoulder.

'I'll see you at ten.'

'Jen.' Nick hurried around the bed and reached for her hand. 'Tell me before you go off doing anything crazy. Okay?'

Jenny stared into his clear blue eyes and melted. Her resolve fading away. He was her partner. The man she wanted to spend the rest of her life with. She needed to be honest with him, but first, she needed to be honest with herself.

To do that, she needed to be sure. Because if she wasn't right, she could tear what was left of her family apart.

'See you at ten Sam.'

She strode past the kitchen bench and out the front door without making eye contact.

'What the...'

Sam's astonished words followed her.

Dialling, she shut the door and waited for the call to connect.

'Jen. What are you doing out and about?'

'My job.'

'O....kay.' Penny's voiced was muffled.

Jenny could hear background noise fading. She assumed Penny was removing herself from anyone else.

'Do you have the ballistics report on the bullet that hit Sam?'

'Jenny. You're supposed to be on leave.'

'Geoff is dead. Sam was shot. Someone is targeting people close to me Penny and I'm not going to sleep away any chance of catching them.'

'I get that. But you're upset. You might not be thinking straight.'

'I'm fine. Ballistics. Can you go over the report with me?'

'What do you need to know?'

'The bullet was spent, a ricochet fragment, but what calibre? Did they get the calibre?'

'I could lose my job telling you this. Grave gave me orders.'

Jenny could hear the tension in her friend's voice.

'What were they?'

'You were off the case until further notice.'

'Those words exactly.'

Jenny unlocked her car and slipped in behind the wheel, tossing her backpack on the passenger seat and waited.

'No, not exactly.'

'What was the order?'

'To let you rest. You experienced a terrible shock.'

'So not specifically to not tell me about the ballistics report?'

Jenny heard Penny's smile in the next few words.

'When you put it like that.'

'So?'

'The bullet fragment was too broken up to provide a calibre, but they found traces of corrosion on it.'

'What sort of corrosion? Like oxidisation? From age?'

'Not oxidisation, but corrosion. Like rust.'

'From steel?'

'Exactly. But bullets aren't made of steel. They have lead and copper and brass, but not steel.'

'Unless they are World War Two 303 rounds.'

'What?'

'It's just something my granddad mentioned. He and my dad, and Uncle Pete were all gun nuts. My Granddad collected books on war journalism and military weapons, and still watches every news show on every war going on.

When we were kids, granddad used to make guns for us. Geoff had…'

Her mind swam with memories of her three brothers and her playing with the toy guns her granddad used to make.

Replica miniature scale models of the real deal. It was strange how she was the only one of the four of them who ended up using a weapon for her job.

'Jen. I'm so sorry about Geoff. You did everything you could have done.'

'Not everything. I'm going to find the bastard who ran him off the road and kidnapped Mel and Tristan.'

'About that.'

'Yes.'

'We found trace evidence in the car. I'm running DNA now.'

'What DNA?'

'I think it's Tristan's.'

'Tell me before you tell anyone what you find. Please.'

'I…'

'Penny. Please.'

'What's going on Jenny?'

'I'll tell you once I'm sure.'

Chapter 39

Jenny hung up. Thoughts began to unjumble in her head as the sedative she was given the night before finally started to wear off.

She needed to check to be sure, but the records she wanted were in the police station and if she went to the station, she'd be sent home to bed or worse – she'd have to share her theory with everyone.

Including detective Dawn Grave and that she shouldn't do. Not until she was sure. And even then, maybe not.

Inserting the key into the ignition, she realised she desperately craved a coffee. There was a good chance she'd be able to meet the person she needed to see and get the help she hoped for at Niko's coffee shop.

Her mind made up, she tossed her phone on the passenger seat, and turned the key, but stopped. Her phone buzzed on the seat, front screen flashing.

Checking the caller ID gave her nothing. The temptation to ignore it completely and drive away was hard to resist. It could be someone with news about Melanie or Tristan.

'Hello.'

'Constable.'

That was a voice she could do without hearing today.

'Gwen.'

'We need to meet.'

Jenny shoved the phone between her chin and shoulder, selected reverse gear and backed out of the driveway. Placing the phone on speaker, she popped it on to the passenger seat and changed the car into first gear.

'I don't think so.'

She pulled onto the main road in the direction of the café.

'I do. That photo.'

'Is nothing.'

'Is everything. You have a secret you want me to keep. I have a story I want to break.'

'Gwen. I've got nothing for you.'

'So you don't mind if I print that photo in tomorrow morning's paper? Prime suspect in the death of Geoff Williams.'

Jenny sucking in a sharp breath. Her fingers gripped the steering wheel, turning white at the knuckles.

'My brother's body isn't even cold and you're exploiting his death for a headline!'

'Girl's gotta do...'

Jenny's head was spinning. She needed to stall. To give herself time to expose the truth before the reporter did.

'Look. I've got a busy morning. I'll meet you after lunch. Niko's café.'

'What time?'

'Two thirty.'

'Two thirty it is then. If you don't show, I'm printing that headline and taking my copy of the photo to your boss.'

'Which one?'

A chuckle erupted down the line sending a shiver through Jenny's spine. It rivalled a sinister James Bond villain and Jenny couldn't help but make the correlation.

She needed help. She wasn't going to be able to break this case and shield her family if she didn't get some help. That assistance should be at the café by now. She needed to focus and get Gwen off her back.

'I'll start with the most powerful one. Detective Grave I believe.'

'You mean the only one you can't sleep with to control.'

'Touché. Although, you never know. I've done some digging into your detective friend. She doesn't have a man in her life. Maybe she likes to swing both ways.'

'You're a piece of work Gwen.'

'Don't I know it.'

The line went quiet. Jenny's eyes flicked to her phone screen. She was gone.

Her mind drifted to the photo in her pocket. She considered burning it, but not for the reasons most would think.

'How could you?'

She shook herself free of the worst kind of images.

Poor Melanie. Why didn't she come forward and tell her what was going on? Why didn't Aunt Carolyn? Did her aunt even know the truth?

Driving up to Niko's café, the very person she could trust and needed to talk to was walking out the front door with a tray of coffee in hand and an ever-present smile on her lips.

Chapter 40

Jenny parked and stepped out of her rusty Dodge.

'Nellie. Can I have a second?'

'I'm so sorry about your brother.'

Jenny nodded and plunged on. Talking about Geoff wouldn't solve anything and only made her want to crawl into a hole and turn into a whimpering mess.

'Thanks. Can I ask you to do me a favour?'

'Anything.' Nellie opened her passenger's side door and carefully placed the tray of coffee inside.

'I wouldn't be too eager until you find out what.'

Nellie peered around conspiratorially. Then leant in close.

'If someone killed my brother, I'd want their head, so girl, anything you want. It's yours.'

'It might cost you your new job.'

'Job's a job. I've got my blog. My freelancing. It won't ruin me. Even though I do really like it. A lot!'

She grinned widely. Then forced a smooth expression somehow sensing smiling right now was in bad taste.

'I need a copy of Melanie's phone records.'

Nellie's thick brown eyebrows rose.

'I can't risk printing them off. Is a photo okay?'

'Perfect.'

'Anything else I can do?'

'I'll let you know, but I don't think so.'

'I'll send it through as soon as I can.'

'Thanks Nellie.' Jenny squeezed the woman's arm.

'Don't thank me yet. Grave is eagle eyed and nothing slips past O'Connell. Not sure I'll be able to get within cooee of the file, but I'll try.'

'Thanks. That's all I can ask for.' Jenny glanced at her watch. 'I have to run. Sam has a hypnosis session with Nev, to see if he can recall the guy who shot him or anything about his dad's murder.'

'This is all linked, isn't it.'

It wasn't a question.

'Yes. I'm sure it is. Is Grave getting anywhere on the case?'

'Nothing slips past her, so I'm guessing she is.'

'I hate to ask. Can you let me know if she plans on arresting anyone?'

'I'd ask why, but I'm not sure I want to know the answer. This is family stuff. I know how that can get. I'll let you know as soon as I do.'

'Thanks.'

Jenny opened her car door ready to slide back in behind the wheel but stopped.

'Oh, I forgot to ask. Gwen.'

Nellie hovered outside her car.

'Anything you can tell me that I can use for leverage against her?'

A wicked grin crossed Nellie's face. Jenny slammed her door and hurried around the vehicle to Nellie.

****

Ten minutes later she parked outside the hospital, slid out and reached for her backpack. Slinging it over her shoulder, she slammed the door shut with her foot.

Nick waved from the main entrance.

'I wasn't sure you were going to make it. You okay?'

'As well as can be expected.'

'You called your dad yet?'

'About Geoff, no.'

'Is there something else?'

'I'll let you know after Sam's session.'

She'd never been into Nev's office. In fact, she didn't know he had one. The curtains were drawn closed. A reclining chair occupied the corner. A bookcase alongside. A wide faux wood Laminex desk occupied the full width of the small room.

'A consulting room.' Nev answered Jenny's unasked question. 'Used by visiting professionals.'

'Ah.' Jenny sat on the edge of the desk. Nick joined her. There were no other spare seats. Nev rolled the office chair over to sit in front of Sam in the recliner.

'I'm going to lay this back a bit mate. Just relax. Honestly, there's nothing to worry about. Hypnosis is like meditation. I'm going to guide you into a safe place where you can relax and let your mind wander.'

'My mind is always wandering,' Sam grinned.

'We aren't talking about girls Sam.' Nick's tone was firm.

'Easy for you to say. You've got one.'

'I'm right here.'

'Sorry Jen.' Sam suddenly grew sheepish.

'It's okay. When you're nearly thirty, you'll no doubt have a permanent partner too Sam.'

'I'm not sure I want to wait that long.'

'Focus Sam. Close your eyes.' Nev laid the chair back.

'We don't all have a permanent partner even at thirty.'

Sam laughed.

'Now, I want you to do a few exercises for me. Listen to my voice, nothing else. Focus on each breath in, and out.'

Nev spoke so calmly. Jenny found herself breathing with Sam.

'That's it. Your body is weightless. Your arms light as feathers, drifting in the breeze. I've tied a helium balloon to your right hand. That's it. The balloon is lifting your arm up, floating, hovering in the air, slowly rising.'

Jenny nearly made a sound as Sam's right arm left the chair rest.

'Now the other arm.'

Sam's arms floated in the air like a spaceman.

'Your mind is clear, light, drifting on the summer breeze. Nothing can hurt you. That's it. Keep breathing. In….out….in…..out….'

Nev turned to Jenny and nodded, then gave her a thumbs up. It was like reading one of his text messages. He always used emoji.

'I'm going to take you back. Your mum is wearing a white shirt, with small yellow daisies all over it.'

It was the shirt she was found in when they uncovered her body.

'She's in the yard, working on her new veggie garden.'

'I can see her. Her hair is tied back. She looks so nice.'

Sam's smile was wide. His face relaxed.

'Is anyone else with you Sam?'

Jenny watched Sam's features wrinkle.

'A girl.'

Nev glanced at Nick and Jenny. They shrugged in unison.

'Is she your age?'

Sam shook his head like a little boy. His entire body wiggled with his head.

'Nah. She's older and pretty.'

'Okay. You're doing great Sam. Where's your dad?'

Sam's hands gripped the armrest of the recliner. His body stiffened.

'It's okay Sam. You're safe. You can wake up anytime you want to, but you're safe and don't you want to know where your dad is?'

Jenny could see Nev focussing on maintaining a calm, slow, methodical voice and rhythm.

Sam's head shook from side to side vigorously.

'That's okay. You're doing great. Find a safe place Sam. Can you find a safe place in the Homestead?'

'We have. We're hiding,' Sam whispered.

Jenny and Nick leant forward to hear.

'Hiding from who Sam.' Nev lowered his voice to match Sam's.

'Scary man. He's going to hurt her!' Sam's hands clasped together, under his chin, up against his chest like he was praying.

'He's going to hurt your mum?'

'No, the girl.'

Nev glanced over his shoulder again.

Jenny's heart-rate quickened. Nick's hand wrapped around her shoulder.

'What's the girl's name Sam?'

Nick let Jenny go and stepped forward as Sam threw his head so hard from side to side he nearly flipped the chair backward.

'That's enough.'

'Mum. Mum!' Sam's voice was shrill.

'I said that's enough.'

'Sam. You're swimming at the waterhole now. The water is cold, the sun warm, the breeze light.'

Sam's features relaxed. Nick stepped back. Jenny reached for his hand to reassure him.

'Mick's diving off the slippery rock at the top. You know the one. Can you see him?'

'Yep. Dumb arse.'

Sam chuckled.

'Okay. Sam. Your arms are feeling heavy. The fabric of the chair is a little scratchy.'

Sam wriggled in the seat.

'I'm going to count to ten slowly. I want you to move your fingers and open your eyes when you're ready.'

Nev counted. Sam's eyelids flickered. His fingers slowly gripped the armrest. Nev reached the end of his counting.

Sam's eyes slowly opened.

'Do you remember what you saw?' Nev wheeled the office chair back away from the recliner.

'Yes.'

'Do you feel okay? Not scared?'

'I'm okay.'

Nev nodded to Jenny who was sitting back down on the edge of the desk, desperate to ask a question.

'Sam. Do you recognise the girl?'

Sam nodded slowly. Jenny fought the urge to press him. She knew what he was going to say, but she needed to hear it from him. She needed to make sure she recorded it in case she needed the proof later.

'It was Mel, your cousin. I'm sorry I didn't tell you before.'

'Did you remember before?'

He shook his head.

'Then how could you tell me?' Jenny rose from the desk and crossed the room to lean down and hug him.

'Thank you. I think I know what's been going on. I think I know who killed your mum and dad.'

'Mel?'

'No. Not Mel.'

'Then who?' Sam leant forward in the chair with curious eyes.

Jenny turned to leave.

'I need to confront him myself.'

'Like hell you do.' Nick stepped into the doorway, blocking Jenny from opening the door.

'Nick. You need to get Sam somewhere safe.'

'How are you going to find whoever it is you're looking for?'

'I think I have his phone number.'

'How?'

'I need to make a call first.'

'To who?' Nick stepped aside but followed Jenny from the office.

'My dad.'

'Why?' Sam scurried up behind, joining the conversation.

Jenny turned back to see Nev leaning against the office door frame. 'Thanks Nev. Please keep this to yourself for now.'

'Client confidentiality.' He held his hands up in mock surrender.

'I'm already bound.'

'Thanks Nev.' She smiled and turned to leave.

'Jenny. Don't ignore me like that.' Nick hurried after her.

She spun around. Planted her hand firmly on his chest and pressed him to a halt.

'Nick. This could get dangerous. I don't know how he'll behave when I confront him with the truth. I don't know if he has Mel, Tristan and Aunt Carolyn. If he does, I think I'll be the only one to talk him down.'

'Your Dad?' Nick gaped.

'No. Not my dad. But give me a minute. I just need to call him before I do anything else. I need to check I'm not jumping to the wrong conclusion.'

'Jen. You need to tell Detective Grave. You need to tell Sarge. You know how much he hates it when you go rogue.'

'Nick. If I'm wrong, I'll have dragged my family through the mud for no good reason.'

'Then let me help you.'

Jenny bit her lip until she drew blood. Her eyes glanced from Sam to Nick and back at Sam. He nodded.

'I want to help too.'

The last thing she wanted was to put the Johnston boys in harm's way, but they had as much of a stake in this investigation as she did. Maybe more.

'Okay. Here's what I think we can do.'

Chapter 41

As the dial tone rang, Jenny's heart picked up pace. Sweat made her hands slippery. The called connected.

'Dad. I'm so sorry.'

A ragged breath greeted her. Followed by a sniff, then a choking sound.

'You didn't put Geoff in that car Jen.'

'I should have figured this out earlier. Then maybe Geoff would still be alive.'

'Figured out what?'

Her father's bewildered voice threw her a minute. Did he honestly have no idea what went on right under his nose for all those years?

'Do you know anyone with a dark coloured Nissan Navara ute dad?'

'Jenny, what's this about?'

'It's a lead I'm following up on.'

'The Adelaide detectives who came to tell us about Geoff didn't ask about a car.'

A muffled voice made Jenny strain to hear what was being said behind her dad's hand over the receiver.

'Dad. Who's with you? Is it mum?'

'Jenny…' She heard her father sigh. '*We* own a dark coloured Nissan Navara ute.'

'We. You mean you and mum?'

'No. Jenny, what's this about?'

Jenny's mind raced. Did they own a dark coloured Nissan or not? What did her dad mean? Her stomach knotted. Her hand held tightly on the phone as more pieces fell together in her head.

'Dad. Do you still have that old Boer War 303 rifle?'

'No. I handed mine in during the amnesty. I'm not interested in having guns in the house.'

'You said mine. Did Uncle Pete hand his in?'

'I don't know Jenny. What's this all about?'

Her dad didn't bother to hide his frustration.

'Who drives the Nissan dad?'

'It's a company car.'

The words were almost spat out.

'What company?'

'The farm's. The employees use it.'

Her father rushed to add.

'Who else uses it dad?'

Deep down she already knew the answer, the blurred photograph Gwen gave her became very clear. But she needed to hear it from her dad. She needed her dad to join the dots he should have joined a decade ago.

'Everyone.'

'You know who I mean dad? Where is Uncle Pete right now? Is he home?'

'I don't know.'

Jenny fought to keep her composure and not scream at her father to stop putting up a wall between her and the answers she wanted.

Needed!

'Did he take any time off when Aunt Carolyn and Melanie went missing?'

'Jenny. What's going on?'

'Just answer the question.'

'Don't take that tone with me.'

She could have told her father what she feared. She could have explained how Aunt Carolyn, Melanie and Tristan were all missing. Possibly kidnapped. But she needed answers and didn't have time for long explanations.

'Don't tell me you never suspected anything.'

Silence greeted her.

Her blood pressure pounded in her ears. If she were in the room with her father right now, she wasn't sure she could stop herself from slapping him silly.

'Did mum know? Did Aunt Carolyn?'

'Jenny. What are you on about?'

'Let's get this straight. I need to know dad. He's already killed Geoff.'

A decision was made. The only way she was getting what she needed from her dad was to spill the whole truth now.

'He could kill Melanie or Tristan or Aunt Carolyn.'

'He'd never hurt them.'

And there it was. Her own father knew all along. For a decade she'd been looking for her missing aunt and cousin.

For ten years her family tried to dissuade her from her search.

In that time, Aunt Carolyn was in contact with her mum and dad. They knew Melanie was alive and they knew why she ran.

'I'll deal with you later.'

'Jen?'

She ended the call. With shaking hands, she fumbled to shove her phone back into her pocket and checked the time.

She had a meeting to get to. Now all she needed was that call from Nellie. Then everything would be ready. Tristan's father, the man who raped her cousin would finally know she wasn't to be messed with.

Chapter 42

The café wasn't busy. She picked the time hoping to have the place to herself.

'Constable.' Niko smiled as she entered. 'The usual?'

'Only one for me thanks Niko, take away cup would be great. I won't be staying long.'

She glanced around the café, her eyes resting on Gwen, sipping a latte in the corner as far away from the counter as possible.

The reporter lifted her cup in salute.

'Can you bring it over when it's done? No hurry.'

'Sure.' Niko took her payment and turned to his coffee machine, one eye watching her as she crossed the creaking timber floor to join Gwen.

'Constable.'

Jenny pulled out a chair and sat.

'Let's get down to things Gwen. I know you know who is in that photo.'

'Of course I know. It was one of two people. They look similar, don't they?'

'Why haven't you gone to Sarge, or O'Connell?'

'I'm not exactly in their good books right now.'

'No. But that's never stopped you from getting what you want.'

'Smart girl.'

Gwen's attempt at a smile came across as a sneer.

'What do you want Gwen?'

Jenny was fairly certain she knew, but needed to know for sure. Otherwise, her plan wasn't going to pan out.

'I want an exclusive story. I think it will be far more lucrative if you break the case. You're getting quite a name for yourself you know.'

Jenny knew. But she wasn't asking for any sort of attention.

'Was it Al who tipped you off about Sam?'

'It was. It got me thinking. Like any good reporter, I could smell a story, especially when I found out the Johnstons used to take in abused women and their children to relocate them. And then you started trying to track down your cousin.'

'You know all this information would have saved the police a lot of legwork. It might have saved my brother's life.'

Gwen had the good grace to drop her eyes to her coffee.

'I'm sorry about your brother. If I'd known…'

'I doubt it Gwen.'

Jenny knew what the woman was about to say.

The reporter glanced up with a tiny curve on her lips.

'You could be right.'

Silence grew between them. Until Gwen finally broke it.

'So what now?'

'A little quid pro quo. I need you to run a story for me. Then I'll give you a full interview on my ten-year hunt for my cousin and catching the man who raped her.'

'Sounds like a deal Constable. I hope you'll consider this relationship once you make detective.'

'Don't count on it Gwen. Here's what I need printed.'

Jenny rose, thrusting a typed article onto the table before turning away in time to intercept Niko as he delivered her coffee.

'Thanks Niko. See you in the morning.'

'I'll have the usual order ready for you Constable.'

'Jenny, Niko. It's been nearly a year. Time to call me Jenny.'

She crossed to the door, glancing at her coffee lid and smiled. Niko never called her by her first name out loud, but her caramel latte always bore a heart and the letter J on it.

The screen door creaked then slammed behind her.

Now to get everything ready. She opened the door of her vintage truck, placed her coffee on the dash and slid behind the wheel.

With no coffee cup holders, she needed to drink before she drove, so she used the time to check her messages.

A text from Nellie sat on her home screen. Clicking it, she read the message, then opened the picture of the phone records Nellie snuck without anyone noticing. At least that's what the text said.

There it was. The number she subconsciously recognised earlier but wasn't sure why. Until now.

She typed it into her phone and sent the text she hoped would set the wheels in motion. If he got it. If he had reception. If his phone was on.

That's what the newspaper article was for. Back up. But would he take the bait?

And was she willing to make Sam that bait? To risk his life to catch Melanie's rapist? To find Mel and bring her home for good?

She knew Sarge would haul her over the coals once he found out. Then there was Detective Grave. The woman warned her not to go off on her own – that her career could be on the line if she did. But this was personal. This was between her and her family. And now Nick's family.

This needed to end now.

Chapter 43

Jenny opened her eyes as early morning light streamed through Nick's bedroom window. For a moment she thought the last few days were a dream, but then realisation hit.

Her brother was dead. She'd never hear his half-stoned laugh or watch him surf again.

She rolled over to find the bed empty. Nick was always an early riser. Slipping out from under the covers, she dressed, and dawdled across the room to peer out the window.

Watching, she saw Sam brush Honey down and place a worn, well-loved stock saddle on her back.

Nick adjusted his Akubra, bent down and lifted Prince's foot to inspect his shoe. Scraping it clean, he let the leg go and moved on to the next.

Light breeze brushed the leaves on the one tall gumtree offering shade over the yards.

The world was oblivious to her plight. Sighing, she set her shoulders and prepared herself for what needed to be done today.

They talked and planned into the night. The only explanation that made sense about Sam's attack was he must have been tracked from the homestead when he left with Honey.

Whoever shot him, knew the area well enough because they killed Nick's parents and took the time to bury his mum in the vegetable garden.

Sam's hypnosis revealed he witnessed it all. Hidden away with Melanie, who carried that secret all these years, deep inside.

Why didn't you tell me Mel?

If she had, none of this would have been necessary. The murderer would have been arrested and Melanie and Aunt Carolyn wouldn't have needed to stay in hiding all those years.

Turning, she strode to the door. Opening it with renewed determination, she went downstairs. Everything needed to appear like business as usual because the text she sent last night – if it was seen, made her certain he'd be watching her every move.

As she typed the message yesterday afternoon, she considered how much it sounded like a line from a horror movie.

I know what you've done.
I'm coming for you.

She checked her phone. There was no response. If she were honest with herself, she didn't expect one. If her father was right – Melanie and Aunt Carolyn, even Tristan should be safe for now.

Her training told her most domestic violence situations were about possession and control. Fear was the motivator. If they were all in his possession, he would keep them scared and they'd play his game.

If she kept her cool and waited for him to come and eliminate any threats, then she'd be able to help her cousin once and for all.

Opening Nick's tablet on the kitchen table, she checked to make sure Gwen kept up her end of the bargain.

The local Saturday morning paper headline read the words she was hoping to see.

LOCAL BOY RECALLS CRITICAL EVIDENCE

The story went on to outline how Sam was not being taken seriously by the Coober Pedy police, *again*. After a decade of their incompetence.

It seemed Gwen decided to add a little of her own poetic licence to the article. No doubt she'd say it was to give it credibility, but Jenny cringed as she read the details.

Sarge was going to be furious.

It didn't matter. She became a cop to find Melanie. She was willing to put her career on the line to make sure her cousin could live without fear.

Jenny's stomach ached with hunger pains, but nausea prevented her from eating anything.

The front door opened. Her senses were instantly alert, but the footfalls down the hallway were smooth and confident.

She smiled. When did she become so familiar with how Nick walked?

'Hey. You want something to eat?'

'No. I'm not hungry.'

Her infamous stomach disagreed loudly.

Nick chuckled. 'I'll get you a piece of toast, something light. You can't take today on with an empty stomach.'

Jenny didn't argue. Nick was right.

'Is everyone ready?'

'Everything is in place. Are you sure about this Jen?'

'Are you? It's Sam's life on the line.'

'Your plan is a good one. We all agreed on it. It's the only way to get this done.'

'I feel like a vigilante though. I'm supposed to be a police officer.'

'It's how we do things in the bush Jen. Besides. You didn't print the article.'

'True.'

Voices on the stairs drew their attention.

Two figures, dressed in moleskins and Akubras appeared in the hallway.

'Ready!' they said in unison.

‘Okay. Let’s get this show on the road.’

Chapter 44

Nick passed the hot buttered toast to Jenny and sat opposite on the long bench.

'How long do you think it will take before Detective Grave catches up with the evidence?' he said.

'She's smart. I'd be surprised if Nellie snapped that photo of the phone records without her noticing. Unless she wasn't in the office. But then O'Connell never misses a thing either.'

'And they all know the chance of you sitting on your hands, even after Geoff's death, is very slim.'

'Even slimmer *because* of what happened to Geoff.'

'True.' Nick reached for her hand and squeezed. 'How are you doing anyway?'

'I'm okay. I'm just focussed on getting this sorted.'

He let her hand go and sipped his drink.

Jenny nibbled a tentative bite of toast, chewed and swallowed. The food went down like cardboard in her dry mouth.

'How long a head start should we give them?' Nick asked.

'An hour. They aren't travelling too far, for good reason. He'll need to keep them in sight, and we need them to be far enough away he won't notice us coming.'

'How do you think he tracked Sam last time? With a vehicle, keeping your distance is hard to do.'

'He's a proficient hunter. I used to go roo shooting with him. He never drove around wildly like some. The spotlight sat in his hand, and he waited patiently for hours. Then bam. The light would flick on, and he'd take aim.'

'Then we need to be even more patient.'

'Hard, especially if Sam ends up in his sights.'

Nick drained his drink. Checked his watch and paced the kitchen.

'You're right. Waiting is hard.'

'It will be worth it.'

Jenny wasn't sure of her own words, but Nick seemed to relax.

****

Jenny peered out the passenger's side of the bubble shaped helicopter windscreen as red dirt and saltbush passed by under them. Flying low, Nick kept the chopper away from the skyline.

Air whizzed past the open doorway, flicking Jenny's hair across her face as Nick banked around in a circle, stirring up a light dust cloud.

Carefully he selected a landing site close enough to get a vantage point, but not too close to give away their position.

The chopper touched down on the rocky terrain lightly. Nick turned the motor off and pulled his earphones away from his ears.

Sweat soaked her armpits despite the early morning temperature.

'Here. Take these.' Nick handed her his binoculars.

'And here's your rifle.'

'Thanks.' Jenny checked the weapon to ensure the breech was empty, then shoved the magazine into place.

'You know these are illegal now, don't you.'

'Luckily dad never registered it then.' He gave one of his rare grins, checked his own weapon then exited the helicopter.

'Where did Sam say he'd be?'

'It's about a twenty-minute walk from here.' He pointed north.

'Over the hill. We should get a good vantage point from there. Hopefully we'll see the vehicle before he sees us.'

Nick started walking. Jenny followed. A tickling sensation made her stop and scan the horizon.

Nick noticed.

'What's up?'

Jenny shook her head. 'Just a little up tight. All good.'

She passed him as he continued scanning the ridge circling their landing spot. Satisfied, he followed.

Jenny picked her way carefully, desperate to not dislodge any loose stones and risk giving away their position. So much depended on stealth.

A few steps from the ridge, she hunched down and slid along with her rifle. The fully automatic weapon held twenty rounds in the clip and was outlawed after the Port Arthur massacre in April nineteen-ninety-six.

The amnesty on guns was a contentious move, but it appeared to be effective in minimising gun violence.

Jenny felt bad for holding an outlawed weapon, but right now, setting this trap and ensuring Sam and the others were safe was her focus.

Nick slid up alongside.

'Do you think he fell for the decoy?'

'Rebecca is about my height and as long as he didn't notice Ed's skin colour, we'll be okay.'

'Ed pulled his collar up. Kept his hat down low.'

'Then let's keep our fingers crossed.'

Jenny laid her rifle down and swung the binoculars around so she could see.

Sam sat on an old burl next to Rebecca, his back between them and her. Ed kept his hat low, but his hands were exposed.

Would it give him away?

Jenny followed the ridgeline with her binoculars, trying to see where he might be hiding, trying to get a shot off.

The sound of stones rolling loose made Jenny and Nick turn as one. She reached for her rifle.

'Leave it munchkin. You know I'm a crack shot.'

Chapter 45

Nick wrapped his arm protectively over her shoulder.

'That's so sweet.' The man stepped forward, weapon aimed at Nick's head.

'Push the rifle away, slowly. Was a nice idea munchkin, but I've outsmarted you. Again.'

Jenny made eye contact with Nick as she rolled over, slowly sliding her weapon to the side.

'Don't call me that. I know what you've done.'

'So you said. In your text.'

Jenny focussed on the rifle barrel, then on his eyes.

'How could you?'

'She's mine. I can do whatever I want with what's mine.'

Jenny moved to rise.

'Slowly now. You, Lover Boy.' The rifle aimed at Nick's chest pointed to their right and back again to Nick. 'Step away. Slowly.'

'I'm not leaving Jenny.'

'Sweet. I'll shoot you where you stand then.'

'You wouldn't.' Jenny wasn't sure as the words left her lips.

He ran Geoff off the road. He raped Melanie and who knew what he put Aunt Carolyn through.

'Don't test me girly.' He waved the barrel of his rifle around. 'Both of you, start walking single file.'

Jenny hesitated. Did he intend to *kill* them? It was what she expected wasn't it? For him to pick them off one by one?

'That's it. Slowly.' He collected up the two rifles and slung them over his shoulder, all while keeping his aim on Nick, then followed.

'What were you thinking Jenny? I've kept tabs on your investigation for years. Melanie told me how close you were getting.'

Jenny's stomach ached. Of course. Her Uncle's number was on Melanie's phone records in the past three months. It was her search that drew Melanie out of hiding. Whatever happened from here on was her doing. Her mum and dad warned her to stay out of it.

They should have told me the truth.

She wasn't sure she would have backed off if they had. But she could have gotten the evidence needed to put the bastard behind bars.

The idea she should have told Detective Grave what she planned crossed her mind. The plan to get him on his own, to get him to give up Melanie's whereabouts was solid. But he was smarter than she remembered.

Smarter than she hoped.

As they picked their way down the incline toward Sam's group, her heart sank. Now Rebecca and Ed were in danger too. All because she wanted to keep this in the family.

'Put your hands up where I can see them.'

Sam rose, keeping his back facing Jenny. Rebecca's wide eyes peeked over his shoulder as she rose. Ed adjusted his hat back at the crown and rose to full height, eyes squinting.

'What's the plan Uncle Pete? Kill everyone here? Wasn't killing Geoff enough for you?'

Jenny took the last few steps toward Sam and stopped.

'That kid was never too bright.'

Jenny stiffened. Nick wrapped his arm around her and squeezed her shoulder.

'It's okay Jen. Keep your cool,' he whispered as he steered her around.

Nick was right, but in that moment, as she glared at the man who made her cousin's life a living hell, she wished she held her gun in her hands.

If she did, she would have blown her uncle's head off. Not a good thing, she knew, but he was a monster in her eyes now, and monsters needed to be put down.

'That's it girly, do as your boyfriend says. Go join the rest of them.' He signalled them back with his rifle.

How did she miss the signs? Melanie was always the life of the party. Miss popularity. Pretty, blonde, petite. But she started acting out in her high school years. Getting drunk, missing the bus, hanging around town with the less desirables.

Then there was the way Melanie flinched away whenever her uncle tried to cuddle her.

'What's the plan?' Jenny scowled.

'I'm sorry I missed last time. If I didn't miss, and I hardly ever miss, this would have been over with a bullet in his head.'

Uncle Pete pointed to Sam who finally turned to face the man who filled his childhood nightmares.

Drawing his shoulders back, chest heaving, Sam glared into the face of fear.

His hands shook. Jenny wasn't sure if it was anxiety or anger. Either way, he needed to keep his cool or things could get very messy, very quickly.

She stepped between Sam and her uncle, blocking any line of sight.

'Yeah. What was with that?' Her tone was intentionally mocking.

'You're usually a very good shot. Your ammo was a dead giveaway by the way. My boss will figure it out very soon. I spoke to the forensic scientist about it earlier today.'

'Why aren't they out here then?'

'Maybe they are.'

Her uncle scanned the surrounding flat land. His eyes darted around the ridge until finally, a sinister smile crossed his lips.

'You're playing with me now.'

'Maybe. Or this is an elaborate plan to get you away from Melanie. Where is she anyway?'

'Nice try. *You'll* never find her.'

Jenny forced away the sinking feeling her uncle could be right. She played this all wrong. Nick stepped up alongside her, wrapped his arm around her once more. Together, they'd protect Sam, whatever it took.

He couldn't shoot them all at once.

Nick's grip grew firm, she resisted his pull for a heartbeat before searching his eyes and reading something in them.

It was rare, but this time she followed his lead as he pulled her to the ground.

The sound of gunfire made her heart leap into her throat.

Chapter 46

Red dust rose into the air. Jenny scurried on her hands and knees on the hard, rocky surface.

A crack like lightning shook her to the bone. Searching for the source, Jenny struggled to see through the smoke and haze.

More cracking exploded, with bright lights and piercing sounds.

Someone set off fireworks.

A shadow disappeared in the haze.

Uncle Pete. He was on the run. Jenny jumped to her feet, only to be pulled back down by Nick.

'Let him get a head start. I've got the chopper.'

Jenny pulled away again.

'That's if he doesn't shoot the fuel tank or blow it up. He watched us land Nick.' She jumped to her feet and ran, turning only to call over her shoulder.

'Get Rebecca and Ed out of here Sam. Call the station.'

But as the words left her lips, she realised the horses bolted with the fireworks. Who on earth let those off? Rebecca? She'd stayed hidden behind Sam.

Now wasn't the time to think about it. Now was the time to catch her uncle, but she was unarmed.

Stopping, she backtracked and frantically searched the ground in the haze. She needed the triple two semi-auto rifle Nick gave her, but instead she found his twenty-two-lever-action. Grabbing it, she levered a bullet into the breech and ran.

Her uncle must have kept the other long-range rifle. She scanned the ridge, a sense of being watched washed over her again.

'I'll go for the chopper.' She heard Nick call over the thudding of her own heartbeat.

The sound of a plane overhead made Jenny stop to scan the sky. Probably wishful thinking she told herself, then set off at a steady jog.

The outline of her uncle's silhouette against the morning sun as he reached the ridge spurred her on. But sanity kicked in and overrode her adrenalin. He could be planning to set up a shoot, picking them off one by one as they approached, and the smoke haze settled.

She scanned over her shoulder at Sam, judging the range. Watching as they tried to coax the horses back.

Her uncle's old army 303 had a range of nearly two and a half kilometres. She was a sitting duck. They were all sitting ducks.

Think Jenny. Think.

The sound of a vehicle starting made her change her mind. He was running. Not what she expected. Putting on the pace, Jenny scurried up the hill, loose rocks rolled down behind her, but she ignored them until she nearly lost her footing.

Shaking off the near slip, she carried on. Speed was all that mattered now. Catching her uncle was the only way she was going to find her cousin.

She needed him alive, or she would never know where he left Melanie. They could all be tied up somewhere, with no food or water. They could die while Jenny tried to figure out where they were.

She needed to be smart.

Reaching the top of the ridge, she watched on as the dark coloured Nissan disappeared in a cloud of dust.

I'm too late!

He was gone, just like that. Everything she planned was a waste of time. Stomping her foot down, she kicked a loose rock with frustration.

The buzz of Nick's chopper blades made her look up as dust rose into the air. Expertly, he manoeuvred the chopper lower and set it down close by.

Waving, he called her over.

'Keep your head down.'

Jenny crouched, held her hair to one side and hurried over, jumping into the passenger's side as Nick lifted off.

'Over there.' Jenny pointed to the retreating trail of red dust.

'We'll get him. He can't shoot and drive at the same time.'

'I wouldn't bet on it. Be careful Nick.'

The chopper gained ground, quickly closing the gap between them and the speeding vehicle.

'He killed mum and dad.'

'He did. I'm not sure we have enough evidence to convict him unless Melanie backs up Sam's story.'

'That's if he survives for trial.'

'We need him alive Nick. Believe me, I'd rather shoot him myself after what he's done, but I don't know where he's hidden my family.'

Nick studied her face a moment, then nodding, he returned his intense gaze to his prey.

The chopper flew in over the top of the vehicle. Dust rose all around them, making visibility difficult.

'I might be able to jump down into the tray.'

'No way Jen. This isn't some Lethal Weapon movie. That's madness.'

'How else are we going to stop him?'

'I've got an idea.'

Nick steered the chopper forward, over the cab, as turbulence buffered them sideways.

Her heart thudded in her chest. Sweat seeped from every pore, running down her back.

She knew bush pilots were known for their flying skills and Nick was no exception. The helicopters used out on this station country were super-fast and extremely nimble.

Still, chasing down a speeding vehicle over rough terrain was a huge risk, but one they needed to take, or lose their chance of finding Melanie.

'It's like bringing in a bush bull.' Nick spoke to himself more than Jenny.

The chopper tapped the top of the Nissan cab as they passed over. Jenny grabbed her seat, fingers gripping on as Nick tapped the cab once more.

'He's not slowing down.'

Jenny yelled over the wind and chopper rotors.

'He will.'

Nick pushed the lever forward. The chopper sped ahead of the ute and spun around so they were going backwards, facing the windscreen. Jenny could see her uncle's face. Stern and set, he wasn't stopping.

Instead, the barrel of his rifle peeked over the dash. Nick pulled back on the stick as the ute windscreen exploded.

'He's off his tree.'

'You got that right.' Jenny agreed.

Beads of laminated glass spilled from the vehicle as the windscreen disintegrated.

'He's not going to stop.'

Nick kept pace with the Nissan, lowering down to the cab for another attempt to halt her uncle's rampage.

A bullet pierced the bottom of the chopper, right behind Nick's seat.

'Pull back, before one of those bullets connects Nick.'

'Just one more try.'

Nick nudged the chopper forward, lowering down to thump the top of the roof. A jolt pushed the chopper away. Nick corrected. Jenny braced herself, expecting another shot to ring out, but instead, the vehicle lurched and rose in the air.

'He's hit something!'

Nick wrenched the stick back and to the left. The chopper veered away in time to watch the dark coloured Nissan leave the ground.

It seemed like slow motion as the vehicle rotated like a corkscrew. The driver's side window wound around under the chopper as Jenny watched through the glass floor. Her uncle's eyes were wide with fear.

Nick hovered the chopper as the ute flipped into the air once, landed on the bonnet, then flipped again to land on the rear. The tray crumpled under the impact, creaking and groaning as metal popped and snapped.

'Damn. We need him alive.' Jenny craned over her shoulder to see if the vehicle stopped flipping yet.

Nick circled the chopper back around.

'Get that gun ready Jen.'

The chopper touched down about ten metres away from the rear of the vehicle. The tray was crushed, the rear wheels dislodged completely, holding the vehicle at an odd angle, but right side up.

Jenny jumped down from the chopper to approach the wreck, rifle at the ready. An arm lay out through the open window on the driver's side. Her stomach knotted as a sense of deja vu struck her.

Blood trickled down the limb.

Her heart sank.

A moan made her catch her breath. Sprinting, she reached the window without due caution, just in time to find herself staring down the barrel of her uncle's gun.

The threat lasted a heartbeat, before he lost consciousness, his head flopping over the steering wheel, the weapon slipping from his hands.

She reached inside the vehicle to find a pulse, then called out to Nick, but he was already reaching into the other side of the vehicle to retrieve the rifles.

'You should have gloves on.'

'Now she thinks about doing things by the book.'

'Pete. Where are Melanie and Tristan? Where did you take them?'

Her uncle's eyes fluttered open. Then closed. How anyone could look evil when they were unconscious was beyond her, but as she considered him now, that's exactly what she saw.

If he was dead. All hope of finding her cousin would be lost with him.

Chapter 47

Jenny wrestled her uncle back into the driver's seat and rechecked his pulse. It was strong. There wasn't much blood. But he could still have internal injuries.

'I'll disconnect the battery.' Nick reached for a jimmy bar dislodged during the crash and pried the bonnet open.

'Do you have a first aid kit in the chopper?'

Nick glanced out from under the hood.

'What the hell did you think you were doing?'

Jenny spun around to see the last thing she expected to see out here, in the middle of the outback.

'Did you know Sarge could ride?' Nick's voice sounded oddly amused.

'No idea.' Jenny tried to open the door to the vehicle, but it was crumpled and jammed shut.

'You are going to pay for this Williams.'

Sarge's horse trotted up alongside the vehicle. Grave joined him, a stern frown creased her brow.

'You might just have blown your chances of a promotion Williams.'

'I'll live with that. Meet my Uncle Pete. Rapist, child molester, murderer. I think we might need the R.F.D.S.'

'Already on the way.' Sarge awkwardly swung down from Honey.

'Why the horses?' Jenny glanced back at her uncle.

'Al met the plane. Thankfully you two weren't too far from the homestead, but we could only go so far in the vehicle and Sam had the horses saddled and ready to go when we got to him.'

Sarge held the reins out to Nick and accepted the two rifles in exchange.

'Is Penny with you?' Jenny checked her uncle once more – his colour wasn't looking good.

'She's with the plane. Ready to roll. It took a bit to twist her arm, but she and Nellie gave you up, about two minutes before Nick did.'

Jenny spun around to face her boyfriend who was back trying to remove the battery. He glanced up, bit his lip, obviously not sure how that little piece of information was going to go down.

'You didn't.'

'I had to.'

'But it was family. You said so yourself.'

'It was. But your uncle raped his own daughter Jen. He shot my brother.'

Nick pulled the battery out, placed it on the ground and left the bonnet open as he scanned the engine bay.

'He was more than you could handle on your own anyway Williams.' Sarge was unusually calm.

Jenny was certain that wouldn't last long.

'Well, I think I might have to disagree.' Jenny waved her arm at her uncle, still unconscious. She noticed his breathing wasn't as steady as before.

'You need to get back to town. You've got visitors and you were ordered to leave the police work to us. You were supposed to be off duty.'

'I was.' Jenny's eyes were still on her uncle.

Where were the R.F.D.S.?

'And we'll put that in the report.' Grave grabbed her by the shoulders and steered her around, away from the vehicle and her uncle.

'I can't leave him. He might tell me where Melanie is and he doesn't look too good.'

'He's not coming to anytime soon. The medical crew will be here soon.'

As if in answer, the R.F.D.S. plane flew low overhead. They all scanned the sky for a moment.

'Besides, we're tracing your cousin's phone and your uncle's now Nellie revealed the number. We'll know everywhere he's been for the last week. We'll track her down Jenny.'

A gurgling sound caused all eyes to turn toward the front seat of the vehicle.

'He's choking on blood.' Jenny wriggled free and rushed to her uncle.

'We'll find your cousin without him.'

Grave hovered next to her as she ripped her uncle's shirt open and searched for chest injuries.

'He's still my uncle. He's my dad's brother. He can rot in prison, but he's not dying on my watch.'

'No one dies on her watch.' Sarge tapped Grave on the shoulder and indicated with his thumb to leave her to it.

No one except my brother Jenny thought, but said nothing as she wrestled with the door, trying to get it open once more.

It wouldn't budge.

'This one opens.' Nick yanked the passenger side door open.

Jenny ran around, climbed in, laid the seat back on the Nissan and began clearing her uncle's airway.

'Hang in there Pete. I'm not letting you get away with it that easily. Do you hear me.'

A gurgling, fluid filled groan told her he did.

Chapter 48

Jenny studied her red and sore hands as she slid into the seat. Struggling, she forced away images of her uncle's blood running red as it flowed over the white porcelain and down the drain.

She wondered over her decision to save him, but not for long. There was just no way she could stand by and let him die.

A mixture of rage and fear boiled inside her gut. She fought the nausea, head in hands leaning on the table.

Two sullen faces stared across at her. She couldn't meet their gaze.

They drove all night from Adelaide, to get to Coober Pedy – only to find she was gone. It was her parents' panicked arrival that broke Penny and Nellie's resolve.

'I didn't know Jenny. You have to believe me.'

Finally, she glanced up and locked on to her father's eyes, struggling not to shake her head. Her mother sat alongside him, shoulders sagging, yet holding her husband's hand reassuringly.

Silence hung heavy. It was her mother who broke it.

'Carolyn told us it was Geoff.'

'She what!'

Jenny sat back in the chair.

'It was why we let him live at home still.'

Her father's eyes pleaded with her.

'And you believed her? Did you ever ask him about Melanie?'

'We did. He said he didn't want to talk about it.'

'So you took that as an admission of guilt?' Jenny paced back and forth, then sat back down so heavily the chair in the interview room slid on the lino floor.

It reminded her where she was. Were her bosses on the other side of the glass? Probably. She would be if she were Grave.

The idea of being Grave one day slipped away. Shaking her head, she reminded herself her career was her least worry today. She'd likely already blown it anyway. Today she needed to find Melanie.

'Did Uncle Pete ever say anything about being out this way, when he was supposedly looking for Melanie?'

Her father and mother exchanged looks. Then collectively shook their heads.

'He must have mentioned something. He's taken Aunt Carolyn, Tristan and Melanie. They could die of dehydration before we find them in this weather.'

It wasn't summer yet, but spring in Coober Pedy could be brutally hot. Today's temperature was climbing.

'I'm sorry Jenny. I didn't know. Carolyn never said…'

'Not now dad. Now we need to think where he might have taken Melanie.'

Her father nodded, drew his shoulders back and rubbed his nose like he used to when he was agitated.

The action put the situation into perspective for Jenny. These were her parents. Not suspects in an investigation.

'I'm sorry dad. It's just this is…' she rubbed the back of her neck trying to think of a word to describe exactly what it was.

'He said he liked it out here. He joked about getting a mine and going off the grid one day, if he could ever find Melanie and Carolyn.'

Jenny leapt from her seat. 'God that's it dad. I never even thought of a mine title search.' She rushed from the room, down the hall and into the main office.

'Mining rights! We need to search the database for anything in the name of Pete, Carolyn, Melanie Williams and throw in Aunt Carolyn's maiden name, in case. Francis.'

Philips was already typing before she finished. Grave and Sarge wandered down the hall.

They were watching.

Grave crossed the room to O'Connell's desk and hovered. 'Anything on the phone coordinates yet?'

He tapped keys on his keyboard and hit print.

'There you go.'

The laser printer whirred to life. Jenny waited for the printout, snatched it up and met Grave in the middle of the office.

Both women scanned the details.

'It only pings the towers intermittently, so this isn't exactly a road map.' Grave pointed at the list of coordinates on the page.

'Email that to the tech team O'Connell. I'll make a few calls and see if we can speed this up.'

'We need to find them soon. Aunt Carolyn has been missing for days. If she's been without water all that time, she could die.'

'Jenny, your uncle took them because he wanted to possess them. He won't have left them without food or water.'

Jenny's stomach ached to find her missing family. Tristan would be terrified. His own grandfather – no, father – was terrorising his mum and grandma. The thought turned her stomach.

'Got something.' Philips called from the front counter.

Jenny rushed over. Nellie reached for Jenny's arm when she drew within reach.

'I'm sorry I gave you up.'

'It's okay. So did Nick.'

Nellie's surprise was precious.

'What have you got Philips?' Jenny pranced from foot to foot next to her partner. Sarge strolled over and Grave hovered close by.

'A mine, in the name of Carolyn Francis. Could it be where Melanie has been this last month?'

Jenny rubbed her chin. 'When was it purchased?'

'Title changed hands on the twentieth June two thousand and six.'

'The year they disappeared. That makes sense. It must have been Aunt Carolyn's, not Uncle Pete's. So why did she claim to not know where Melanie was when she came here earlier this week? Surely she suspected Mel would go to the mine.'

'She probably checked there first,' Philips said.

'Maybe. Either way, Aunt Carolyn lied to my mum and dad and said Geoff was Tristan's father, knowing my parents would keep him away from Melanie. I think Geoff knew what Melanie knew.'

'Your uncle claimed he hadn't seen Melanie since she went missing, but your cousin said he visited every month.' Grave started walking toward the interview room. 'I think I need to ask your dad something.'

Jenny scurried after the detective.

Grave flung the door open. Her father and mother jumped in unison.

'Sorry. Didn't mean to startle you. I've got a question, if you don't mind, before you go?'

Jenny's dad and mum glanced at one another, then nodded.

'Did your brother take a break each month, for a few days?'

'I didn't keep tabs on him, but yes, we rostered alternate long weekends off when we covered supervision on the farm so we could get a few extra days off.'

'Thanks.' Grave turned to leave.

'What's happening?'

'You can go now Mr Williams. Jenny is safe, your brother is in surgery and then he'll be in custody. You can head back to Adelaide if you like.'

'I'm not going anywhere until you find my sister-in-law and niece. And her son.'

Her father was on his feet now. Jenny wanted to tell him how he should have stood up for them years ago, but kept her mouth shut.

'Suit yourself.' Grave strode toward the doorway. Jenny stepped aside.

'Williams. With me.'

'Yes…Detective.' She was never going to get used to that.

Grave strode down the hallway, glanced over her shoulder then leant in close so only Jenny could hear.

'I think your Aunt Carolyn might not be as innocent as she seems.'

'What do you mean?'

'Just a hunch.'

Grave took off so fast Jenny needed to jog to keep up.

'Will someone track Carolyn Williams' mobile, and I want S.E.S. on standby in case we need help. Then we need to get out to that mine.'

'Who?' Sarge crossed his arms over his chest.

'Everyone. Nellie can hold the fort here. Right Nellie?'

'Yes Dawn.'

'Dawn!' Philips gawked at Nellie. 'Since when have you been on a first name basis.'

'Since I'm a civilian and she doesn't like Ma'am.'

'Let's go Philips. Grab your weapons everyone,' Grave ordered.

Jenny rummaged through her jeans pocket for the key to her locker as she hurried over.

'Where do you think you're going?' Sarge uncrossed his arms to reach for the Landcruiser keys.

'With you.'

He shook his head.

'You're on suspension.'

'Since when?' Jenny scanned the room.

'Let her come Sarge.' Grave carried on out the door like she was in charge.

Sarge scowled, glanced at O'Connell who was putting on a utility vest he rarely wore and offered no support. Sarge huffed when he realised he was out voted.

'Keep your head down Williams.'

'Will do Sir.'

Chapter 49

Jenny sat in the back seat of the Landcruiser Phillips drove. Grave in the passenger's seat. Sarge and O'Connell were in the other vehicle.

She wished Penny were there, for moral support more than anything, but the forensic scientist was busy processing her uncle's vehicle for evidence that could help them find Melanie.

Grave's words puzzled her. Like Melanie, her aunt was a victim. She ran to William Creek Station. She wouldn't have done so if she was covering up for Uncle Pete.

But Ed never saw *her* at William Creek Station. Could Mrs B. have got it wrong? Did Ron only pick Melanie up from the William Creek Pub? Did Aunt Carolyn disappear looking for Melanie?

She'd lied about Tristan's father. First the teacher, then Geoff.

But why? Why would any woman stand by and let her daughter be abused by her own father?

No. Grave was wrong. Way off beam. She had to be.

'Nearly there.' Philips called over his shoulder.

The police Landcruiser slid sideways as they left the bitumen highway for a rutted dirt road. Piles of white and ochre coloured dirt dotted the desert all the way to the horizon. Yellow signs indicated abandoned mines were prevalent in the area and crossing the land was unsafe.

Grave drew her eyes from the landscape and glanced at Philips.

'How on earth do you find your way around out here? Every hole in the ground looks like the last one.'

'Some of these mines are just shafts into the ground where miners blast and dig, but others are habitable. I've probably visited nearly every one of those over the years.'

'People live out here?'

Grave sounded unconvinced.

'It's a life,' Philips said.

'Not much of a life.'

Jenny agreed, but kept her mouth closed. Her mind was too busy trying to figure out what the hell was going on with her family.

The Landcruiser reached the top of an incline, then began the descent. Philips slowed the vehicle down, taking the washed-out ruts one wheel at a time.

Jenny held the handle above the window. Grave did the same. Each rut jostled them sideways.

'Remind me before I leave this town that I don't want to take another assignment out here.'

'Do you get a choice?' Jenny asked.

'Not likely, but I'm sure I can play the monthly cramps card if another one comes up.'

Jenny laughed.

Philips blushed.

The windscreen smashed.

Philips hit the brakes for a split second.

'Move!' Grave yelled. 'That was gunfire.'

The vehicle lurched forward, bounding over ruts and salt bush.

'Where did it come from?' Philips scanned the area, eyes frantic.

'Keep your eyes on the road. I'll look for it.' Grave kicked the remaining glass out of the windscreen with her Doc Martins. Keeping her head down, she peered out over the dashboard searching the ochre landscape trying to spot the shooter.

'There!'

Jenny pointed out her side window as Philips turned toward the direction she was pointing.

'What are you doing?' Grave's voice was shrill.

'Keep your heads down.' Philips' face was set and focussed.

The vehicle dropped back a gear. The wheels spun. Gravel flicked up and the car sped up.

'Philips. What are you doing?'

Jenny could hear the terror in her own voice now.

Another gunshot rang out, but this time it passed high over the vehicle. Philips didn't slow down. The Landcruiser roared past the makeshift iron front of a derelict dugout. It disappeared from Jenny's view in a blur.

Philips floored the accelerator and dropped back another gear. The all-wheel drive vehicle climbed the embankment behind the shed front before the brakes jammed on hard.

The seat belt dug into her collar bone. Ignoring the pain, she pushed the door open and unclipped the seatbelt in one frantic and uncoordinated move.

Out the corner of her eye she saw Philips do the same. Detective Grave grabbed the radio from the dashboard.

'Shots fired. Shots fired. Keep back.'

Jenny heard a crackling reply but didn't make out the words as she and Philips peered over the edge of the hillside to see where the entrance to the dugout was.

Glancing at Philips, she saw his chest heaving, much like hers.

'Can you see another way in?'

'No. Do we call a tactical team in?'

Grave sauntered up to join them. Raising her hands, she patted them on the back simultaneously.

'Take a deep breath. Both of you. We are out of gun fire range up here. Sarge is putting a team on standby, but I'm confident we can de-escalate this on our own. Jenny. Talk to your aunt.'

'And say what?'

She fought for calm.

'Tell her Peter Williams is in custody. Tell her it's over.'

'What's over? I don't understand why she's shooting at the police.'

'Think about it Jenny.'

Grave's calm, patient voice drilled into Jenny.

Thoughts tumbled around her head so fast it was giving her a headache. She considered what Grave mentioned before – that Aunt Carolyn wasn't ever seen at the William Creek Station.

'She went back to him.'

'Exactly. You've done domestic violence training, think about how many women fail to leave at all and of those who do, how many go back?'

'Too many.' Jenny blew out her cheeks.

Realisation finally hit her. Her aunt went back, and probably gave up Melanie to her father. It was almost too difficult to comprehend, but it made so much sense in retrospect.

Uncle Pete must have kept them hidden all these years. Maybe so no one would work out Tristan was his son.

Leaning over the edge, Jenny watched for any movement below. Only in Coober Pedy could you effectively drive a vehicle on top of a house.

'Kudos for quick thinking Philips.'

Jenny eyed her partner as she scanned the top of the dugout, looking for a possible way in.

He turned back to her, his eyes sparkling, a grin curved his lips.

'They can't shoot you if you are on top of them.'

'You got that right Philips.' Grave joined Jenny to peer over the edge.

Faint sounds echoed up from behind them. She turned to see Philips already walking toward the air vent in the top of the dugout.

The plastic pipe protruded a metre from the roof line. She watched as Philips peered in.

Hot sun belted down on them. The dugout roof was warm to the touch as Jenny laid down on her belly to peer further over the edge, looking for the doorway in.

Sweat pooled at the small of her back. Shielding her eyes, she focussed on the hillside they drove down when they came in. Without her Akubra, it was difficult to see against the glare.

The Landcruiser roof was barely visible against the ridgeline. Waiting, watching their progress. She needed to get everyone out safely. Even her crazed Aunt.

Jenny jumped to her feet, checked her safety was back on her Taser and clipped it to her utility vest. Cupping her hands, she called down over the edge of the dugout.

'Auntie Carolyn.'

'Go away. Leave us alone girl. You've done enough damage.'

Jenny bit her lip to keep tears at bay. She never intended to cause her aunt and cousin any trouble. She just wanted them back safely.

Was this all her fault?

'You've got this Williams.' Grave patted her shoulder and waved for her to go on.

'Aunt Carolyn, you're safe now. Let Melanie and Tristan out.'

'Go away. Where's Pete?'

'Uncle Pete is under arrest. He can't hurt you anymore.'

Jenny checked over her shoulder. Philips wore a frown as he tried to focus on something inside the air vent.

'It's too late.'

Jenny's stomach tightened. Bile rose in her throat, assaulting her taste buds.

'What do you mean Aunt Carolyn. Are Melanie and Tristan okay?'

'Jenny!' Philips hissed in a hushed tone.

She turned. Philips pointed down the pipe. He could see something. She waited as he flicked his flashlight on and shot a beam of light down the pipe.

'You don't understand,' her aunt continued, her voice shaking.

'Put the gun down Aunt Carolyn and we can sit down and talk about it.'

'He'll find a way.'

'Uncle Pete? No, he won't Aunt Carolyn.'

Jenny hesitated, but her mind was made up. Her gut assured her she would be safe – her aunt wouldn't shoot her. The police in general, maybe that was possible, but her.

Her feet were moving toward the slope before she realised. Sliding down the hillside toward the front of the dugout.

'What are you doing?' Philips called after her.

'Leave her Philips.' Grave grabbed his arm as he made to follow. 'What's down the pipe?'

Jenny heard his answer. It filled her heart with hope. Melanie was down there, with Tristan and they were alive.

'Aunt Carolyn. I'm going to put my weapon down.' Jenny drew her gun from the holster at her hip. Grabbing the butt, she carefully laid it on the ground.

A rifle barrel appeared between cracks in the dugout iron-clad wall. The door was impossible to see until it creaked open a few inches.

'And the Taser,' Carolyn ordered.

'Can I come in and check on Melanie and Tristan?'

The barrel shook from side to side.

'I want to help Aunt Carolyn. I've got evidence Uncle Peter tried to kill my boyfriend's brother. It's enough to put him in prison for a very long time, but we can keep him there forever if you let me talk to Melanie.'

'He'll get a lawyer. He'll tell lies and everyone will believe him.'

The hopeless tone in her aunt's voice nearly broke her heart. What did her uncle do to the woman to make her so afraid? How could her parents have no idea? Surely the signs were there.

A voice from behind startled Jenny.

'No, we won't Carolyn. We won't believe him ever again.'

Jenny swallowed tears as she heard the words leave her mum's lips. On the hillside, her father watched on.

Sending her mum in was risky, but it was the right choice. If her aunt saw her dad, things could have escalated quickly. The brothers looked too much alike.

'We know he lied to us Carolyn. We know he forced you to lie for him.'

'I wanted to tell the truth.'

Her aunt's words came out in a sob.

‘We know.’ Jenny waved for her mum to step behind her. ‘My brother is gone Carolyn, but we can keep Melanie and Tristan safe. I promise.’

The gun barrel lowered. The door creaked open wide enough for Jenny to see her aunt, covered in sandstone dust, shaking from fear or adrenalin or both.

‘He told me to keep Melanie here, even if I had to shoot her in the leg. He said we were his property. His!’

‘He was wrong Aunt Carolyn.’

Jenny held her hands high and tentatively stepped toward her aunt. The thudding in her chest echoed in her ears, making it difficult to focus as she inched her way forward one cautious step at a time.

‘I need you to put the gun on the ground. Can you do that?’ She snuck forward another two steps, but halted as her aunt’s hands shook and the barrel of the rifle quivered.

A tense silence grew. Jenny opened her mouth to say more but stopped herself. Rolling her lips together and breathing deeply through her nose, she waited.

Patience wasn’t usually in her skillset, but she pictured Melanie and Tristan, in the dugout, terrified and continued waiting as Aunt Carolyn’s expression went from fear, to concern to reluctance and finally, the gun barrel was shakily lowered all the way to the ground.

Jenny let out a slow breath. She didn’t allow her limbs to relax yet. Fighting the temptation to move forward, she gave a final request she hoped with all her heart her aunt would comply with.

The woman was exposed, and Jenny knew Sarge or O’Connell would be staring down the scope of an assault rifle, ready to take the shot if the need arose.

‘Can you put the gun on the ground and walk toward me Aunt Carolyn?’

The woman studied her surrounds as she opened the iron gate wider and peered around into the brightness. Jenny waved her hand at her back to keep her mother behind her. Her aunt squinted to watch the hillside. Sarge and O'Connell would still be out of view.

What was she waiting for?

Then it dawned on Jenny. Aunt Carolyn was still expecting her husband to rampage over the hill, guns blazing at any moment.

'Can I show you a photo Aunt Carolyn? It's Uncle Pete, after a crash, in hospital and handcuffed to the bed. You don't have to worry about him.'

Aunt Carolyn shuffled toward Jenny, her eyes wary. Her body rigid. The gun still in her right hand. But she nodded yes.

'I just need one hand to get my phone out. Okay?'

Another nod.

'Here.' Jenny dug into the front pocket of her vest, not far from where her cuffs hung. They jingled as she pulled her phone from the snug fabric.

Aunt Carolyn's eyes focussed on the cuffs, then grew wide with fear. Jenny glanced up, as Philips leapt from the top of the dugout.

The air left his lungs with a gush as he impacted against her aunt.

Dust rose in the air. Arms and legs flung in every direction.

Her mother squealed. Grave appeared at the edge of her vision. Jenny's heart skipped a beat. She was glued to the spot, unable to think, unable to move for a split second.

The scene slowed. Jenny heard words coming from her mouth but had no idea what she said. Everything sped back up in a blink of an eye.

She was on top of her aunt, cuffs in hand as Philips held the squirming woman down as best he could.

Jenny clipped the cuffs in place, being careful not to over tighten them as her aunt howled like a feral cat.

'It's okay Aunt Carolyn. It's okay. We won't hurt you. We just need to secure Melanie and Tristan. I promise. We won't hurt you.' Tears sprang to her eyes before she realised it.

Philips made eye contact, shuffled to his feet and grabbed her aunt's cuffed hands.

'I've got her.'

Jenny didn't wait to ask if he were sure.

'Mel!'

She was inside, flashlight in hand, gun drawn and safety off before she could take another breath.

A shuffle behind her told her Grave was running back up.

'Mel! Tristan!'

Jenny aimed her flashlight and gun in unison. The beam flitted from wall to wall, floor to ceiling. The dark dugout was silent except for the sound of her own footfalls and her hammering heart.

'Mel!'

A shuffle of coarse fabric on rock made Jenny spin to her right. Huddled in the corner, with dirty tears streaming down her face and duct tape over her mouth was the one person she longed to see.

Everything else in her world blurred as she rushed forward. Holstering her gun, she ripped the tape from her cousin's lips and hugged the bound woman tightly.

'Tristan.' Melanie's voice cracked as she uttered that one motherly word.

'I've got him.' Grave carefully scanned the dark cavernous dugout one more time, gun still in hand, before holstering the weapon and untying Tristan.

His body was limp, his colour pale.

'Clear!' Grave yelled toward the entrance.

'Get an ambulance.'

'Is he going to be okay?' Melanie's voice was barely a whisper.

Jenny untied her and pulled her close as Grave searched Tristan's neck for a pulse.

The detective's hand searched, trying to pick up anything. Finally, in the dim light of the flashlight on the ground, Jenny saw Grave's lip turn up.

'He's going to be okay.'

Jenny let out a breath, released Melanie from her tight hug and helped her to her feet.

Sarge appeared, gun in hand, flashlight beaming into their eyes.

'Grab the kid Sarge.' Grave clamoured to her feet, collected her flashlight and cast the beam over Tristan.

Sarge jumped forward, holstered his weapon and swept Tristan into his strong arms in one easy lift.

Jenny staggered as Melanie fell against her, but she didn't care. Melanie and Tristan were safe.

Her joy was short lived.

As they exited into the light of day, Melanie collapsed to the ground. Was it the sight of her mother, covered in dirt, cuffed arms at her back? Or was she hurt? What did she miss?

Chapter 50

The pale greenish grey walls of the hospital ward were less welcoming than usual. Jenny licked her lips and swallowed bile as they rushed through the hospital entrance.

A warm hand squeezed hers.

She glanced over to Nick.

'It will be okay Jen.'

'But my uncle killed your mum and dad and nearly killed Sam.'

Nick stopped and pulled her to him.

'I don't blame you Jenny. I can get past it.'

She wasn't sure she could. Pushing the thought aside, she tried to focus. Grave was about to interview Melanie. Right now, all she needed to think about was supporting her cousin.

All the worries about Nick and staying in Coober Pedy and her career needed to go on hold for now. Right now, her family needed her.

Drawing a slow breath, Jenny nodded and stepped into Melanie's room, pulling Nick with her.

'Constable. We've been waiting for you.'

'Sorry to keep you.' Jenny let Nick's hand go and joined her cousin at her bedside.

Melanie was pale and weak. Dehydration and anxiety took their toll over the past few days, but Nev said he expected her to make a full physical recovery.

Her housemate's words echoed in her head.

'I can't vouch for her mental state of mind. That's going to take some serious professional help.'

And it was. Jenny could see it in Melanie's eyes. Her cousin was broken.

Would she ever be the same again?

'Okay Melanie. This isn't going to be easy. We don't need a full statement yet, but we do need to know a few things so we can lay formal charges against Peter Williams. Can you help us?

Melanie's eyes were wide, but she nodded slowly.

'I'm going to need you to speak up for the recording. Can you do that?'

Grave's voice was calm, not exactly friendly, but not intimidating either.

Mel's eyes searched round the room. Sarge waited by the door. O'Connell and Philips were busy with Aunt Carolyn back at the station. Nev hovered close by in case a sedative was required.

They all hoped it wouldn't be necessary. It was the main reason Jenny was allowed to attend the interview, to give Melanie a sense of calm and safety.

'Okay.' Mel's voice was so soft. So vulnerable.

Jenny reached for her hand and held it, firmly, but carefully.

'I'm here Mel. Say the word and we can take a break.'

Melanie's head bobbed up and down once.

'Can you please state your name for the recording?' Grave continued.

Melanie obliged.

'When you booked to go to the William Creek Station, did you intend to run away from your father?'

'Yes.'

'Did your mother know?'

'Yes.'

'When Ron Johnston collected you from the William Creek Pub, did your mother go with you?'

Melanie shook her head gently. A tear rolled down her cheek. Jenny patted her hand softly.

'Can you answer for the recording.' Grave's voice was soft, encouraging.

'No. She was gone when Mr Johnston arrived.'

'What happened at the William Creek Station?'

'Ron and Patricia took me in. I stayed there while they tried to find somewhere safe for me to go.'

'Did you and your mother intend to stay at the mine we found you in?'

Melanie shook her head. 'Only if we had to. Mr Johnston was going to find us a place.'

'Okay Melanie. We need to know what happened the day Ron and Patricia died.'

Another tear rolled down Melanie's face. Jenny wiped it away with her thumb. Her cousin locked eyes with her, begging her without sound to not make her say what needed to be said.

Jenny held back her own tears.

'Mel. We need to know. Sam was only young. Your testimony will add a life sentence to the table. He'll never see outside prison walls again. He'll never hurt you or Tristan again. I promise.'

Jenny glanced at Grave, hoping against everything she wasn't lying to her cousin.

Grave nodded. But Jenny knew it would all come down to the court, the judge and a final verdict. They needed every piece of evidence to get the maximum sentence.

'I came back when I heard about Ron's murder investigation. I'm sorry. I'm so sorry.' Melanie's eyes locked onto Nick.

'It's not your fault.' Nick stepped forward. 'You're a victim too Mel.'

Jenny's heart leapt with his words. He could have held her cousin responsible. He could have taken his grief out on her, but he wasn't going to.

'Let's go back to the day Ron and Patricia died.'

Melanie glanced back at Detective Grave, then held eye contact with Jenny.

'I was out helping Patricia in the vegetable garden. We were carrying a lime tree, in a plastic bag. It was so heavy, Patricia stopped me from lifting it because I was pregnant.'

Melanie rubbed her tummy, lost in a memory or feeling.

'As she lifted it to the edge of the garden, the bag split open. The tree exploded. We were so surprised, then…' Mel swallowed tears. 'Then Patricia collapsed. Blood was everywhere. I screamed. I ran, like a coward for the homestead.'

'You ran for your life Mel. It's okay.'

A tissue box appeared on the bed. Jenny pulled one out and handed it to Mel. She ignored it, so Jenny gently dabbed the tears from her cousin's cheeks.

'Ron met me at the doorway, grabbed my arm, dragged me inside and shut the door. He held a rifle in his hand. I was so scared.' Her cousin sucked in a gulp of air and rushed on.

'He pushed me through the kitchen, up the stairs and told me to grab Sam and hide in the servant's stairwell. He said Sam would know where it was.'

Jenny nodded. Nick led her to the same place when the homestead was set on fire.

The smell of ash touched her senses despite it being months since the homestead was rebuilt.

Nick's hand squeezed her shoulder. She peered over to see worried crystal blue eyes assessing her. She nodded she was doing okay. His hand slipped away.

'Go on Mel. We know the spot.'

'He started screaming out my name. It made my blood run cold.'

'You need to say who he is Mel.' Jenny coaxed, knowing what Grave would need on record.

'My dad…' the title caught in her throat. 'Peter Williams screamed my name. There was arguing, then another gunshot. Then what sounded like furniture being dragged around.'

Melanie's chest was heaving. Tears were streaming down her cheeks too fast for Jenny to catch. The sodden tissue was useless. Snot dripped from Melanie's nose.

'I think that might be all she can handle.'

Jenny checked with Nev, who nodded he agreed and reached over to draw up a syringe ready to add to Melanie's drip.

'No. No Jen. I need to let this out.' Melanie's voice was shrill, desperate.

Jenny glanced back at Nev who bit his lip, considering his patient's well-being. Finally, he nodded for her to let Mel go on.

'I was so frightened. He came right into the room we were hiding in. Sam was with me, but he seemed to have gone into another world. I thought I might need to keep him quiet, but I didn't, and it was me who nearly gave us up.'

'But you didn't?' Jenny asked.

'No. He opened drawers, the wardrobe, threw things around the room, but never found the entrance to the stairwell.'

'How long did you stay in there?'

'I don't know. An hour? Maybe more.'

Long enough to bury Patricia.

Silence grew as Melanie composed herself, accepted a fresh tissue and finally blew her nose. She carried on giving her statement. By the time she was finished. They were all exhausted, but Melanie was spent.

So much so she drifted off to sleep without a sedative and before she explained why Geoff got involved. It took all Jenny's self-control not to press her cousin.

Why did her brother turn up to help Melanie? How did Aunt Carolyn's car end up on the side of the road?

'Okay team. We are done for now. I'll go check in on what your aunt shared with Philips and O'Connell. I think you best call it a day Williams.'

'Yes Sarge.'

Jenny wanted to find out what her aunt's interview revealed, but she also needed a shower and a few minutes to decompress.

Her boss ushered everyone out of the room. Grave followed Jenny out.

'You did a good job today Williams, despite ignoring my order not to go it alone.'

'Sorry about that Detective. But it's...'

'Family. I get it. Nevertheless. I nearly decided not to recommend you for a detective position, but I convinced myself we need more passionate cops like you in the job.'

'Detective position?' Nick glanced from Grave to Jenny and back.

'It's just a recommendation Nick. It doesn't mean anything.' Jenny slipped her hand around his waist.

'Actually. It's a job offer Jenny. The state government is pushing for more female detectives, and I've put your name forward. The job is yours if you want it.'

Grave's phone pinged with a text. The detective glanced down at the screen, frowning as she read.

'Everything okay?' Jenny didn't try to read the message but got a glimpse of a few words about someone being missing
.

'It will be.' Grave slid the phone back into her suit pants pocket. 'Now where were we? A job offer. That's right. It's yours if you want it.'

Jenny could sense tension in Nick's body without looking at him.

'I'll need to think about it Detective.'

'What's to think about. You've solved your cousin's case. It's what you came all the way out here for. Right!'

'It is, but things have changed.' She turned to look at Nick. His eyes were fixed on Grave.

Grave nodded. A smile crept across her lips.

'I understand. The offer is there. You've got my number. If you decide to take me up on it, I'll put you in contact with the right people to make it happen.'

Grave held out her hand.

'It's been nice working with you Williams.'

'You're leaving?'

'I'm done here, and I need to chase something up.'

'Anything to do with all those text messages?'

Grave studied Jenny a moment.

'You'll definitely make a great detective one day. The texts are a family thing. Like the saying goes, *you can choose your friends, but you can't choose your family*. Be seeing you Jenny.'

The detective turned and strolled down the hallway toward the hospital entrance, leaving Jenny staring after her.

'A shame she couldn't join us for a celebratory drink.'

'She probably feels like she doesn't belong.' Nick's tone said he was beginning to believe she didn't.

'I hope you don't leave us in the lurch Williams, but if you have to, we'll understand.' Sarge spoke from the doorway of Melanie's room.

'I'm not planning on going anywhere in a hurry Sir.'

'Are you sure?' Sarge joined them in the hallway. 'It's a great career opportunity.'

'It is, but I don't think I'm ready.'

'Let's grab a bite to eat before we head back to the station.' Nick's arm wrapped around her.

'Don't be too rash.' Sarge called out as they reached the end of the hallway.

'Leave her be.' She heard Nev say as they strolled past the nursing station and out the automatic glass doors.

A cool evening breeze touched Jenny's cheeks. Her stomach growled.

'Food it is then,' she agreed.

Chapter 51

The smell of Nick's spicy aftershave made Jenny's skin tingle as she lay on the burnt orange bedspread in the hotel room Nick often used when he was in town. The very same one she stayed in when she first arrived in Coober Pedy.

It seemed like a lifetime ago now.

'Ready?' he asked as he appeared from the cramped bathroom.

'I'd rather stay here and lay with you, but my stomach won't let me.'

'Come on. Getting out will do you good.'

Jenny poked her cheek with her tongue, seriously considering not going anywhere but then she realised the case was over. Getting together was a ritual for her now.

'I'm stuffed, but it's Penny's last night and I need to at least grab some food, a drink and debrief with the team. I still can't work out how Geoff got involved in all this. Maybe the interview with Aunt Carolyn revealed something.'

'Always the cop.' Nick reached for her hand and pulled her to her feet into his chest. His eyes scanned her face a moment. She could see a question in his gaze, but now wasn't the time to let him ask her about the future.

'Let's go. I'm starving.' She pulled him toward the door.

A voice called from along the veranda as Nick pulled the door closed.

'What a day!'

Penny linked her arm in Jenny's.

'What a week.'

Jenny's earlier anxiety disappeared with Penny's wide grin.

'And I didn't even have to use my holiday pay up to help. How good is that!'

Her friend strode toward the motel entrance, dragging Jenny along at a cracking pace.

Two minutes later they were picking out food from the motel restaurant menu.

'I'll order. What do you want?'

Nick collected the menu from her hand knowing she would have selected one of two regular meals she always ate.

'Pesto chicken pasta. I need the carbs.'

'And you Penny? This one's on me, as a thanks for solving my mum and dad's case.'

'It's our job Nick.'

'I know, but still, how many cold cases get this much attention?'

'It helps to have friends.' Penny grinned at Jenny. 'Tenacious ones at that. I'll grab a steak and chips, no salad, thanks.'

Jenny was glad Nick left the table. Finding out why her brother was involved was eating away at her. The idea he might still be Tristan's father sat in the back of her mind, even though Melanie said her father was the one who raped her.

Incest was a horrible thing. It could affect other family members. Could her uncle have encouraged Geoff? She forced the thought down. She needed facts, not speculation.

'Did the DNA on Tristan come back?'

'Not yet. Why?'

'Just wanting to confirm Tristan's father.'

'Didn't Melanie say her dad molested her from the age of thirteen?'

Jenny swallowed her question, then shook her head. She wouldn't sleep until she was sure.

'Yes, but my brother, where does he fit in all of this? Melanie was too exhausted to elaborate.'

'Ah. Haven't you read your aunt's interview transcript yet?'

'No. It's been a long day.'

Penny grinned mischievously.

'Lucky I snuck a look then.'

Jenny wanted to hug her friend, at least she hoped she did. The smile on Penny's lips said Geoff did nothing wrong.

'Tell me.'

She leaned closer, eyes searching around to make sure no one else could hear.

'Geoff heard we were tracing the panel van. *His* panel van.'

'Who told him?'

'Carolyn didn't know, but your parents could have said something.'

'Maybe. But why did he go and get Melanie? What was their relationship?'

'Your aunt left Melanie to go back to your uncle. They met at the mine you found them at. Carolyn caved, told him everything she planned and gave Melanie up. He went to William Creek Station and you know what happened there.'

'He killed Nick's parents.'

'And left empty handed. He never found Melanie.'

'So where did Geoff come in?'

'Your aunt called him. Told him to go and pick Melanie up and bring her to Adelaide, to keep her safe from the schoolteacher.'

'They lied to Geoff?'

'They lied to everyone. Melanie went with Geoff, thinking he was taking her to safety, to her mum.'

Jenny pictured her nature loving brother doing a favour for his cousin. It explained why he knew Melanie was alive, but not why he never told her.

'He must have reconnected with Melanie when he found out the police were looking for him and his car.'

'Why didn't he phone me? Everyone thought Melanie was staying with me.'

'Only he knows that.'

Penny didn't say the obvious. That the answer to all the unanswered questions died with her brother.

'I don't understand why Aunt Carolyn let Melanie stay with me if Uncle Pete was controlling them – abusing them?'

'She played along with your uncle. I guess she was afraid of what he might do otherwise.'

The terror in her aunt's actions out at the mine explained a lot.

How did they all miss the signs?

'He wanted Melanie staying close to you in case you found out anything about the investigation.'

Jenny's mind went over some of the things Melanie said. At first, it appeared she was helping them with the investigation. But it didn't take long for Melanie to ask questions, rather than offer help.

Then the comment she made to Nick, when she apologised for his mum's death. Everything made sense now. It was shortly after that when Mel said she was going back to her mum.

'Where did Mel go when she left here?'

'Her phone pinged at various locations around town. She never left the area. And your brother's phone pinged here at the beginning of the week, when we started looking into the link between Ron's death and his panel van. There were also other calls between his number and hers going back a long way.'

'My head is spinning. He must have known about Uncle Pete all along?'

'He knew he'd been accused of sleeping with Melanie. He knew his car was seen and the police were chasing him, but I guess he was probably worried your uncle would come looking for Melanie after the police said she wasn't with you anymore.'

'I guess we'll never know exactly what Geoff did or didn't know.'

'No, but we do know he did everything he could to keep your cousin safe.'

'Yes.' Jenny studied her hands a moment as she fought back the tears.

'He died to keep her safe.'

'Exactly.'

A jug of beer and a tray of cold glasses appeared in front of Jenny.

'I'll be back in a second.' Nick turned to leave.

'Who are these for?'

'Them.' Nick nodded toward the door as Nev, Tim, and Philips entered with his son Tommy and wife Dianna.

'Party time!' Penny grinned. 'I'll give you a hand Nick.' She slid her chair back and joined him as he returned to collect her wine and a few other drinks and snacks.

Jenny watched them huddle together in quiet conversation as they crossed the dining room to the bar.

Something was going on. And she had no idea what it was.

Chapter 52

Philips sat down opposite Jenny at the long table in the middle of the dining area.

'Hey. Hero of the day.'

Dianna sat down next to him. Their son ignored the seat his mum patted and headed for the kids' game room.

'No way. You're the one who leapt out of nowhere.'

Dianna used sign language. Her fingers moved rapidly, but Jenny had been practising.

She signed back.

He jumped down from on top of the dugout and arrested my aunt.

Dianna signed some more.

Jenny shook her head and signed back.

No. He wasn't in danger and didn't do anything stupid.

Technically, her aunt still held the rifle in her hand, but Philips came from nowhere. It was a solid move.

'Hey you two. I'm not liking this talking about me when I'm right here.'

Philips signed as he spoke.

It was something Jenny was still working on and was going to take a lot more practice.

'Detective Grave sends her apologies. She said a family thing cropped up she needed to deal with. I know that feeling.'

Nev, Tim and Philips laughed.

Jenny noticed Tommy's blonde hair bounce as he disappeared behind the long glass wall in the play area.

'He's getting so big.'

Jenny watched him ask a boy if he could join him to play a game. The idea of kids crossed her mind. Was she ready to settle down to be a full-time country cop?

Nick returned with a wide smile. He rarely grinned, let alone smiled. Jenny scanned his face, then frowned at Penny who wore a similar expression.

They are definitely up to something!

Sarge appeared with another jug of beer, O'Connell two steps behind him. But what caught Jenny's eye was the short, buff, ash blonde man at O'Connell's side.

His tight muscle shirt showed every ripple of his abs. Jenny was momentarily distracted. But when the unnamed visitor sat next to O'Connell and leaned in for a kiss on the Senior Constable's cheek, so much about his aloof manner suddenly made sense.

Jenny smiled. O'Connell tipped his head.

Standing, she reached down the table, her hand extended.

'Hi. I'm Jenny. I don't believe we've met.'

'I'm Gary. Nice to meet you.'

His soft voice and gentle handshake made Jenny smile broadly.

'Nice to meet you too.'

Nick buzzed around the table, filling glasses like a waiter. Jenny watched him with growing suspicion. Finally, he returned to his chair, but didn't sit.

'Okay.' He cleared his throat.

'Can I have everyone's attention please.'

He glanced around like he was looking for someone. A frown formed on his brow, then disappeared as his eyes fixed on three people entering the restaurant.

Jenny's heart-rate kicked up a notch as Sam guided her mum and dad across the room and found them seats at the end of the table.

Nick held his beer aloft.

'Sorry we're late.' Sam reached for a glass. His grin matched his brother's and Jenny squirmed with discomfort.

'Now we are all here, except Mel of course.' Nick glanced at Jenny.

She knew her expression was one of pure anxiety. He was up to something. Something Penny knew about but intentionally kept to herself.

'First of all. Thank you to everyone. You all helped solve my mum and dad's case in some way or another.'

Jenny relaxed.

'Dinner and drinks are on me and Sam tonight. You've put so many demons to rest this week, not only for me, but I think I speak for Jenny and her family too.'

Nick held his beer glass toward her mum and dad. They lifted theirs in salute and nodded their agreement.

Jenny's eyes stung. Her stomach knotted as her dad's gaze met hers. There was a softness in there she'd not seen for a long time. Nick's voice snapped her attention back to him.

'But what I've really called you all here for is something very special. Actually, someone very special.' Nick rummaged in his pocket.

'But first, let's toast to the future.'

A chorus of *cheers* and *here here,* erupted around the room. Jenny noticed Gwen standing with the local paper's photographer on the far side of the room. A Cheshire cat grin plastered on her lips.

Surely she didn't expect her exclusive interview now?

'Now. For the moment of truth.' Nick put his beer down after nearly draining it dry. Then pulled something from his pocket. Jenny's stomach did a summersault.

His eyes fixed on hers and sweat broke out under her arms.

'I know you've been offered a big promotion. I know you said you didn't want it, that you weren't ready.'

What did he have, some sort of medal of honour or something?

'Did you mean what you said. About staying here?'

She nodded, suddenly aware of what might be in the dark blue velvet box.

'In that case.'

Nick dropped to one knee and opened the box to reveal a white opal and diamond ring.

The entire restaurant stopped. Jenny could sense them holding their breath. She knew she was. Her cheeks turned a dark shade of red. A hot flush threatened to overwhelm her.

This was so unlike Nick. He was private and sullen and emotionally retarded at the best of times.

She turned to Penny, her eyes drilling her friend with an accusing stare.

'You put him up to this show.'

It wasn't a question.

'Oh God it took some coaxing. Hurry up and answer the poor guy. You know you want to.'

Jenny grasped the ring box in one hand. For a moment, Nick held his breath. She saw the sudden anxiety in his eyes. He thought she might close the lid, but he soldiered on.

'Jenny Williams. Would you do me the great honour of becoming my wife? My soulmate. My companion for life?'

She rolled her lips to hold back the emotions.

'Yes.' The word came out softly, just like the tears rolling down her cheeks.

'What was that?' Sarge bellowed. 'Speak up constable.'

'Yes! Yes Nick. Yes!'

She dragged him from his knee, as she rose, then wrapped her arms around his neck to plant a firm kiss on his lips.

'I'm not going anywhere Nick Johnston. Coober Pedy has grown on me. You've grown on me.'

Nick pulled back, lifted the ring from the satin interior and slid it on her shaking finger. Cameras flashed and cheers erupted. Hands touched her shoulders, pulling her around and away from Nick's embrace.

He let her go reluctantly.

Expecting to find her mum or dad, she was surprised to be face to face with bright orange hair, dark red lipstick and the soft warm hug of her mum away from home.

'Oh Luv. We are so happy you decided to stay and take this bachelor off the market.'

Jenny' eyes sought out Nick's. His crystal blue eyes twinkled with the same happiness filling her soul.

'So am I Marj. So am I.'

****

This isn't the end for Jenny, but I'm taking a break to pursue a new series starring Detective Dawn Grave. Find out what family business dragged her away from Coober Pedy in such a hurry in *Grave Regret*, book one in the new *Dawn Grave Crime* series, available from all good bookstores.

In the meantime, why not follow Jenny's career as she becomes a detective in Adelaide. You'll meet Detective Williams in book 2 of the *Foxy Mystery* series. If you don't mind a little sizzle with your mystery, then check out the five-book series online or ask your local bookstore.

Thank You!

I hope you enjoyed reading the *Opal Fields Series*.

If you did, why not tell your friends, or better still, leave a review with your favourite retailer so others can make an informed decision about buying into the series.

If you leave a review, I'd love to see a copy, but most of all, I'd like to thank you for reading my stories. You're awesome, really! Without you, I'd be a lot less motivated to get in front of my computer screen and dream up these crazy crime/mystery adventures. Without you, I'd have never bothered to publish. Thanks!

I promise, I'm not finished with Jenny. In fact, I have a few ideas in mind including a Christmas special, but for now, I'm really keen to follow Dawn Grave to Far North Queensland and find out more about her family, her past and her future.

I always love to hear what readers think, so if reviewing isn't your thing, I'm open to an email message or comment on my website. You'll find my books and more about me including how to sign up to my readers club at www.fionatarr.com

Don't want to miss out on any new releases? Follow me on Amazon or Bookbub, just search Fiona Tarr

Books by Fiona Tarr

Opal Fields
Her Buried Bones
Her Broken Bones
Her Scorched Bones
Her Hidden Bones
Her Lonely Bones
Her Covered Bones

Foxy Mysteries
Death Beneath the Covers
Presumed Missing
Deadly Deceit
Twisted Vendetta
Dead Cold

Or the full collection
Foxy Mysteries Complete Collection

The Priestess Chronicles
Call of the Druids
Relic Seeker
Shiloh Rising

The Eternal Realm
The Jericho Prophecy
Delilah and the Dark God
Reign of Retribution

Covenant of Grace
Destiny of Kings
Seed of Hope

Legacy of Power
Heir of Vengeance
The Ehud Dagger - Prequel

Printed in Great Britain
by Amazon

40580106R00159